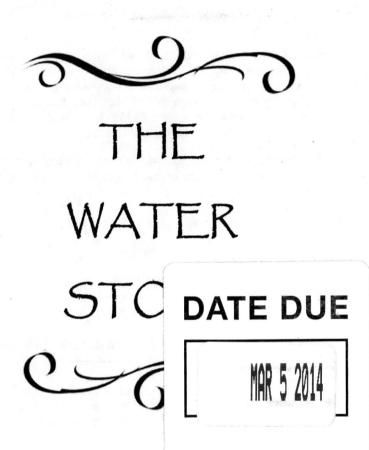

THE

WATER

STO

BOOK TWO

THE REIGN OF THE ELEMENTS

RILEY CARNEY

First Edition

Printed in the United States of America

ISBN 978-0-9841307-3-3 (pb)

The Library of Congress has catalogued the hardcover edition.
ISBN 978-0-9841307-2-6 (hc)

Summary: Matt, Samsire, and their friends, set off on another quest, following the clues of a long-dead dwarf adventurer as they desperately race against time and Malik's forces to find the Water Stone before it's too late.

Visit www.booklightpress.com

This book is dedicated to Mom, Dad, and Nick for always being there for me, and to Ben, the most amazing dog and companion there has ever been, who will live on in Samsire

A portion of the sales from this book will go to Breaking the Chain to help eliminate the bonds of illiteracy and poverty.

MUNDARIA

SAMSIRE

PROLOGUE

Beyond the grasses of the Endless Fields and south of the dark trees of Northwood Forest, a single tower loomed above the city of Marlope. The town was large, but seemed to shrink in the pillar's shadow like an animal cowering from a predator.

A lone man walked up the cold, winding marble stairs of the tower. He was tall and dark-haired with a sharp chin and ears that stretched into long pointed tips. His dark eyes glinted dangerously.

When he reached the top of the steps, he turned down a long marble hallway that led to two massive black doors. He paused, breathing in deeply before placing both palms on the doors and pushing them open into the large room beyond.

The room was empty except for a tall, misshapen figure, staring out the windows that glared down on Marlope. He wore dark robes which dangled loosely from his body.

From the back, his head appeared to be bald, but the skin was crusty and scarred, molten black and white, swirling into an ugly gray hue. His ears protruded from his head like a bat, blackened and charred. His limbs were long and crooked, and one leg was slightly longer than the other.

He did not turn as the doors opened, but stood motionless, as if riveted by the scene beneath him.

The dark-haired man walked across the room, appearing to lose confidence and height with every step. He fell into a kneeling position as he drew closer to his master.

"My lord," he whispered, his voice reverberating across the large room.

The figure still did not turn. "I do not sense that you bring me good news, Kerwin."

Kerwin licked his lips nervously, but did not rise from his reverent position. "The scouts report that the boy has survived, my lord."

A chilly silence followed. Kerwin cringed as he waited for his master to strike out angrily, but instead, the misshapen figure before him merely clasped his hands together behind his back.

"The scouts have also reported that he does indeed have possession of the Fire Stone," Kerwin continued.

"That is ill news, indeed. Tell me, Kerwin. Is this how you repay me for all the gifts I have given you?"

"No...no, my lord," Kerwin sputtered, his face now pale.

"No, I think not. I am the Commander of Shadows. The Stones of the Elements belong to me! I will have them once more."

"Yes, my lord."

The Commander began to pace along the windows.

"Does the boy know of the prophecy spoken so long ago?" he asked.

Kerwin hesitated before speaking. "He is accompanied by the Wizard of Light. I have no doubt that he will tell the boy. But, my lord...surely this boy cannot be the one-"

"Silence!" The Commander spoke with such ferocity that Kerwin jumped to his feet in alarm.

"I meant no harm, my lord," Kerwin muttered.

"The Wizard of Light," the Commander spat in disgust.

"Yes, my lord. If...if this wizard tells him of the prophecy, then it is likely that he will also teach him the magic of the Fire Stone and...and other magic as well."

"Only I have true control of the elements, Kerwin. This boy will not succeed."

Kerwin bowed his head, "Yes, my lord."

"Still, he could be dangerous if he were to find the second stone," the Commander said, almost to himself. "I must have it before he does. Send out your best spy."

Kerwin seemed startled. "But, my lord. Surely I should be the one to look for the stone."

"No. As incompetent as you may be, I need you here. Send your lieutenant to trail the boy. I have no doubt he will lead us to the stone. And have an Aguran trail your lieutenant. Send him to me before he leaves. Call for Vivona too, and tell her I need her. I must be in peak condition."

"Yes, my lord," Kerwin said, bowing even though his master was still turned away.

Kerwin moved quickly to the door, but he stopped when he heard the Commander's low, threatening voice.

"Do not fail me again, Kerwin."

Kerwin left without another word. As he closed the door behind him, he breathed deeply, his black eyes glinting. He straightened his spine, regaining his composure, and walked down the winding stairs until he reached the base of the tower.

The guards pulled the doors open and Kerwin stepped into the cold night. Ignoring the soldiers that lined the street, he did not stop until he had reached a large stone building with a sharply slanted roof.

He flung open the door and entered a large room with a roaring fire in the fireplace. A single man sat beside the fire, running a polishing stone along the blade of a sword. He looked up as Kerwin entered, his brown eyes stared at him defiantly before returning to his work.

Kerwin glared at him angrily. "I expect you to show more respect to your commander."

The man seemed unfazed by Kerwin's anger, but stood up, the firelight revealing a long burn down the left side of his neck. He looked at Kerwin coldly.

"You are not my commander," Rock Thompson said dangerously.

Kerwin's jaw twitched, rage rising inside him at his lieutenant's insolence.

"I represent the wishes of the Commander of Shadows and hold his trust, thus I am your commanding officer. You will obey my orders."

The man nodded slowly, his eyes brimming with defiance.

"The Commander wants me to stay here, so you are to trail the boy. Undoubtedly he will lead us to the next stone, but you must have patience. It may be some time yet before he searches for it. Do not kill him."

The other man sneered.

"Do not harm him until he has led you to the stone. Then you must kill him."

The man smiled cruelly. "Shall I take others with me?"

"Yes," Kerwin answered. "Garans, not men. And listen closely. There is something else you should know."

Kerwin glanced around and then spoke quietly in his ear, placing a small container in his hand. The lieutenant's smirk grew more sinister, and he nodded briskly.

"Go, now," Kerwin instructed him. "The Commander wishes to see you."

Rock left the room and after a moment, Kerwin followed. He walked quickly to the garan pits, where the twisted black creatures were fighting ferociously, battling for authority amongst themselves.

At the edge of the pits, three tall figures were watching the garans fight. They were Agurans, their bones protruding grotesquely beneath their dark gray skin. They watched the garans without expression.

Kerwin beckoned to one and it slithered over to him, its long spindly limbs dangling at its sides.

"Trail the man following the boy," Kerwin whispered. "Do not let him know you are there, but keep an eye on him and the boy. Gather as much information as you can and report back to me."

The Aguran disappeared down the street.

Kerwin smiled to himself. He would not disappoint the Commander of Shadows this time. His man would bring back the stone and the boy would pay for the trouble he had caused. The boy would die.

CHAPTER ONE

Matt fumbled for the reins as his horse whinnied shrilly.

"Whoa!" he yelled.

The horse would not be calmed. It whinnied again, and before Matt could react, it reared up onto its hind legs. Matt's feet flew free of the stirrups, and the reins slipped through his fingers. He was thrown from the saddle. For a moment, he hung in the air, then came crashing down. He slammed into the river bank and began to slide down the bank, unable to get traction in the mud. He slipped into the river, and the current pulled him into the icy water. His hands scrambled to grab onto the long grasses that grew along the bank, but it was too late. The river wanted him and it quickly swallowed him up.

Matt sucked in a breath of air just as his head was dragged under and his entire body was submerged. Matt fought against the water, but his clothes weighed him down and he didn't know how to swim. The water buffeted his body from all sides, violently forcing the air from his lungs and pushing him down the river with terrifying speed.

He thrashed wildly as the current began to pull him down into the dark depths of the river. He could not see and he could not hear. He struggled to scramble upward, but he was trapped below the surface. He was drowning.

Despair clawed at him. He was on the verge of surrender, and then, incredibly, someone was grabbing his arm. He reached desperately for it as he felt another hand clutching at him. He felt himself being lifted.

Finally, his head broke the surface, and he gulped in giant mouthfuls of air. Hanging limply in the arms of his rescuer, he allowed himself to be dragged to the bank where his fingers groped the moist earth. Coughing, he rolled over onto his back, breathing heavily. His rescuer slumped onto the shore beside him, his breathing labored as well.

"Are you all right?"

Matt turned and saw Galen lying beside him. His dark hair was plastered to his head and the long jagged scar down his right cheek was clearly visible.

"Galen," Matt sputtered. "You saved me."

Galen grinned. "What'd you expect me to do? Leave you to drown?"

"Are you two insane?" someone exclaimed.

Matt pushed himself onto his elbow. Emmon was running toward them, his unruly golden hair flapping in the wind and his eyes wide in concern. Arden followed close behind him. Matt and Galen climbed to their feet, their clothes heavy with water.

"We're fine," Galen assured them. "Luckily, I got him before he reached the rocks."

Matt looked at him gratefully, shivering in the cool forest air. He glanced back at the river, at the rapids and rocks that lie ahead. A wave of nausea washed over him as he realized the fate he had almost met.

They all turned at the sound of pounding hoofs as Lucian galloped to where they stood and then pulled sharply on Innar's reins. The wizard's face was fierce, and he held his staff aloft as if expecting an attack. His eyes swept over Matt and Galen's dripping clothes.

"What happened to you two? I was only gone a few minutes! I thought you were being attacked," he demanded.

Matt looked past Lucian at the black horse he had been riding. Striker whinnied happily and trotted over to him.

"Something spooked Striker when we were crossing the river," Matt explained. "He threw me and Galen jumped in to save me."

Lucian sighed, running a hand through his gray-peppered black hair. "And you're both all right? Why is it, Matthias, that even a peaceful of journey becomes troublesome for you?"

Matt grinned. Lucian shook his head before pulling Innar back around. Emmon and Arden sent concerned glances in Matt's direction before they mounted their horses again.

Matt's wet clothes clung to him heavily, but despite the coolness of the Amaldan Forest, summer was nearing and his clothes would soon dry from the warm sun piercing the canopy of leaves.

He patted Striker's neck and checked to make sure that his pack was still fastened firmly to the saddle. Everything, it seemed, was still safe in his pack. He started to pull it shut when panic rushed through him, and he reached for his chest. The black pouch he always wore around his neck was still there, with the Fire Stone inside. He could feel the warmth of the Stone seeping through the fabric. Releasing the pouch, he sighed. The Fire Stone's warmth was comforting, but Matt's feelings toward it were mixed since it was also an unrelenting mystery that intrigued him to the point of torture.

"Come on, Matt!" Galen called. "If you stand there much longer, you'll freeze."

Matt reluctantly mounted Striker. The horse whinnied nervously, and Matt gripped the reins tightly in case the horse tried to throw him again. He patted the horse's neck reassuringly and scanned the area around them. Something had definitely spooked the horse before, but Matt saw only the broad, soaring trees of the Amaldan Forest.

Striker was still nervous, his ears flattened against his skull. Matt turned in his saddle, holding on tightly. In the gaps between the trees, he could see something large and colorful streaking through the air above them. Multicolored feathers and black leathery wings gleamed in the sunlight.

"Samsire," Matt said with a smile.

The other horses whinnied nervously, as well, sensing the alorath's approach. Matt watched Samsire streak over the forest, circling several times before plunging gracefully through the upper branches of the trees and landing heavily a short distance ahead.

"Hello, Sam," Matt said after Sam lumbered over and leaned over him protectively.

"What happened to you?" Samsire demanded. "I saw you stop. How did you manage to get wet?"

Matt grinned at him sheepishly. "I fell in the river. Striker threw me."

"I leave you alone for an hour and you find a way to get yourself into trouble?" the alorath scolded. "If you had been riding with me instead of that horse, things might have been different."

"Yeah, it would have been a much longer fall," Matt said, laughing.

Sam flashed his teeth in a dangerous grin. The horses stepped backward.

"Don't worry, Sam," Galen said. "I'm here to make sure he survives in your absence."

The alorath turned to Galen and lowered his head so that his leathery, blue-green snout was only feet from, and then he flung his large, clawed foot in front of Galen in a mock bow, exhaling loudly. Galen's horse responded by throwing his front legs high in the air, nearly unseating Galen, but the mergling shifted quickly in his saddle to stay on and laughed at the alorath.

"Go on ahead, Sam," Matt said, laughing. "I'll be okay without you."

Samsire nodded at Matt grudgingly, casting a sidelong, jealous glance at Striker. Without a word, he huffed into the forest.

Galen laughed. "I'm not sure that Sam and Striker have gotten off on the right foot."

Matt rolled his eyes and watched Sam disappear from sight. If he was being honest, he would prefer to be riding Sam rather than Striker, especially after what had just happened in the river. Since they were riding to meet the elves, though, Lucian had suggested that Matt arrive looking as normal as possible.

More than a week ago, a hawk had arrived bearing a message for Emmon from Lady Can of the elves, instructing him to return to Amaldan since his quest to find the Fire Stone had been successfully completed. Emmon and Arden had pleaded with Matt, Lucian, and Galen to join them, and after weeks in Ridgefell, Matt was savoring the freedom of traveling again.

The time they had spent in Ridgefell had been hard for Matt. It was difficult for him to adjust to his new identity. For days he puzzled over many questions, most prominent of which was who his parents really were. And always lingering at the back of his thoughts were questions about the Fire Stone. He had tried many times to create fire from his palm the way he had when he rescued Emmon from Kerwin's knife, but he had not been able to repeat it.

Whenever Matt pestered Lucian for answers, Lucian would tell him to be patient, that the time would come for him to understand. To Matt, the Fire Stone was a reminder of the destiny he felt that he could not avoid. Traveling with his friends again during the past week, though, had given him a break from his muddled thoughts.

"You're lucky that Hal's not here," Arden told Matt, riding up beside him. "He would have gone off on a rant about proper riding style after you fell."

Matt laughed. The older boy had chosen not to accompany them to Amaldan, but had remained in Ridgefell, instead, to train with the soldiers there. His first choice would have been to return to Hightop to see his one true love, Cadie, Duke Rellin's daughter. Unfortunately, Barrum, Duke Rellin's former lieutenant and Malik's servant, had overthrown Duke Rellin, and was now the self-appointed leader of Hightop, so it was dangerous for any of them to venture near the city.

"He'd probably lecture you on proper chivalry while he was at it," Galen said, never one to pass up the opportunity to take a jab at Hal. "He'll be an expert on it by the time we meet up with him again."

Everybody laughed. Even Lucian smiled. Poking fun at Hal was always an excellent source of entertainment because of his desperate attempts to be dignified.

"It's a shame he's missing, Amaldan, though," Emmon said without sympathy. "I am very happy to have trees surrounding me again."

Arden scowled. "I can't say that I'm all that excited to be back here, though."

"Why not?" Matt said.

Arden's eyes, the color of melted chocolate, narrowed. "I tagged along with Emmon on his quest without getting permission. I am in loads of trouble!" She nibbled at her lip. "Also, I'm fourteen now. It's time for me to be assigned a craft. That means no more adventuring for me."

"Come on, now Arden. I'm sure you'll be assigned a good craft," Emmon said.

Arden made a face. "In my dreams. No, my grandfather will send me to knitting school or something like that."

"Counselor Lan's not that bad. He's quick to forgive," Emmon replied.

"He'll forgive you, maybe, but he's so darn protective of me. He'd probably call an armada of healers if I cut my finger!"

Emmon shrugged, conceding defeat. Matt sighed as he looked around the forest. It was a place that he had dreamed of visiting since first meeting Emmon and Arden. He had read and heard many stories about the elves, and although he had known Emmon and Arden for many months, he was curious to see what the rest of their race was like.

He had read one legend that described the elves as thieving liars who had stolen their magic from Mother Nature. Matt did not believe it, because he knew how trustworthy and true his friends were, but he was fascinated by how many different perceptions there were of the elves and he wondered why.

To Matt, the elves represented an unlimited source of wisdom and inexplicable power. He was excited to learn about their culture, and he was especially excited to learn about their magic. The elves were masters of the magic of the earth, one of the four elements that Matt was destined to be the master of. He didn't yet understand how he would be able to master the earth, though, since there was not a stone with that power like there was with fire, air, and water. Maybe the elves would be able to teach him how to control it.

"Let's stop for a moment," Lucian said. "The Heart is not far from here, but we should rest so that we can be at our best when we greet the elves."

Feeling a shiver of excitement, Matt climbed off of Striker's back. The others reached for their water skins and parcels of food.

Emmon tossed Matt an apple, but before he could bite into it, Lucian laid a hand on his arm.

"May I speak with you for a moment, Matthias?" he said quietly.

Matt looked up at Lucian curiously and followed him away from the others. Lucian glanced around.

"Wear your sword today, Matthias," he said in a low voice. "And, of course, you are wearing the Fire Stone, aren't you?"

Matt nodded, giving him a questioning glance

The wizard added, "The elves are difficult to win over and since you are the one in possession of the Fire Stone instead of Emmon, you must make a stronger effort to show them that you are courageous, clever, and judicious. We must convince them that you are worthy of the Fire Stone. The elves can be either powerful allies or frightening enemies."

Matt nodded and felt a knot forming in his stomach.

"Right," he said.

"When we are in the Heart of Amaldan, be aware of your surroundings. Do not let the elves intimidate you. You have already done many great things, Matthias. Do not forget that."

Lucian smiled at him warmly, but Matt barely heard the praise. The excited curiosity he had felt about visiting the elves had instantly been replaced by apprehension. He reached for the Fire Stone without thinking about it. Its warmth seeped through the pouch into his hand, and he felt a surge of power. He forced himself to ignore the strong impulse to remove the pouch from his neck.

Lucian patted him on the shoulder and walked back to the others. Before Matt could follow, he heard heavy footsteps behind him and turned to see Sam looking down at him.

Matt smiled weakly up at him, relieved to see his friend. As he stroked Sam's feathered leg, the alorath leaned down to him.

"Don't worry, Matt If the elves start in on you, they'll have to deal with me."

Matt nodded, Sam's words restoring his confidence a little. Together, they walked back to the others. Emmon and Arden were talking excitedly and had already mounted their horses. Galen, however, was silent. His normally cheerful and mischievous face was serious, and his blue eyes gleamed dangerously.

Glancing sideways at Galen, Matt retrieved a bundled cloak from his pack and carefully unwrapped it to expose his sword, Doubtslayer. The leather scabbard revealed the sword's unique shape, slanted in on one sid e near the point. Its silver hilt was wrapped in a brown leather grip, worn from use.

Matt belted on the sword and his two throwing knives, and climbed into the saddle. He noticed that Galen was also wearing his sword. He felt very uneasy as he followed Lucian through the trees. He had fastened his bow to the outside of his pack for easy access, and his hand moved to it. Emmon saw the movement and sent him a reassuring look, but Matt was not comforted.

"Hey, Matt," Arden said behind him.

Matt twisted in his saddle to look at her, and she smiled at him.

"Relax."

Matt nodded. If only he could meet the elves when he looked and felt less bedraggled. They had been traveling for a week and his clothes were still damp and muddy from his fall in the river.

He forced himself to relax, but he could not stop thinking about the elves. Next to him, Galen's face grew pale when his eyes rested on the imposing line of trees twenty feet ahead. The trees towered above the rest, and their intertwining branches formed a tight, impenetrable wall, stretching as far as they could see on both sides.

"What is that?" Matt breathed in amazement.

Emmon smiled proudly. "That is the entrance to the Heart of Amaldan."

Samsire approached the grove curiously. His feathers glittered in the strange luminous light of the forest, and his eyes shone in wonder. Emmon dismounted and everyone followed suit. Emmon and Arden placed their hands on the nearest tree trunk.

"Allow us to enter trees. Open your heart," Emmon said in a voice scarcely above a whisper.

The intertwining branches of the trees began to move, slowly breaking loose from each other. Matt felt his breath catch in his throat as a doorway was revealed.

Emmon turned to Matt with a grin. "Come on, Matt. Let's go in."

CHAPTER TWO

Emmon and Arden strode through the arched foliage, leading their horses, and Lucian followed closely behind. Matt glanced up at Sam, and the alorath stepped forward, smiling at Matt reassuringly. The boughs of the archway separated some more, forming a much larger archway so that the alorath could pass through. Taking a deep breath, Matt, Galen, and Sam walked through together.

Emmon, Arden, and Lucian were waiting for them on the other side of the archway inside a tunnel made of hundreds of enormous trees in two straight parallel lines.

"Emmon! Arden!" they heard a startled voice yell.

A young elf with brown hair and brown eyes rushed up to them.

"Rankin!" Emmon cried.

The elf embraced Emmon and then Arden. "You left without saying goodbye."

Emmon looked at him apologetically. "I'm sorry, Rankin. When Lady Can assigned me my quest I had to leave as quickly as possible. I ran into Arden as I was leaving, and she followed me."

"Good thing, too," Arden muttered under her breath.

Rankin smiled. "I understand. I'm just glad you are back. You've been gone for more than four months. I heard that you were successful."

"We did what we needed to," Emmon said, and then he looked back at Matt and the others. "Rankin, these are our friends. This is Lucian, the Wizard of Light. This is Galen and Matt, and that's Samsire, Matt's alorath friend."

Rankin's eyes grew wide. "You've been traveling with an alorath? They can be fierce creatures. I've heard that they can be unpredictable and dangerous."

"Actually, I'm pretty predictable," Sam rumbled. "I fly, I eat, I sleep. And I'm only dangerous when I'm hungry, but that's why I keep all these puny midgets around. Just in case."

Matt could not resist smiling at Rankin's suddenly terrified expression.

"Don't mind Sam. He just gets a little defensive sometimes."

He offered his hand with a grin. "I'm Matt."

Rankin shook it half-heartedly. "Nice to meet you. Nice to meet all of you." He looked warily at Sam, who grinned toothily. "Come on. I'll show you all to the Gathering Hall."

As Matt followed Emmon and Arden, his spirits began to grow lighter. Rankin seemed to welcome them. Perhaps Lucian's warning would mean nothing. Matt glanced at the wizard walking beside him, his eyes thoughtful as they scanned the walls of the tunnel. Galen was also studying the trees, but his face was uncharacteristically hard to read.

After walking in silence for ten minutes, the tunnel widened and opened onto a glorious view. Before them was the Heart of Amaldan.

Buildings made entirely of vines and plants were woven within the branches of the towering trees and on the ground, blending into the forest landscape as if they were not there at all. Instead of stairs, branches of adjacent trees had been bound together so tightly by vines that they formed inclined ramps. The ramps connected the separate huts and buildings which were nestled within the sheltering boughs.

Elves were walking across the forest floor and along the ramps connecting the huts. Some held smooth, curved longbows and were dressed in light traveling garb, others wore long, elegant robes. Elves, young and old, wandered in and out of the huts and buildings. They seemed peaceful, yet proud, respectful of the forest, yet very much in command of it.

Rankin led them away from the center of the city to a structure with two enormous carved doors wedged between two trees. The carvings depicted a large tree with elves bowing at its trunk. Matt remembered why Emmon had left on his quest in the first place, to find the Fire Stone before Malik did to protect the Great Tree of Amaldan. The carving on the door must represent the Great Tree, which the elves honored above all other things in the forest.

Elves stood on either side of the door, and without a word, they pulled the doors open and motioned for the group to enter.

Samsire remained outside, but gave Matt an encouraging nudge with his snout.

"You'll be fine," he breathed.

Matt expected the Great Hall to be similar to the one in Hightop, with tall marble pillars and grand polished floors, but it was quite different. Instead, it was an open room with walls made entirely of the trunks and boughs of trees. There was not a roof overhead, only the open sky, and the floor was the soft grass of the forest floor.

At the end of the strange hall, a number of elves sat in chairs made of twisted boughs. Two elves sat alone in the center. The lady had fair white skin and long brown hair. Her blue eyes sparkled kindly as she gazed upon Matt and his friends. The elf beside her was tall and proud, with black hair and a sharp chin. He did not look quite as pleased to see them. Rankin bowed to them briskly and retreated to the door.

"Welcome, friends," the lady said and rose to her feet, as did her companion.

Emmon and Arden stepped forward and bowed low. Matt, Lucian, and Galen followed their lead.

"Lady Can, Lord Balor," Emmon said.

"Rise, Emmon, son of Drathen. Rise niece, Arden, daughter of Michain. I welcome you home to Amaldan," Lady Can said. "Rise guests. You are welcome here."

They rose to their feet and Lord Balor spoke. "It brings us great joy to witness your return, Emmon and Arden, and to meet the guests who have aided you on your quest."

"Yes," Lady Can said. "Welcome, Lucian the Wizard of Light. It has been some time since you have walked among our trees."

"It is a pleasure to be back in Amaldan again," Lucian said, his gray eyes twinkling.

"And you, Galen," she continued quietly. "You are welcome here again, as well."

Galen bowed his head but did not speak. Matt could not see his face, but he wondered when Galen had been in Amaldan before.

"And young Matthias, as well. You and your alorath friend are both welcome here, however, I must request that the alorath not mar the forest or our dwellings, magical creature though he may be." She paused. "You carry great power with you. Emmon has honored you with a great gift."

Matt bowed and his mouth felt dry as he spoke. "Thank you, my lady."

Matt sensed that she was gently reprimanding him for having possession of the Fire Stone. He looked at her kind face, so similar to Arden's. He could feel the elves at the periphery of the hall looking at him curiously. Lord Balor was staring at him with disdain. Matt's cheeks burned with discomfort.

"You and your companions have done well, young Emmon. As have you Arden, though the manner in which you participated in this quest is less commendable," Lord Balor said.

"Nevertheless, I commend you for your deeds. Guests, you are welcome to stay in Amaldan for as long as you wish. The Heart and the forest are yours to explore. We hope you enjoy the wonders of the magic that reigns here. Rankin will show you to your quarters."

Matt felt a rush of relief that the encounter had proven to be so brief and painless. They bowed, and as they turned back toward the two great wooden doors, Lady Can's voice spoke from behind them. "Stay, if you will, Emmon."

Matt glanced at his friend and saw that the happiness in his green eyes had turned to apprehension. Emmon watched them as they followed Rankin through the doors, and then he disappeared from sight.

As soon as the doors of the Gathering Hall had closed, Rankin began to lead them away.

"I will show you where you will be staying if you will follow me, please," he said.

Lucian and Galen followed Rankin, but Arden grabbed Matt's arm.

"Come on, Matt," she said. "Don't you want to see what's going on with Emmon?"

"What do you mean?" he asked.

She smiled mischievously. "I know a place where we can watch what's happening. Come on."

Matt wrenched his arm out of her grip. "No, Arden. I don't want you to get me in trouble before I've even made an impression."

"Don't worry! Come on!"

Arden ran off, but Matt hesitated. He thought of Lucian's warning about the elves and the need for Matt to impress them. Matt did not want to create problems, but he also very much wanted to know what was happening to Emmon.

He looked over his shoulder and noticed that Galen was watching him with a slight smile on his face. He winked at Matt and then quickly struck up a conversation with Rankin as they walked away. Matt grinned, glancing around for Sam, but the alorath had disappeared while they were inside the Gathering Hall. Matt sprinted after Arden.

"Where are we going?" Matt asked Arden, as she skirted around the corner of the building.

"A place Emmon and I found a long time ago."

Matt followed her along the seemingly impassable wall of trees that encircled the hall until she stopped at particularly tall tree. Placing her feet on its base, she grabbed a thick knot that protruded from its trunk, and pulled herself up onto the lowest branch. She waited until Matt was balanced beside her.

"Can you do a shield invocation?" she asked.

Matt nodded. "I haven't done one since Hightop, but-"

"Good. When I tell you, make one around both of us. It'll be easier for me to disguise us if we have a shield first."

Arden scampered further up the tree, and Matt followed her, unable to see anything through the thick leaves and branches except the bottom of her legs and her feet. They reached an outcrop of branches that overlooked the inside of the Gathering Hall and Arden stopped. They were about fifteen feet above the forest floor, looking down at Emmon, Lady Can, Lord Balor, and the other elves in the hall. Matt quietly crawled up next to Arden, and she gestured with her hands for him to create a shield.

Taking a deep breath, Matt cleared his mind and felt a tingle in his fingertips. He focused on the area around them and muttered the word, 'shield' under his breath, picturing the invisible protection in his mind until it materialized.

Arden put a hand on the inside of the shield and shut her eyes for a few moments, focusing intently. When she opened her eyes, she smiled at Matt and began to watch the scene beneath them. Matt tried to watch, but he could feel his energy drain when he turned his attention away from the shield, so he listened instead of watching.

Lady Can was addressing Emmon in a kind voice.

"It was most careless of her to burden you, Emmon, and I apologize for my niece's rash behavior," she was saying.

"I enjoyed the company," Emmon replied. "And I probably wouldn't be here if Arden hadn't helped me."

Lord Balor grunted disapprovingly. "We shall address it with her grandfather, but now there are other things we must discuss. First and foremost, we accept your quest as complete. You have done as we asked, and since the other two Stones of the Elements are still hidden and Malik does not appear to know where they are, Amaldan is currently safe from his evil."

Emmon's face grew flushed at the praise, but he said calmly, "Thank you Lord Balor, but-"

"I must ask you, however, why you gave the Fire Stone to that boy?" Balor interrupted abruptly.

The color drained from Emmon's face, but he did not respond.

Lady Can filled the silence. "It was wise of you, Emmon, to see the power that young Matthias can wield. For he is, incontrovertibly, the one of the Prophecy of the Elements. You have shown great insight and your choice was well made."

"Be that as it may, the words of the Prophecy are clear," Lord Balor said sharply. "The boy is dangerous. Keep your distance from him, he could be destructive."

Matt nearly dropped the shield as his anger mounted. Lucian was right, the elves had already made their assumptions about him, or at least Lord Balor had.

Emmon lifted his head and looked Balor in the eye.

"Thank you, Lord Balor. But I will not consider my quest complete until the two remaining Stones of the Elements are found. If Malik finds them first it will not mean anything that we found the Fire Stone. It is crucial that we find all of the stones before Malik."

Emmon bowed low to Lady Can and nodded at Lord Balor. "Thank you, my Lady."

He left the hall without another word.

Matt sat very still until Arden nudged him. Relieved, he let the shield drop and took a deep breath. He felt slightly tired, but his energy quickly returned, and he followed Arden down the tree as silently as he could.

They reached the ground and scampered around to the front of the hall. Emmon was walking slowly across the clearing in the direction Rankin, Lucian, and Galen had gone. Matt followed Arden, but was hesitant to approach his friend. He felt badly that Emmon had been chastised because he'd given the Fire Stone to Matt and was traveling with him.

Matt bowed his head as Arden tapped Emmon on the shoulder. The elf turned in surprise, and his face brightened visibly when he saw them.

"Hey," he said.

"Hey," Matt responded uncertainly.

Emmon was staring at him curiously. Matt felt anger and frustration building inside his chest again. . Could Emmon actually believe some of Balor's accusations?

"What?" Matt finally demanded.

"I'm just waiting for you to transform into the essence of evil," Emmon replied without smiling.

Matt stared at him for a moment, and then they grinned at each other.

"Come on. Do you really think that I would ever believe the ridiculous things that Balor said about you?" Emmon said, still smiling, and then added rather matter-of-factly. "I've been around you long enough to know who you are, Matt. Besides, if you suddenly become evil, I'll just have Sam eat you."

CHAPTER THREE

Matt walked with Emmon and Arden through the Heart of Amaldan. Rankin joined them and led them through the maze of ramps to a group of huts. Emmon had been told that he could go back to his old sleeping quarters in the scout barracks and Arden was expected to return home to her grandfather, but they had both decided to stay with Matt, Lucian, and Galen for one more night.

They were staying in a large hut made of leaves and branches with a soft floor made of ferns. There was no furniture except for the beds and a small table in the corner that was constructed of what appeared to be fallen branches.

That evening, Galen made an amazing stew from root vegetables given to him by the elves, and they all talked for several hours. Samsire flew in to say good-night but he did not stay for long, since he was finding the Heart to be an unwelcoming place for an alorath. Sleep came quickly to Matt, who was exhausted from his ordeal in the river and the emotional stress of meeting the elves.

He awoke early the next morning, just as the light began to squeeze through the branches of the forest, and he found he was alone in the hut. He yawned, rolled out of bed, and rummaged around in his bag until he found a clean tunic. He slipped it over his head and washed his face with cold water in a wooden bowl on the floor.

Reluctantly, he placed the black bag that held the Fire Stone around his neck, and pulled aside the thin fabric that covered the doorway. Emmon and Arden were walking toward him dressed in fresh clothes and looking more relaxed than he had ever seen them.

"Come on," Emmon said. "We'll show you around."

Matt buckled his knives around his waist as a precaution, and followed his friends down the ramp. Elves moved around serenely, taking no notice of the three teenagers. Many were entering the city from the tunnel of trees that they had come through yesterday, all bearing bows and full quivers.

"Those are scouts," Emmon said. "They have the largest training center in the Heart since it is such an important craft."

"How many crafts are there?" Matt asked craning his neck to look around the upper level of the city.

Arden shrugged. "Too many. Anything can be made into a craft. Only the major ones have training centers, though."

"The nine important crafts are diplomacy, magic, scouts, scribes, guards, architects, smiths, creature trainers, and healers," Emmon explained.

"What's the difference between a scout and a guard?"

Emmon smiled. "Guards are basically the foot soldiers of Amaldan. Scouts are the most skilled warriors. They have to be much quicker and smarter than the guards, and they need to have perfected their abilities."

"So basically, you're the best," Matt said.

"Basically," Emmon grinned, and Arden shoved him, laughing.

They led Matt all through the city, pointing out landmarks and certain elves that were particularly talented or had unusual crafts. Matt was happy listening to their eager ramblings

"What's that?" he asked as they approached an open clearing in the trees.

"This is the scout's training center. We learn everything here, archery, magic, self-reflection," Emmon answered.

There were several different sections of the field where elves were practicing different fighting skills. There was an archery range and fighting dummies, as well as an area where elves appeared to be meditating.

Matt noticed a slightly older looking elf with shoulder-length brown hair and thoughtful eyes adjusting another elf's bow arm and watching over the archery range with authority.

"How old is that elf?" Matt asked curiously. "He doesn't look older than twenty, but he's teaching all of the scouts."

Emmon followed his gaze and laughed. "He really is ninety-two."

Matt laughed, remembering that Emmon had jokingly claimed that he was ninety-two when they first met.

"Funny you should pick him out," Arden said flatly. "That's my grandfather, Counselor Lan."

"Come on, Arden. You'll have to see him eventually," Emmon said, pulling her forward.

Matt followed them as they tromped across the fields. Counselor Lan did not notice them at first, but when he caught sight of Emmon pulling Arden across the field, he began walking toward them.

Lan was taller than Matt had realized and his face, though free of wrinkles, gave the impression of years of memories. He stopped a few feet from them, and they all stared at each other in silence for a moment.

"You have returned at last, Emmon, as have you, my granddaughter," Lan said without emotion. "And you must be Matthias, the bearer of the Fire Stone."

"Yes, sir, I am."

Matt squirmed under the elf's keen gaze, and finally looked down at his hands, waiting until the probing eyes moved away from him. Lan stared at Emmon and Arden with such intensity that Matt was amazed they did not retreat into the shelter of the trees.

"I am disappointed with you, Emmon," Lan finally said.

Emmon held his teacher's gaze, but Matt saw his jaw clench as Lan continued to speak.

"You should have known better than to let Arden accompany you on your quest. It was unwise of you to allow her to accompany you. You were assigned a dangerous task. I am disappointed in your judgment."

"I am sorry, master," Emmon said. "I-"

Lan cut him off and turned to Arden. "The fault does not belong to you alone though, Emmon. Granddaughter, I am more disappointed with you than I have ever been before. What possessed you to join Emmon on this dangerous quest? It was foolish beyond measure. The dangers were vast."

Arden was defiant as their brown eyes met. "I wouldn't have it any other way! I don't regret going!"

Counselor Lan glared at her. "You are fourteen now, Arden! It is time for you to be assigned a craft. You cannot spend your life running around looking for trouble."

They stared at each other, the anger between them palpable. Matt glanced uncomfortably at Emmon. After a few moments, they both seemed to relent, and Lan turned to Matt abruptly.

"Would you like to see the training fields, Matthias?"

"That would be…great, sir," Matt stammered.

Lan nodded and set off across the field. Matt, Emmon, and Arden followed, struggling to keep up with the elf's long stride.

"As you can see," Lan said. "Scouts must be experts in archery, and they must know how to use it in all types of combat. Of course, other forms of combat are also taught. Over to the left is where the scouts practice magic."

"What type of magic?" Matt asked, suddenly very interested.

Lan looked at him curiously. "Elven magic. Our magic is one form of elemental magic. It is the magic of the earth. Nature's rules control our lives, and through earth magic, we can control nature. It is the great bond between elves and nature."

"The magic of the earth includes abilities such as camouflage or disguise. Scouts must always be able to hide themselves and blend into their surroundings. We teach the scout candidates how to develop their natural gifts."

Matt was already amazed at how the elves seemed to disappear into the surrounding trees. He wondered what else they could do with the power of the earth. Earth magic was the only elemental power that he could not achieve with one of the Stones of the Elements. Matt would need to learn how to use it. Lucian had learned magic from the elves, so maybe Matt could too.

"Can you teach me how to use earth magic?" Matt asked.

At first, Counselor Lan looked annoyed, but after studying Matt for a moment, he said, "It is not your time yet, Matthias."

Matt wanted to protest, but he stopped himself. It was important that he not appear rude and impatient. He knew that if he had any hope of defeating Malik, he needed to master all four elements, the earth included, but it was also important that he not anger those who could teach him that skill.

Matt reluctantly focused his thoughts back on the scouts, marveling at the rigorous training and their innate abilities. He began to realize how talented Emmon was that he had been chosen to train as a scout at such a young age, and then complete his training in only two years.

When they reached the end of the field, Lan turned to Matt. "You are welcome to visit and train if you wish, though I doubt you could keep up with the scouts."

Emmon looked at Matt and rolled his eyes, but said nothing.

"I am not finished with you, Arden," Lan said as they turned to leave. "We must talk. And, Emmon, although you have officially completed your training, I expect you to report to me tomorrow morning."

Arden did not respond, but Emmon bowed his head respectfully. Counselor Lan nodded politely at Matt and returned to the training fields. Arden's eyes shot daggers at Lan's departing back.

"He doesn't seem that bad," Matt said to her, and she turned the daggers on him.

Matt and Emmon laughed, and even Arden could not resist smiling.

"Come on, Matt," Emmon said. "We'll show you around some more."

Matt followed his two friends, listening to them banter back and forth as Emmon teased Arden playfully and she quickly retorted. Although Lord Balor's words still bothered him, and he was uneasy about his destiny, Matt felt the peace of Amaldan calm him, until a harsh voice called out to them.

"Emmon!"

"Great," Emmon muttered under his breath.

They turned to see a tall elf with closely-cropped brown hair and intense green eyes rapidly approaching them. Matt looked at Emmon, wondering who this was, but his expression was impossible to read.

"Come here, Emmon," the elf said brusquely.

Emmon's jaw clenched as he turned apologetically to Matt and Arden. "That's my father, Matt. I have to go." He started to walk toward the elf, and then added, "I'm really sorry," before following miserably after his father.

Arden watched him go. "Whenever I'm feeling sorry for myself because my grandfather is difficult, I think about Emmon's father and I feel pretty lucky."

"What about Emmon's mother?" Matt asked.

"She's a master at the diplomacy center. They both put a lot of pressure on Emmon to be perfect. Thank goodness he was assigned to be a scout when he was only thirteen. I'm pretty happy I was able to assist with that," she said, grinning broadly.

Matt smiled, but he felt a knot form in his stomach as he was reminded of his own unfortunate father and mother, or at least the two people who he had thought were his parents, and their continual cruelty toward him. Absently, he rubbed the tender, elevated scar on his side from the stab wound he'd received from Kerwin, the man he had grown up thinking was his father, but was really Malik's right hand man. He could still vividly recall Kerwin's murderous expression as he stabbed him.

"It's all right," Arden said, as if sensing Matt's feelings. "Emmon's used to it. He avoids them most of the time. And his father's really harsh and unemotional, but he's not evil. Come on. Let's go find something to eat."

"All right," Matt replied, following her. "But, first, I want to find out where Sam is."

He pulled Sam's shimmering blue and green feather from his pocket, and squeezed it, scanning the treetops, as it grew warm in his hand. He waited for a moment until he could see Samsire diving through the trees. The alorath landed heavily nearby, and a flock of birds lurched into the sky.

"Where have you been, Sam?"

The alorath grinned. "It's a big forest, Matt, which means there's an abundant supply of food."

Several elves stopped to examine Samsire, suspicion and curiosity on their faces.

"Hmm. Aloraths are supposed to be the most magical and powerful of creatures. I don't see anything special about this one," one pale elf said.

Sam turned his large head to face the elf, and then, with mischief in his eyes, he rubbed his feet together to create a small jet of flame that circled around the elf in a whirling, flaming ring.

The elf gasped, his face alarmed.

"Look again, you may be missing something," Sam said smugly to the elf, and then turned to Matt and Arden, still grinning. "Personally, I don't see what's so special about these elves. I'll meet up with you later, Matt. I want to see what's so fascinating about these rude creatures"

The alorath leapt into the air, flying dangerously close to the elves' heads. Matt struggled to suppress a laugh as the elf grew even paler.

"Temperamental creature," the elf grumbled as he stepped over the fading ring of fire with exaggerated dignity and hurried away.

Arden giggled as she led Matt to a large hut situated above the ground between several trees. There they found a table full of food, fruit, nuts, fresh meat, and drinks made from spices and fruit. When they had finished eating, they returned to the hut where they had slept, sitting on the high balcony with their legs dangling over the edge, while they watched Sam fly in and out of the Heart.

Sam appeared to be enjoying both the attention from the elves. Matt watched the elves, amused by the differences in their attitudes toward Sam. Some were in awe of him, and others were exceedingly unimpressed, though Matt felt like those elves might be jealous of Sam's status as one of the most magical creatures in the land.

One elf with long silver hair, her face crinkled with age, straightened her frail, crooked body to see Sam flying back and forth. When she lifted her face to watch, her green eyes suddenly locked on Matt's face. She stared at him with a strange expression of shock and disbelief. Matt looked at her curiously, and she quickly averted her eyes, but she glanced at Matt repeatedly during the next few minutes.

"Do you know who that is?" Matt asked Arden, looking down at the elf.

She shrugged. "I have no idea. Why?"

"She's staring at me," Matt said, puzzled by the strange mixture of sadness and amazement that he saw in the old elf's eyes.

"That's strange. I don't think I've ever seen her before," Arden said, getting to her feet. "I should probably go see if anyone needs me. Someone always seems to have an odd job for me. Do you want to come with me?"

CHAPTER FOUR

Matt decided to look for Lucian and Galen instead, and he found Lucian walking along one of the ramps on the way back into their hut.

"Ahh, Matthias, I was just searching for you," Lucian said. "How are you enjoying Amaldan?"

"It's amazing," Matt replied enthusiastically.

"I agree. Every time I return, I feel that there is no place in Mundaria that equals the beauty of this forest," Lucian said in agreement. "A good deal different than the underground cavern of Gremonte, isn't it? But that city is a wonder of its own.

"I believe that Alem would like it here. He was afraid that the elves would not take kindly to his presence since elves and dwarves are not fond of each other, but I think the elves would have welcomed him. Of course, Alem is also very comfortable in Gremonte, since it was originally a dwarven city."

Many weeks ago, when they were sure that Matt was out of danger from the knife wound, Lucian and Alem had gone to Gremonte to meet with Chief Golson about Gremonte's defenses after the attack on the underground city. Matt's old teacher Alem had remained in Gremonte with the promise to see them soon.

"Matthias," Lucian said, his gray eyes twinkling, "I assume you wish to continue your lessons in magic?"

Matt's heart skipped a beat. Ever since he had found the Fire Stone, he had wanted to learn how to use it, and he wanted to learn more about using his other magical abilities, as well. He nodded, trying not to look too eager for fear that Lucian would change his mind.

"Good," Lucian replied. "Follow me, then."

Matt followed Lucian across the ramps that connected the various buildings of the city. They weaved through clusters of huts and the web of ramps. They did not stop until they reached a large complex of huts interconnected by narrow walkways.

"What is this?" Matt asked.

"This is the elves' training center for magic. The huts are specially designed to accommodate various types of magic."

They passed a number of elves, many of whom nodded respectfully at Lucian, but scowled at Matt. Matt fell back behind Lucian. His discomfort subsided only once they were inside a hut, tucked into the farthest corner of the training center. The hut contained only two chairs and a small, low ledge protruding from the wall. The walls were lined with thick, lush vines, and the floor was coated in moss.

Lucian looked around the room in satisfaction and sat down in the chair. He waited for Matt to speak, as if sensing that something was bothering him.

Matt hesitated, but then said, "Lucian, why do the elves seem to hate me."

"Hate is a strong word, Matthias. It is not that the elves hate you, rather, it is the opposite. They admire your skill, but they are jealous, especially that you possess the Fire Stone."

"You've told me that before," Matt said slowly. "But what does that have to do with anything? Is it just because they want the power of the Stones themselves?"

"Yes and no. Obviously, for magical beings like the elves, the magic of the Stones of the Elements is desirable. But there is another reason. You see, Matthias, the elves of Amaldan have been searching for the Stones for quite some time. They have always prided themselves on their ability to know the general whereabouts of the Stones. That is how Emmon knew where to go when he was searching for the Fire Stone."

Lucian paused. Matt had an idea what Lucian might say next.

"There's a reason we came to Amaldan, isn't there?" Matt said.

Lucian smiled. "Yes, Matthias. There is a reason why we came to this forest. The elves can help us find the remaining Stones of the Elements. They have information that could be very useful to us."

"How do we find out?" Matt asked eagerly.

Lucian frowned slightly. "I have already asked the elves for their assistance, but they are reluctant to give it to you."

"Then how do I get it?" Matt exclaimed.

"Patience, Matthias," Lucian said. "I think, perhaps, you must show them that you are worthy of their help by earning their respect."

Matt had more questions, but Lucian held his hand to stop him.

"That's enough talking for now. We have work to do. The elves have prepared this room specifically for our purposes. The walls and floor are fireproof so that we can experiment in any way we wish," Lucian explained. "Your magical career has taken a new turn. Now that you have the Fire Stone, your training will be different."

"In what way?" Matt asked before he could stop himself.

"Patience," Lucian scolded gently. "I will explain if you will give me the chance. I have no doubt that Kerwin has already reported to his master, Malik, that you have the Fire Stone. I would also guess that they have realized that you are the One told of in the Prophecy of the Elements. We can assume that the Commander of Shadows will be searching for you and the Fire Stone. Do you remember what I told you about how I first recognized your magical power?"

Matt nodded. "You said that I had an aura surrounding me that marked me as someone with magical abilities."

"Exactly, but although I am trained in recognizing auras, I could only see yours in times of peril. Once you began your magical training, however, it began to glow around you constantly. Your aura is very bright, and now, with the Fire Stone, it glows like the sun to anyone who is experienced in detecting auras. It would be very easy for Malik, or any of his minions, to track you down with magic."

"Is there anything I can do about it?" Matt asked, feeling panic rise in his chest.

"Yes," Lucian answered. "That is what I will teach you, beginning today. First, you must learn to detect an aura around someone else. It is a sight invocation, similar to the revealing invocation that I taught you in Hightop. I have unmasked my own aura so that you can see it. Now, clear your mind and listen to what you must do."

Matt stood up and closed his eyes as he always did when he wielded magic. He forced all thoughts from his head and breathed deeply. He quickly felt the pleasant tingling in his fingers that occurred whenever he focused on the magical part of himself.

"The sight invocation is rather simple, but it may be difficult for you to accomplish at first. It requires you to open your senses to everything magical around you. Feel the magic flow within you and imagine it forcing away the blindness that clouds your senses. Focus your mind. Let your magic fuel you. Then, say or think 'sight' and open your eyes."

Matt sighed, wondering how he was supposed to do what Lucian asked, but he knew complaining would get him nowhere. He had no idea where to start, but remembered Lucian's most frequently repeated advice: focus.

He focused on the tingling in his fingers and felt it spread like warm liquid up his arms and into his chest. It spread through his entire body, until he felt like he had woken up for the first time, like his entire body was alive. He savored the feeling for a moment and then murmured the word 'sight', concentrating all of his newfound magical energy on the concept of the word rather than the word itself.

Matt opened his eyes and stepped back in surprise. Lucian was surrounded by a bright haze of white light. His aura. Matt gasped and blinked several times, but his focus began to weaken and the haze disappeared.

"Well done," Lucian said approvingly. "If you practice daily, you will soon be able to maintain the sight without even thinking about it and release it only when you wish to. You will also not have to use the actual word to start it.

"Now you must focus on recognizing your own aura so that I can teach you how to mask it. Try it again, this time attempt to maintain the sight for longer."

Matt nodded and focused once more on the tingling sensation. He tried to get it to spread through his body like it had before, but failed.

"Focus, Matt."

Matt tried again, and this time he let the magic flow on its own instead of trying to force it. He felt the same energized feeling he had felt before. He opened his eyes and stared at the shimmering haze surrounding his teacher.

"Excellent. Now look down at yourself."

Matt looked down at his hands and arms, and he was surprised to see that they were glowing with the same light that surrounded Lucian. He looked down at his legs and saw that he was completely surrounded in the white light. He gasped again and Lucian chuckled.

"Now that you are aware of your aura, you can see that it is very obvious. Do you understand now why it so important for you to learn to mask it?"

"How?" Matt asked, still concentrating on maintaining the sight.

"Draw it in. A bit like sucking water into your mouth, but without using your mouth. Focus on the light flowing back into you," Lucian instructed.

Matt looked back at his hands and focused on the strange white light. Experimentally, he breathed in deeply until his lungs were too full of air to take in anymore air.

"I hope you aren't planning to breathe in your aura, because it won't work!" Lucian laughed. "Let's try it another way. Try to draw upon your magic the way you did when you achieved the sight, but then focus on calling your magic into yourself."

Matt sighed, struggling to hold onto the sight invocation and call in his aura at the same time. He cleared his mind of all thoughts and tuned his senses toward the magic surrounding him. Slowly, he began to pull it in, and he could see the light around him diminish to shimmering specks until it had disappeared altogether. He felt no different, but his aura was no longer shining.

"Well done, Matthias!" Lucian exclaimed. "With a little practice you should be able to keep it masked constantly, with the occasional adjustment, unless you lose control. For instance, if you were to become unconscious your mask would fall, but during natural sleep it will stay hidden. Very well done, Matthias. Excellent, in fact!"

"Thanks," Matt said, happy to receive some of Lucian's rare praise.

"Practice both the sight invocation and masking your aura every day. Eventually you will be able to maintain both without concentrating at all."

"I will," Matt said, pushing in the chair. "Thank you, Lucian."

Matt began to walk toward the door, but Lucian's voice stopped him. "Where are you going, Matthias? We are not done yet."

Matt was surprised. In every magic lesson they had had before, they had only practiced or learned only one invocation.

"There is something else that you must learn. Something that cannot wait much longer," Lucian said seriously.

Matt sat down facing his teacher. They sat in silence for a moment.

"I have let you live the past few weeks in peace, but now you must begin to learn of the power of the Fire Stone. If you wish, we can postpone it for a bit longer-"

"I don't want to wait," Matt interrupted.

Matt felt an urgent need to know how to use the Fire Stone. It was a constant presence in his thoughts.

Lucian nodded. "I think that is a wise choice, but I do not wish for you to start today when you are travel weary."

Matt tried not to show his disappointment. "So, what are we going to do, then?"

"I thought you could begin by learning a little about the Fire Stone and the other Stones of the Elements," Lucian replied, smiling. "Do you have any questions you would like to ask me?"

"What can the Stones of the Elements do? I mean, what is their power?" Matt said eagerly.

"Many things, Matthias," Lucian replied. "Obviously the Fire Stone gives its bearer the ability to control fire, meaning that you can create fire, manipulate it, multiply it, and suppress it. Wizards have speculated that it might even be possible to harness just its heat and use it for many tasks."

"The other two stones have similar powers. The Water Stone is the strangest of all of the three stones. It allows control over water, like the Fire Stone controls fire, but the Water Stone also has the power to heal. We do already know a relatively weak non-elemental invocation that we commonly use for healing, but the Water Stone is said to be able to heal any ailment. This ability makes it very valuable. Of course, there are some things that are not meant to be healed.

"The Wind Stone harnesses the power of the wind, since it is the element of air. Anything to do with air, such as clouds, wind, cold, storms, and things of that nature, can be controlled with the Wind Stone."

Matt marveled at the enormity of the power the Stones of the Elements. The Water Stone was particularly amazing to him. The ability to heal was very appealing, but seemed impossible. He decided that the Wind Stone was probably the most powerful of the stones, since air was the most prominent element, except perhaps the power of the earth.

"You have more questions?"

"If the Stones control three of the elements, what controls the power of the earth?"

"Earth is the most mysterious element," Lucian said. "Those who have the power of the earth, such as the elves, can make things grow, and they can communicate with the animals of the woodland, but they cannot control all aspects of the plants and animals. And there is no stone for this magical power, so we must hope that you can learn it from the elves."

"I asked Counselor Lan today if he could teach me, and he said that it wasn't my time."

Lucian nodded. "Then we must honor that. For now we must focus on honing your innate magical abilities, and then we will work on controlling the Fire Stone."

"Lucian," Matt said uncertainly. "What if…I can't control it?"

The wizard smiled at him, but Matt saw a flicker of worry in his eyes. "We shall see, Matthias. Do not underestimate your abilities. You have considerable talent in magic."

Matt nodded and stood to leave, but stopped before he reached the door.

"I have one more question. What happens when the stones merge? When Malik merged the Stones, even though it damaged him, he gained complete control over all of the elements, didn't he? So, when he disappeared after the Battle of the Endless Fields, did he still have the Stones' power, and if he didn't, how could he have survived? Pryor and Cosgrove found the stones separate and intact, right? How did that happen? And what happened to the Immortality Scroll?"

"You ask the questions that haunt us all. We do not know how Malik lives or what power he has. I do believe, however, that Malik has been able to keep the power that he once possessed over the elements, but for some reason he needs the stones again.

"As for the Immortality Scroll, we do not know its location, but I have no doubt Malik searches for it, as well. Though he still has power, possessing the Stones of the Elements and the Immortality Scroll are his only hope for total and complete domination. But you must not dwell on this, Matthias. For now you must focus only on your training."

Lucian patted him on the shoulder. As they walked together through the magic center, Matt was intensely aware of the warmth of the Fire Stone against his chest. He left Lucian to look for Emmon and Arden, and he found Arden dragging a bulging sack of flour down one of the ramps. She looked up at him as he approached and pushed her hair off her forehead.

"They want me to drag these sacks down to one of the lower huts," she said disgustedly. "Why not store them down there in the first place? I should know better than to offer help here. They always find meaningless chores for me to do."

Matt grinned at her. "Here, I'll help you."

They both grabbed a corner of the sack and dragged it down the ramp. Even between the two of them, it was very heavy and Matt wondered how Arden had managed on her own.

"Over there," Arden told him, tilting her head toward a sad-looking, empty hut near where the trees grew thicker.

They managed to drag the bag into the small storehouse and Arden sat down on the bag.

"Phew. Thank goodness there weren't more of these. Thanks for the help, Matt. Say, how was the lesson with Lucian?"

Matt pulled her to her feet. "I learned some new invocations, but mainly we just talked."

Arden looked at him questioningly, but before he could explain, he was interrupted by Emmon's voice.

"Matt, Arden!"

The elf was walking toward them, his quiver and bow slung over his shoulder. It looked like his father had finally let him go.

"I've been looking for you," Emmon said. "Counselor Lan wants me-"

He stopped short, his expression puzzled.

"Emmon?" Matt asked curiously.

"Behind you!"

Matt looked over his shoulder and saw a dark shape emerging from the trees behind him.

Immediately, he recognized the black spindly limbs and vacant white eyes, fear shot through him.

A garan!

It lunged at them, claws outstretched. Matt acted instinctively, yelling as he grabbed Arden and pulled her to the ground. Something whistled overhead and just before the creature could reach them, it fell dead with Emmon's arrow embedded in its chest.

"Did it touch you?" Emmon said, rushing to Matt and Arden.

"No," Matt gasped. "Thanks to you."

He and Arden climbed to their feet, staring wordlessly at the garan. He could barely process what he was seeing. The forest was heavily protected by elven magic. It was impossible to believe that one of Malik's mindless, evil creatures could get past those protections.

"How did it get by the scouts? And why didn't the disguise invocations surrounding the Heart keep it out?" Arden whispered.

Emmon shook his head, and Matt suddenly felt very vulnerable. Emmon looked into the trees where the garan had emerged, but there was no sign of others.

"Arden," Matt said. "Can you go find Lucian or Galen? Hurry! Emmon, will you help me lift it out of here?"

Emmon had already unfastened his cloak and, wrinkling his nose in disgust, was beginning to slide it under the garan's body. Matt grabbed the other end of the cloak and they both grunted as they lifted the creature off the ground and lugged its limp form back toward the trees.

Matt glanced around again, but they were still alone. Emmon pulled the arrow from the garan's body and then paced back and forth between the trees until Arden appeared with Lucian.

"Matthias!" he exclaimed. "What happened?"

Matt gestured to the dead garan. "It came out of nowhere. Emmon killed it as it tried to attack us."

"Did you see where it came from?"

They all shook their heads and Lucian frowned. "Perhaps it followed us yesterday into the Heart, waiting until it could attack."

"Followed us?" Matt echoed.

Lucian nodded gravely. "Yes, Matthias. It is rare for garans to wander freely. They are controlled by Malik, so, though we cannot be sure, it is very likely that he sent this garan to follow you. You must realize that, although you dealt Malik a terrible blow by recovering the Fire Stone, he remains very powerful and more vengeful than ever."

Matt slowly digested Lucian's words. "Then I shouldn't have come here," he finally said. "If I'm putting everyone in danger…"

"Don't even think that way," Emmon said. "This wasn't your fault. We're all Malik's enemies, now. And it's like Lucian said, we really don't know why the garan came here or where it came from."

"An excellent point, Emmon," Lucian remarked. "You were meant to come to Amaldan, Matthias. We must regroup, you must learn, and then we will strike. But for now, the most important thing you can do is to keep your eyes open. Always be aware of your surroundings.

He bent down and touched the flattened grass around the garan.

"I will check amongst the trees for others. It is rare that a garan travels alone. I guarantee there are others nearby."

"We should go with you then, Lucian," said Matt. "You can't go alone if there's a chance that there are others. What if there are a lot of them? You wouldn't stand a chance on your own."

Lucian smiled. "I appreciate your concern, Matthias, but you cannot venture into the woods right now. If a garan captured you and took you to Malik, we would be at a serious disadvantage. I will not venture too far in, for now, but I must be sure that there is not an entire army of garans lurking just beyond our sight, ready to grab you if the opportunity arises.

"Do not speak of this incident to the elves, yet," he said. "Perhaps Samsire will help us dispose of the body."

He gave Matt's shoulder a reassuring squeeze before walking away. Matt watched him go, knowing that Lucian felt the same sense of foreboding that was creeping through him. His enemy was

following him and waiting to strike. Whether Matt liked it or not, he could not ignore that Malik was still out there waiting for him, and even a place as magical and safe as Amaldan was not truly safe.

CHAPTER FIVE

Galen crouched to the ground, running his hands through the dirt. He glanced around him, watching the cluster of bushes that surrounded him for any movement. Looking ahead, he could just barely make out the thin, almost imperceptible trail that wound through the broad tree trunks.

"Just a little farther," he said quietly to himself.

Straightening, he repositioned his scabbard over his back and set off down the trail. The undergrowth of the forest had nearly concealed it after all these years, but Galen scarcely needed the path to guide him. He had traveled this trail so many times that the way was permanently ingrained in his memory.

The days when he used to walk through the forest seemed so long ago, yet also so near. Times were different then, he supposed, but even now, five years later, he was uncomfortable in the Heart with the elves. The forest was the only place that offered him solace.

He continued to walk until the trees abruptly gave way to a small clearing encircled by a thick web of foliage. Careful not to leave a trail behind, Galen wove between the trees and stepped into the clearing. He surveyed it slowly.

It looked exactly the same as he had last left it. The overgrown grasses were as high as his knees, and were no longer flattened from the hours he had spent here when he and his instructors would sneak away for his training. Sighing in remembrance, Galen sat down on the worn tree stump in the middle of the clearing and leaned back to look up at the sky. The sun was setting, but he could still feel its heat. This was one of the few places in the forest where the sun shone freely upon the forest floor, unimpeded by trees.

He placed his hands on the back of the stump as he leaned backward, and his fingers fell into a narrow crevice. He reached inside, his fingers closing around something soft and bendable. He laughed as he pulled it out.

"Still here, are you?" he said quietly.

It was a small leather journal filled with notes, drawings, and every thought that drifted had through his teenage brain. Writing in it was the only thing that had kept him sane while he lived in Amaldan.

He began to flip through the pages, but froze when he heard a sudden rustle in the forest behind him. Jumping to his feet, he silently pulled his sword from the scabbard while whirling around to face the sound.

The clearing was empty, but Galen could hear something moving in the trees. It was large, larger than a man. He scanned the trees, searching for signs of life or movement. He could not see it, but he could sense it and hear it. It moved stealthily, like a cat.

"Samsire?" Galen called. "Are you skulking about in there?"

But his voice startled whatever it was, and there was more rustling as the creature moved away from the clearing and then, silence. Galen did not lower his sword. Something felt distinctly unnatural to him. He had enough elf magic in his veins, and he had spent enough time in the forest, to be able to sense when something was out of place here, and something was not right.

There was another rustle in the underbrush behind him, but this sound was different, and closer. Galen turned around, his sword still outstretched, ready to strike.

"Lady Can," he said quietly, lowering his sword and bowing respectfully, and trying not to look as bewildered as he felt.

"Galen."

The Lady of Amaldan stood in the center of the small clearing, her long, brown hair windblown. She smiled at him, but her face was ashen.

"May I ask why you are out here alone, my lady?" Galen asked as politely as he could, but unable to conceal his surprise. "There is something moving in the forest, and I am certain that it's not a bunny. I don't think it's safe for you to be out here alone."

She smiled at him. "I was merely walking through the forest, my friend. I often do. I think that you, especially, should understand this need, Galen. The forest is my true home, and while the Heart is sheltered in the forest's boughs, I sometimes find that I need to venture further into the forest's natural state."

Galen did not speak, watching her carefully.

She continued softly. "There is something you should know, Galen. Things are changing. In the forest and in the rest of Mundaria. I can feel it. The forest and I are one. Something has begun that we elves cannot mend."

Her eyes were piercing. "Do not forget my words, Galen. It is important that you do not forget where you come from. You will always be an elf."

She sadly looked around at the trees and then back at Galen one last time before she turned and walked back toward the edge of the clearing.

"Lady Can?" Galen said, his voice hoarse with emotion.

"I am proud that you are an elf, Galen. You have the best qualities of elves and humans. You will play an important role in the salvation of both races."

She smiled and disappeared into the trees. Galen stared at the spot where she had disappeared, trying to process what had happened. He lowered his sword and sat back down on the tree stump.

But unease prickled at the back of his mind.

The arrival of Lady Can moments after the creature had fled back into the forest must be connected somehow. She and the forest were one, as she had just reminded him. Did her mysterious appearance and disappearance mean that she had sensed something unnatural in the trees of Amaldan? And her kind words, what of those?

Galen looked up at the darkening sky. He would sleep here tonight, but he knew that he would not sleep easily.

* * *

Matt was startled into wakefulness by a loud clattering outside his hut. He sat upright in his bed and automatically created a shield around himself without speaking. He looked around nervously, but his small room was quiet. Breathing a sigh of relief, he dissolved his shield and rolled out of bed, slipping on his leather boots.

It had been a week since they had arrived in Amaldan, and Matt had been training diligently with Lucian. He could now perform many non-elemental invocations with ease and many without speaking. The training had also made him more alert to sounds and movement because Lucian constantly attacked him with unannounced shocks of magical energy, flying rocks, and other attack invocations.

But still Matt had not tried to use the Fire Stone.

He crept to the cloth covered doorway and poked his head outside. It was very early in the morning, and only the palest light penetrated the thick foliage of the trees. The air had a slight chill, but promised a pleasant day ahead. Nothing seemed to be stirring except for the gentle chirping of crickets on the forest floor.

The morning was beautiful, and Matt did not want to return to his bed. He stepped onto the balcony and leaned on the twisted railing. The forest was magical, just as Lucian had said it was, and it inspired tranquility in even the fiercest of individuals.

He leaned further over the railing, looking at the earth below, and suddenly he was hit from behind. He lurched forward, nearly tumbling from the balcony. Gripping the railing for support, he pulled himself to his feet. Fleetingly, he wished he had his sword, but he quickly flung up a shield invocation.

What had hit him?

He looked around in confusion and fear, his thoughts racing wildly through his head. Hesitantly, he stood up, ready to retreat into the safety of his hut for his sword, if needed. He moved backward toward the hut, his eyes darting around. He had not gone three steps when a deep voice behind him spoke.

"Having fun, Matt?"

Matt smiled, recognizing Sam's voice His fear faded as he saw Sam balanced precariously between two enormous trees behind the hut. Matt took a deep breath to slow his heartbeat.

"Sam! You could have killed me!" Matt cried.

The alorath grinned toothily. "I would have caught you before you hit the ground."

"What are you doing here? Did you run out of things to eat in the forest?" Matt said sarcastically.

"Come on now, Matt. It's the summer solstice. The day of your birth. You've lived sixteen years now."

Matt had not even thought about it being the day of his birth. He only ever remembered it because it was on the first day of summer, but he had been so busy with his training that he hadn't even thought about the solstice this year.

His day of birth had never been acknowledged when he lived in Sunfield. The summer solstice may not even be his birth day, he thought suddenly, but merely the day he had been found by Kerwin and Vivona after Lucian placed him on their doorstep. Matt shook off the thought. What mattered was that he was sixteen, almost a man.

"Yeah, I guess I am," Matt said quietly to Sam.

Samsire flew to Matt and Matt climbed onto his back. The alorath glided through the trees, soaring above the sleeping elven city, and Matt marveled at the craftsmanship of the buildings and the way they blended in with the forest.

Sam flew for a long time and for many miles, and they drank in the landscape, periodically sharing stories from the past week. When they returned to the Heart, the city had awakened, and the elves looked up in awe as Sam glided back to Matt's hut and gently deposited him on the balcony.

"Have a happy day, my friend," Sam said, beaming.

"Thanks, Sam," Matt called as the alorath flapped quietly away.

As he turned back to his hut, he saw Lucian walking toward him dressed in more elaborate clothes than usual. His short speckled hair was neatly combed back and his gray eyes sparkled in the morning light.

"Ah, good morning, Matthias!" Lucian smiled. "And a delightful day of your birth to you!"

"Thanks, Lucian," Matt grinned back, gesturing to the wizard's clothing. "What's the occasion?"

"Every year the elves celebrate the summer solstice," Lucian replied. "It is quite an impressive festival with an abundance of magical displays. Since Lady Can and Lord Balor will attend, I must look presentable, instead of just a ragged, old traveler, as I usually do."

Matt laughed and walked alongside Lucian. They wandered down to the forest floor where the elves were bustling about preparing for the festivities.

"When does the festival start?" Matt asked.

"Not until the sun is at its highest point in the sky. It will take place in the center of the Heart," Lucian answered. "Now if you'll excuse me, Matthias, I must go to the magic training area to prepare for the festival. I wish you a very joyful day of your birth, my young friend."

The wizard patted him on the shoulder and walked off in the direction of the Magic Center. Matt wandered slowly around the city, watching the elves hurry past. Several scouts strode by purposefully toward the scout barracks. Matt followed them, thinking that Emmon might be at the training area.

He would most like to see Galen, who always made him laugh, but Galen had disappeared the day after they had arrived almost a week ago, and whenever Matt questioned Lucian about his whereabouts, Lucian would say that Galen must be the one tell him that when he returned.

There were few people at the training center, except for a few older elves who were peppering targets with arrows.

"Hey, Matt!"

Emmon was walking toward him, green eyes shining. The elf's golden hair was wildly unruly as usual, but he was dressed in clean brown pants and a green and gold tunic.

"Hey, Emmon," Matt said. "What are you doing?"

"Looking for you!" Emmon replied. "Today is the day we celebrate your birth, Matt. You are sixteen! Come on, let's go find Arden."

"Don't you have other things to do?" Matt asked.

He had not seen Emmon much during the past week, since the elf was continually reviewing his scout training with his teacher, Counselor Lan, or accompanying his father. He had only been free to spend time with Matt in the evenings after his training was done.

Emmon shook his head. "No, not on festival day. Lan won't make me train today, and I haven't had to go on patrol or anything since I got back. Besides, Lan is probably doing something to get ready for the festival."

They walked back up into the trees, following the elaborate paths and ramps until Emmon stopped in front of a small hut. It was built differently than the other huts, with two levels, and doorways on all sides. Emmon had only just lifted his hand to knock on the wall beside an open doorway when Arden stuck her head out from around the corner.

"Hi, boys!" she said cheerfully. "It's the day to celebrate your birth, Matt!"

They spent the remainder of the morning watching the preparations for the ceremony. Several elves scolded them for not participating, but they took no notice, feasting happily on the fresh fruit and sweet berries lay out on the tables, instead.

"What exactly happens at the festival?" Matt asked Emmon later as they leaned against the outside wall of his hut with their legs dangling from the balcony.

"It's different every year. Usually there are magical displays, both elven and non-elemental, and music and dancing, and heaps of food. It is a celebration of life and prosperity."

"And of the forest and the earth," Arden added.

Matt nodded happily. There were no impressions to make, no special customs. Only a celebration to enjoy. As Matt sat with Emmon and Arden and the minutes passed, though, he began to think about what Lucian had told him. They had not come here merely to enjoy themselves. They had come to Amaldan to gather information about the other two Stones of the Elements. The elves had the information, but Matt had no idea how to get it.

"Are you all right, Matt?" Arden asked him. "You're quiet."

"I was just thinking about something Lucian told me. There's a reason we came to Amaldan," he said and then told them that Lucian had asked for the information about the Stones on Matt's behalf, but that the elves had not been willing to share it with Matt.

Emmon and Arden listened carefully, and they were both frowning by the time Matt finished.

"They won't give you the information?" Emmon exclaimed. "I'll go over to the Library of Scrolls and see if they have the information there. I'll tell them that I need it in order to continue my quest. Maybe they'll give it to me, and I can pass it on to you."

"Thanks, Emmon," Matt said gratefully. "That would be great."

Emmon grinned confidently and climbed to his feet. Matt and Arden watched him walk through the trees deeper into the Heart. They waited hopefully, expecting him to emerge from the trees triumphant and smiling. When Emmon did return, however, he was scowling and empty-handed.

"What happened?" Arden asked him in surprise. "They wouldn't give it to you?"

Emmon shook his head. "I asked for information about the Stones of the Elements, and the librarians were happy to help me at first. But when I asked where the Water Stone and the Wind Stone might be, they stopped talking, and they practically pushed me out of the library."

He shook his head and looked apologetically at Matt. "I'm sorry, Matt. I think they know something, but they knew that I would give it to you."

"Don't worry about," Matt told him. "Thanks for trying."

Emmon looked angry as he sat back down. Matt tried to spend the rest of the morning thinking about the festival, but locating the Stones was never far from his mind. How would he find them without the elves' help?

* * *

Matt stood by Emmon and Arden as the sun shimmered high in the sky. They stood in the center of the Heart with the other elves, forming a large circle. Matt scanned the crowd for Lucian, but could not see him anywhere.

"Matt, it's beginning," Arden said.

Nine elves moved into the center of the circle, Counselor Lan and Emmon's father, Drathen, were among them, as well as an elf he had often seen at the magic training center. Matt guessed that they were the nine counselors of Amaldan. A hush fell upon the crowd as Lord Balor and Lady Can followed their advisors into the circle.

Lord Balor's sharp chin was high in the air, his thick black hair covering his ears. He looked proud and healthy, but Lady Can did not. Dark shadows circled her calm eyes, her pale skin was sallow, and her expression strained. Her eyes sadly scanned the crowd, and she seemed to be leaning on Balor for support.

The elves did not appear to notice that their Lady was in distress, though, as they looked admiringly upon their leaders and waited patiently for Lord Balor to address the crowd.

"It is the one day of the year, as it has been for all the years our race has walked this earth, that we celebrate the life provided to us so generously by the earth. Summer has arrived. It is a time of joyous prosperity among the boughs of our trees. My friends, let us celebrate!"

The elves erupted in cheers and a group of elves carried in dozens of hollowed-out tree trunks into the circle, each filled to the brim with a variety of meat, cheese, bread, and fruit. They all migrated toward the food, conversing among themselves. Matt followed his friends and stood with them for about an hour, while they talked and laughed with the other elves.

Eventually, though, Matt moved to the outskirts of the crowd. He couldn't help feeling awkward standing with the elves. They seemed so much more sophisticated and formal than he, and Lucian's warning about impressing them still lingered in his mind.

He contented himself with watching them, until he felt someone looking at him. The old, silver-haired elf who had stared at him that first morning in Amaldan, was studying him intently. Their eyes locked, but this time she did not turn away. She smiled at Matt and beckoned for him to join her.

He stepped forward curiously, but collided violently with an elf rushing in the opposite direction. He fell against a group of elves walking by him, and he lost sight of the silver-haired elf. When he regained his footing, he could not find her.

He gave up looking for her when he noticed that the elves were all moving back into a circle. Several elves were in the center again, Lucian among them. The magic counselor stepped forward and placed his hands on the forest floor. After a moment, Matt could see a green stem push through the dirt and rapidly grow into a small sapling. The elf stepped back and another elf took his place. This elf expanded the sapling until a small apple dangled from a branch.

"Do you understand what they are doing?" a voice whispered in his ear.

Matt turned his head, and saw a familiar face grinning down at him. "Galen! Where have you been?" Matt whispered.

Galen held a finger to his lips. "I will tell you later. Watch."

There were now numerous apples hanging from the branches, some green, some red.

"What are they doing?"

Galen's eyes glowed. "I've seen it many times before. It's a tradition. One elf starts it and each adds to it until it is a completed work of art."

The next elf added a whole new level to the tree, with red leaves and pears rather than apples. The magic continued as each elf within the circle added their own magical touch until the tree was now over twelve feet high, and the top level had the needles and pinecones of a spruce.

Finally, Lucian stepped forward and placed both hands on the trunk of the tree. He closed his eyes and breathed deeply. A sudden explosion of white light blinded Matt, and he moved his hand over his eyes until the light subsided to a glow.

The tree glimmered with a pale, white light, and its fruit looked silver under the darkening sky. Each leaf was illuminated, revealing the intricate veins on their surface. The elves were bathed in the silver radiance. An elf began to clap and others joined in until the crowd erupted in tumultuous applause. The tree's creators each bowed in turn, and then they all disappeared into the crowd.

"It will remain there until the winter solstice," Galen told Matt. "Then it will be removed and the elves will wait for the next summer solstice to create a new work of art."

"It's beautiful," Matt said admiringly.

Galen laughed. "It is rather spectacular. Come on, let's get something to eat."

Emmon and Arden joined them and the celebration continued late into the night. Matt was never able to ask Galen where he had been for the past week, and though he continued to look for the remainder of the night, he never saw the silver-haired woman again.

CHAPTER SIX

Matt awoke the next morning to the sound of persistent knocking on the wood door frame of his hut. He groggily pulled himself from bed. His ears were still ringing from the noise of the celebration the night before. He was surprised to see Galen waiting impatiently at his door with a pack slung over his shoulder.

"Let's go down to the guard training center, Matt. Bring your sword," Galen grinned.

Matt grabbed an apple and strapped Doubtslayer to his belt. Though he was tired, he was eager to be with Galen again and was very interested in learning about where he had been since they arrived in Amaldan.

"Where have you been this week, Galen?" Matt asked as they walked.

"I've been wandering in the forest," Galen replied vaguely, taking a sharp right.

Matt hurried to keep up with Galen's long strides. He had not been in this part of the Heart before and he looked curiously at the unfamiliar structures.

"The guard training center's just up ahead," Galen said. "I thought we could practice a bit."

"Sure," Matt replied. "What were you doing in the forest?"

They had reached a large complex of huts similar to the scout's training area. Galen walked to the field and dropped his pack on the ground.

"I was looking around. It's a habit that I've had ever since I first started spying on Malik." Galen said.

He pulled out his sword belt, and fastened on his sword, Lightningstrike.

"Ready?" Galen grinned and Matt nodded.

They drew their swords, knocked them against each other once, and then stepped away from each other. Matt fell into his ready stance, holding Doubtslayer in his right hand. It felt familiar, yet strange in his hand, like a lost friend. Galen's eyes gleamed and Matt felt energy surge through his veins. He shifted his weight from foot to foot, prepared for Galen's assault.

Galen swung his sword down in a graceful arc and Matt watched it move in slow motion, reacting with a swift block. The motions felt awkward at first, but Matt's instincts took over quickly. Soon, their movements grew more rapid, and they began to mirror each other's strikes. Matt reacted automatically, letting his body move without thinking. He fell into a natural rhythm, and he soon felt sweat dripping down the back of his neck.

Eventually, his limbs grew heavy, and it became a struggle to block Galen's blows. The mergling showed no sign of tiring though, and he continued to attack Matt with rapid strikes. A particularly hard blow struck Matt's sword on the tip and Matt lost his balance as he tried to evade it, wobbling forward. Galen saw the opportunity and gently pushed Matt's left arm. Off balance, Matt tumbled backward, landing hard on the ground, his sword flying from his hand. Galen stood over him and placed his sword against Matt's chest.

"Yield," he said with a grin.

"I yield," Matt replied, sighing in exhaustion.

Galen sheathed his sword and pulled Matt to his feet. They rested against one of the towering trees on the border of the arena. They sat in silence, watching a few guards wander through the training center.

"So, now are you going to tell me what you've been doing?" Matt asked.

Galen smiled. "Nothing can satisfy your curiosity except the whole story, can it?" He sighed. "I was exploring my homeland and reveling in old memories. My mother was an elf. I was born here in Amaldan."

"I didn't know," Matt answered quietly.

"Lucian knows, but few others do, except the Amaldan elves, of course," Galen said.

Silence settled between them.

Finally, Matt spoke. "What was it like growing up here?"

"The first five or so years were good years, though I don't remember much. I do have one powerful memory from early childhood, though. My earliest memory, in fact. My mother, Karina, was a prominent member of the diplomacy craft and was always very busy. I never knew who my father was. Another elf took care of me when my mother was busy. Her name was Maia. She was younger than my mother and had a newborn child.

"One day I was with Maia and we were confronted by a counselor and a group of guards. They began to yell at her. I don't really remember what they were saying, but eventually they pointed at me and said that my kind, a mergling, was an embarrassment to elven dignity. They told Maia that she was an outcast also since she was my caregiver."

Galen stared off into the distance, his eyes clouded. "I started to protest. I was too young to understand that I should be silent, and the guards grew angry, eventually lunging at me. Maia protected me, yelling angrily at them, and then carrying me and her baby back to my home, crying softly. The next day, she was gone. My mother later told me that she had been banished to Southwood Forest. I didn't understand why she was banished, but I realized for the first time that merglings were looked down upon in elven society.

"There was one other mergling who lived in Amaldan when I was growing up. His name was Banen, and he was several years older than me. When I was ten, he beat an elf in a magic contest, since merglings are often particularly gifted at magic. There was a lot of unrest that followed, since Banen gloated about his victory, and the elves hated to be inferior to a mergling. Banen disappeared three days later. He was chased out of Amaldan or he ran away to escape the ridicule and disdain.

"During the next six years, I grew bitter and angry about the elves and their attitude of superiority, but I kept my head down and complained only to my mother.

"At fourteen, I was denied the right to learn a craft, though several instructors from the guard and scout centers noticed my abilities and secretly tried to train me. The training was sporadic and poorly executed, but it gave me a basic knowledge of fighting and survival skills.

"When I was sixteen, a group of elves complained that I was an unnecessary burden to the forest. There was much debate, and my mother began to fall apart. She was a strong elf, but she had lived a long life and she had become sickly. The combined stress of her illness and the years' long battle to protect me had made her physically and emotionally frail.

"She and I decided that I should leave Amaldan. I did not want to leave her there in failing health, but she begged me to leave, giving me supplies and wishing me luck. I left before the elves could decide on my future, not knowing where I was going or what would become of my mother.

"I thought that the meager training that I had received from the instructors who had risked so much to train me would be enough to allow me to fend for myself. I had not traveled long when I encountered an expert swordsman, the one who gave me this scar."

He touched the jagged scar that ran down the right side of his face.

"Weak and in pain, I blindly staggered on until I stumbled upon an empty camp. There was food and blankets, and I ate frantically, until I fell asleep in exhaustion and pain. When I woke up, Lucian was leaning over me, tending to my wounds. I panicked, not understanding that he had saved my life, and I attacked him with magic. He quickly shielded and explained that he meant no harm.

Eventually, I grew to trust Lucian, and he agreed to train me in the art of magic. I also began to perfect my fighting skills.

"That was five years ago. I traveled and trained with Lucian for more than a year, and we have stayed in constant contact since. After many discussions with Lucian, I decided to devote myself to finding Malik and ending his vile ambitions. I have been spying on him ever since."

Matt let Galen's words sink in for several minutes. He had not known that the elves harbored such dislike toward merglings. The amazing thing was that Galen did not seem to be bitter about it anymore. He was always so optimistically cheerful.

"I'm sorry about your mother, Galen."

Galen smiled. "It's not all that bad. I made it sound dramatic. Mostly, I had an enjoyable life when I lived in Amaldan. I wasn't sure what it would be like to come back, though. My mother died shortly after I left, and I feared that without her presence, I would not be welcome here. Luckily, Lady Can has never had ill feelings about merglings, and the corrupt council that ruled then has since been dismissed.

"Still, I don't feel completely comfortable being in the Heart. I prefer the forest, it's less trouble. Speaking of trouble, I heard that you have already had some. I can't believe there was a garan in Amaldan. Elven magic has always been too powerful for Malik's evil magic. But that may be changing. I sense that the forest is in danger. I think Lady Can feels it, too. "

Matt nodded grimly, and Galen scowled. "Keep your eyes open, Matt. Try not to think about it all the time, but keep your eyes open.

Focus on your training and on learning as much as you can from the elves. They will make valuable allies if you ever have need of them in the future."

Galen quizzed Matt about his training with Lucian and they talked about different fighting techniques. Eventually, elves began to train in the fields around them, and Galen got to his feet and shouldered his pack.

"You fought well today, Matt, especially considering you haven't trained in more than a month. When you are traveling, you might want to consider wearing your sword on your back. It will give you more mobility and is much more comfortable than leaving it to bang at your hip," Galen suggested as they walked out of the training center. "Practice as much as you can. I have a feeling that you're going to need all the skills you can learn."

Matt nodded. "I will. You're not leaving again already, are you?"

"I'll be nearby in the forest. Before I go, though, I have something for you."

He rummaged in his pack for a moment, before withdrawing a small leather journal.

"I know it's late, but it's to honor your day of birth. It's just a little something that could help you on your quest. It always helps me to keep a journal of my travels."

Matt took the small book, rubbing the soft leather with his thumbs. Its pages smelled like the trees and it felt comforting.

"Thanks, Galen," Matt said, smiling.

Galen patted him on the shoulder. "I'm here whenever you need me, Matt. And be careful who you trust."

* * *

Matt went to the magic complex for his lesson with Lucian. He ducked inside the small hut on the outskirts of the magic complex and found Lucian sitting in the small chair, his stubbly chin resting against his chest as he dozed.

"Hello Matthias," he said with his eyes still closed. "Forgive me. I had a rather late night last night. Come. Sit."

Matt grinned and sat cross-legged on the mossy floor. Lucian straightened up, but did not speak as he studied Matt closely.

Matt took advantage of the wizard's silence to sneak in a question. "What was that magic that you did at the festival last night, Lucian?"

Lucian smiled. "That was Light magic. Do you know why I am called the Wizard of Light?"

Matt shook his head.

"When I was a young wizard, I realized that Malik's magic was surrounded by darkness, both figuratively and literally. I also realized that darkness had an opposite. Light.

"Light magic can be used to light a dark cavern, and Dark magic can suck away the light, but they can both also affect the goodness or evilness in someone's heart. Although it is much more difficult to achieve, manipulating goodness and evil can be a very useful and powerful tool. I have spent a great deal of time learning to control Light magic."

He waved his hand. "But that is another lesson entirely." He paused. "It is time, Matthias. Take out the Fire Stone, please."

Matt stood, feeling dread and excitement, and he removed the Fire Stone from the pouch. He held it reverently for a moment, cradling it in his palms. The semi-transparent black stone wavered for a moment before steadying. Orange, red, and yellow streaks danced like flames at its center. He placed it on the table, and they both stared at it, entranced. Who knew what mysteries were contained in this stone?

"The Stones of the Elements are powerful objects that are not to be tampered with. As you learn how to harness the Fire Stone's energy, you must be careful that you are wielding it, instead of it wielding you. This power should never be taken lightly. Do you understand?"

Matt nodded, his mouth dry. "I understand."

"Good. Then we shall begin. My knowledge of fire magic is somewhat limited, but I understand the basic steps of summoning the power that is trapped within the Fire Stone. My understanding of your connection with the Fire Stone is that you must draw the power out, and then let that power mix with the magic that flows within you. Combined with your own magic, you should be able to manipulate fire to your will. First, though, you must summon the power of fire."

Matt waited for Lucian to continue, but the wizard remained silent.

"How?" Matt finally asked.

Lucian stared at the Fire Stone. "I am not certain, but I have an idea. Take the Fire Stone in your hands."

Matt did so, immediately feeling the surge of energy. "Now, clear your mind and focus. Feel the power of fire within the stone. Let it flow through you, but do not release yourself to it. Rather, let it release itself to you. You have used the magic of fire before, and I believe the stone will react to you again. Let yourself be filled with its magic."

Matt breathed in deeply and closed his eyes. He could feel the warmth of the Fire Stone creeping through his fingers. He focused on the tingle of power, willing it, inviting it, to join with him. It was like trying to coax a nervous, reluctant horse to allow a rider on its back.

After a few seconds had passed, Matt reached within himself to find his own magic as he had done many times before, and he let his magic spread through his body and down his arms. As it reached his fingers, it touched the animated magic of the Fire Stone, and he felt his own magic being pushed back up his arm. Determinedly, he forced his magic gently back into his fingers until it collided with the Fire Stone again.

This time, Matt felt a peculiar sensation. Slowly, he felt the warmth of the fire magic blend with his own. It felt as if his own magic was a handful of snow that had been plunged into a vat of boiling water. The two forces swirled angrily in a wild dance, and Matt's eyes flew open in panic.

He was quickly losing control as the sensation spread through his arms like a powerful whirlpool of magic and raw swirling energy. He struggled to stop it before it consumed him completely. Lucian's words went through his mind: *You must be careful that you are wielding it, instead of it wielding* you. He was remotely aware that he was jerking and twitching uncontrollably.

"Matthias! Don't lose yourself!"

Lucian's voice seemed to awaken Matt's overwhelmed senses. He could suddenly feel the sweat dripping down the back of his neck and smell the damp earthiness of the moss beneath his feet. The magic still raged within him, but he was aware of his surroundings again.

He called on all of his remaining strength to force the magic back. He felt his knees buckling beneath his body. The Fire Stone slipped from his limp fingers, and he fell in a heap beside it.

Abruptly, the magic that had been thundering through his body disappeared. Strong hands were gripping his arms, and Matt looked up at Lucian. His eyes were filled with concern.

"Matthias! Are you all right? Answer me!"

"I'm…I'm fine," Matt croaked.

Lucian helped him into a sitting position and leaned him against the wall. His tunic was wet from perspiration and his legs felt like jelly.

"Are you sure you're all right?"

Matt nodded weakly, closing his eyes as he gathered his thoughts.

"I tried to join my magic with the Fire Stone, but I couldn't control the Fire Stone's magic. It was too powerful," Matt said numbly.

Lucian paced around the hut for a few moments and then turned back to Matt.

"Perhaps you were too aggressive in reaching for the Fire Stone's magic. Perhaps I was too aggressive in teaching you now. Alem thought it was too soon..."

Matt thought of Alem scowling grumpily while scolding Lucian, and Matt chuckled. Strength was returning to his limbs, and his breathing was slower and more even.

"Can you stand?"

"I'm fine, Lucian. Really, I am. Just a little unsteady," he said, allowing Lucian to help him up.

Matt looked down at the Fire Stone lying innocently on the mossy floor. It looked like nothing more than an ordinary black rock. Reluctantly, he reached down and let his fingers close around the oval stone, and quickly returned it to the pouch around his neck.

"I am sorry, Matthias. I should have known better."

Matt shook his head. "I thought I was ready, too. It was much more powerful than I thought it would be."

"I think we are finished for the day," Lucian said. "You should not be concerned with what happened. It will go better next time."

"Right," Matt said, doubtfully. "Thanks, Lucian."

Matt left the hut before Lucian could see how disappointed he was. He needed to learn to use elemental magic, and he needed to learn it soon, or he would not survive. Apprehension and dread engulfed him, sending a shiver down his spine. The forest around him felt ominous. The garan that had tried to attack him at the outskirts of Amaldan was only the beginning of the evil that Malik would unleash. It would not be long before Malik came after Matt again, and Matt had to be ready to face him.

CHAPTER SEVEN

Several days later, Matt walked across the Heart, savoring the cool evening air. Maybe he would find Sam and they could fly to the top of the highest tree to see the sunset. He ignored the usual stares from the elves. He was becoming used to their attitude toward him now, and he accepted it, knowing that he couldn't change the way they felt about him. He reached into his pocket for Samsire's feather, but a shout stopped him.

"Fire!"

Mat whirled around, searching for the source of the shout. A lone elf sprinted out of the trees to Matt's right, sweat dripping down his face. He nearly collided with Matt.

"Fire!" he exclaimed again as he spotted Matt. "There's a fire in the trees! And there are elves in there!"

"Where?" Matt demanded.

The elf struggled to catch his breath. "Two hundred yards into the trees!"

Matt stared into the forest, hesitating for a fraction of a second, and then he turned to the frantic elf.

"Listen," he told the elf urgently. "You have to find whoever you can and tell them what's happening. Bring help."

Before the elf had a chance to respond, Matt was running into the trees. He squeezed Sam's feather, feeling it grow hot in his hand. He kept running, pushing aside branches and bushes. Less than thirty seconds later, he heard the sound of Sam plunging through the trees. He landed heavily beside Matt.

"What's going on, Matt?"

Matt scrambled onto Sam's back.

"There's a fire and elves trapped in there! Hurry and fly, Sam!"

The alorath pumped his massive wings and rose into the air. They streaked above the trees, and Matt immediately saw the plume of dark smoke coming from the trees just ahead. Samsire dove toward the trees and within seconds they were back on the forest floor. A blast of heat hit Matt in the face.

A tight grove of trees was engulfed in flames. Matt climbed down from Sam's back and stared at the fire, paralyzed. He could only think of the last time he had faced a raging fire, when Kerwin had burned down the barn and the rest of the village of Sunfield.

A strangled scream erupted from the grove, bringing Matt to his senses. An elf was scrambling out of the undergrowth on her hands and knees as she tried to get past a burning log. Matt lunged forward and grabbed her arms, pulling her across the ground. There was a crack above them, and Matt watched in fear as a burning branch began to snap, splintering away from the trunk.

"Come on!" he yelled.

Yanking again on her arms, he managed to pull her farther away from the fire. The branch above them snapped away from the tree and fell to the ground only inches behind them. Matt shielded his face from the flying sparks and propelled them both forward.

"Are you all right?" he asked.

She shook her head, terrified. "Nigel is still in there!"

Matt turned back. The fire was spreading, and the flames in the center were higher than ever. Matt had to get in there and rescue the other elf, but how? His hand closed instinctively on the pouch around his neck. He had not tried to use the Fire Stone again since he had failed to control it, but maybe this time, he could. Maybe instinct would take over the way it had when Kerwin was about to kill Emmon.

Matt's heart was pounding. He knew that if he did not act quickly, someone could die. He also might make the fire worse. It suddenly seemed too risky. But before he could even try to think of another solution, Samsire was there. He grabbed Matt's tunic in his mouth and tossed him onto his back.

The alorath rose into the air. As soon as they were above the fire, Sam blew enormous quantities of water onto the raging flames. Parts of the fire were extinguished, but flames still rose upward with the billowing smoke. Samsire did not pause, turning back around to attack it again.

Matt clung to Sam's neck as he wove through the trees. The fire was snaking up the trunks, devouring bark and leaves as is it traveled. Heat and sparks hit Matt's face, and he pressed himself closer to Sam's neck. The alorath continued to send a stream of water down on the fire, but it was difficult to contain. Matt continued to scan the forest floor, squinting against the smoke. After several minutes of futile searching, Matt finally spotted movement in the flames.

"There, Sam!" he yelled.

Sam dove toward the spot, but a wave of fire erupted from the undergrowth. Sam reared back and flew above it. The area where the elf was cowering was too small for the alorath to land. Matt was afraid, but he knew what he had to do.

"Try and put out some of the flames near him, Sam!" Matt yelled in his ear. "I need to go down there."

Before Samsire could protest, Matt slid down Sam's front leg, dangling for a moment before dropping down. He fell through the scorching hot air and landed on the small patch of land between the trees that was still untouched by the fire. Smoke and ash flew into his face and he pulled up his tunic to cover his mouth and nose.

He crouched beside the elf who was coughing violently. Matt looked around frantically. Walls of fire blocked their way on three sides. Their only possible exit was past the enormous burning log to Matt's left, but there was no way over or under it.

He reached down and pulled the barely conscious elf to his feet. As Matt dragged drag the elf toward the log, Matt felt a splash of water and hot steam against his face as Samsire tried to extinguish the fire around them. But it was moving too quickly. He extended his hands toward the burning log. Only two days ago Lucian had taught him a blasting invocation, a burst of magic strong enough to knock someone off their feet. Matt hoped that it would work now.

He tried to calm his pounding heart and focus on the magic. He reached out with his hand, feeling the intense heat of the flames. Matt yelled and unleashed his magic, but the log only quivered.

Panic surged through him as he tried again, but still the log barely moved. They were trapped. Fearfully, Matt looked for another exit, but there was none. Desperate, he reached for the Fire Stone around his neck and felt a surge of power enter his body. He extended his hand again and, with a yell of triumph, blasted the log into a burning tree in a shower of sparks.

Still supporting the elf, Matt staggered through the opening, forcing his way through the flames, until finally they reached untouched trees and entered the cool air of the living forest.

Sucking clean air into his lungs, Matt let the elf slide to the ground and collapsed against a tree so he could catch his breath. Samsire landed beside them and looked at Matt in concern.

"You okay?"

Matt nodded, but before he could respond, he was nearly knocked over by the female elf he had rescued earlier.

"Nigel!" she squealed. Nigel coughed loudly, leaned against her as she turned to Matt. "You saved him?"

"What's going on here?" a voice boomed behind them.

Counselor Drathen, Emmon's father, was walking toward them as a cluster of elves threw buckets of water at the still spreading flames. Matt climbed to his feet, feeling suddenly anxious. He had only met Drathen once, but he knew the Drathen disliked him. Emmon was suddenly standing beside Matt.

"Counselor Drathen, sir!" the girl said. "The...the fire." She glanced at Matt. "Matt and the alorath saved our lives!"

"Saved you?" Drathen said, his eyebrows elevated. "Are you sure he did not have any other involvement in this fire?"

Drathen's eyes locked on Matt's chest, but it took Matt a moment to realize that he was suggesting that Matt had used the Fire Stone to start the fire. Anger began to churn in his stomach, but before he could respond, Emmon stepped forward.

"Father, Matt wouldn't have-"

"Silence, Emmon!" Drathen snapped. "I did not ask for your opinion. I just want the facts from your friend here."

"Excuse me, sir." The other elf from the fire had climbed to his feet, still coughing violently. "He didn't start the fire, sir," he said between fits of coughing. "I did."

"You did?" Drathen repeated skeptically.

"Yes, sir," the boy said seriously, bowing his head. "I just wanted to show Maria some of the wood skills I had learned in guard training. I'm sorry."

Drathen looked at him seriously. "Very well. We will discuss this later, Nigel." He turned to Matt, looking at him appraisingly. "I suppose you deserve our gratitude, Matthias, for saving these witless elves from their own devices."

Matt stared at him wordlessly, unsure of what to say. Drathen turned away from him and walked back to the group of elves fighting the fire. The boy and girl looked at each other miserably, thanked Matt, and walked off. Emmon watched them go, and then turned to Matt with a bemused expression.

"Uh...how did you end up in the middle of this one, Matt?" he said, his eyes twinkling.

Matt grinned. "You know me, Emmon. I try to stay away from trouble, but it just has a way of finding me."

Sam snorted and Matt glared at him. "Why don't you go help them put out the fire, Sam?"

The alorath gave him a toothy grin and lumbered off to help. Elves ran back and forth to the fire with containers of water, while Sam assisted from above, until it was finally extinguished.

News traveled quickly through the Heart, and soon there was not a single elf who had not heard about the fire and about Matt and Sam's exploits. Matt noticed a considerable change in their attitude toward him. Most of the elves had abandoned their customary scowls and several even smiled at him.

The next morning, Matt felt distinctly cheerful as he followed Emmon and Arden across the wooden bridges and ramps to the scout training center. He had not had the chance to practice his swordsmanship or any other skills since he had sparred with Galen a week ago.

He and Lucian had been practicing magic every day, though, and Matt almost felt comfortable enough to fight with only magic. He could create shields without thinking, move objects through the air, send small shocks of energy short distances, and easily reveal hidden objects. He rarely had to use the words to create an invocation anymore.

When the teenagers reached the training area, it was swarming with elves practicing archery, fighting techniques, and magic. Matt and Emmon went to the archery range while Arden went to the sharpening wheel to sharpen her two long, dagger-like knives.

Emmon nodded at two elves who were shooting at targets. They were older than Emmon, but they return his nod respectfully. Emmon grabbed a handful of arrows, and methodically fired them into the center of his target. Matt fitted an arrow into his bow, pulled his string back, took aim at the target in front of him, and let go of the string. The arrow streaked toward the target and buried itself just to the right of the center. Matt frowned. He was nowhere near as accurate as the elves.

"Not bad, Matt," Emmon said, suppressing a grin. "But you might want to work on your speed."

Matt turned to look at Emmon's target. Two dozen arrows were already clustered at its center. Matt shook his head and muttered under his breath, and Emmon smiled while he refilled his quiver. After Matt had worked through three dozen arrows, and Emmon had given him a few pointers, Matt was much happier with his aim and his speed, but he knew that he would never be able to match Emmon's skill.

They unstrung their bows and found Arden systematically shredding a dummy to pieces with her knives. Her long brown hair was pulled back into a braid, but stray pieces stuck to her forehead as sweat trickled down her face.

"Feel like sparring, anyone?" Arden asked.

"I'm game," Matt said.

They moved to an open area of the field, and Matt and Arden pulled on leather jerkins. Matt fastened his sword to his belt and tightened the straps. Emmon sat cross-legged on the grass as Arden drew her knives and Matt pulled Doubtslayer from the scabbard.

"Don't worry, Matt," Arden said, grinning. "My knives aren't all that sharp."

"I wasn't planning on finding out," Matt replied as they moved in a circle, facing each other.

Arden smiled dangerously and flew at Matt, her knives spinning in front her. Matt leapt back and shoved his sword in between them, stopping her momentum. She stepped back, and Matt took advantage of his longer weapon by swinging his sword in a graceful arc over her head and down toward her side.

Arden jumped nimbly out of the way, bringing one of her curved knives against Matt's sword in defense. He quickly responded with a swipe at her opposite side. Arden parried and swung at his left shoulder. Matt caught her blade with his sword and pushed her away. They circled each other for a moment, both their weapons at the ready.

Arden swung one of her knives at Matt's side, and Matt parried it easily, but he did not take into account the other knife which she brought streaking toward him. He dived awkwardly to the ground. Arden stood above him, but before she could call for surrender, he rolled to his other side and pushed himself nimbly to his feet.

Arden did not have time to react before he swung his sword at her right side. Hastily, she held up a knife, barely blocking his attack. Matt sensed his advantage and pushed harder, hammering Arden with a series of quick attacks. She parried each of them, but did not have the chance to retaliate.

Their bout moved further away from Emmon, intruding upon the scouts practicing against the sparring dummies. Matt noticed only the adrenaline rushing through his veins and the clanging of his sword against Arden's knives. They were both breathing heavily and sweat dripped down their faces.

Finally, Matt left too much space between attacks, and Arden took a rapid strike at his side. He jumped back as he parried, but barreled into a sparring dummy. Unable to regain his balance, he fell to the ground. Arden acted quickly this time and bent over him with her knives.

"Yield," she gasped.

Matt glanced at her feet and saw that they were far apart and close to his own.

"No," he replied.

Arden's smile faded to surprise as he looped his foot around her ankle, and pulled it toward him. She fell hard onto her back, and Matt rolled up onto his knees, knocking her knives out of her hands.

He held Doubtslayer in the air above her and said, "Yield."

Arden smiled and held up her palms in defeat. "I yield."

Matt let his arm drop to his side and smiled back at her. He glanced around and saw that a group of elves had gathered around them, and they were glaring at him. Emmon held out a hand to both of his friends and pulled them to their feet.

As he returned Doubtslayer to its scabbard, Matt nodded to the nearest elves and apologized for interrupting their practice. They looked at him coldly, and he quickly walked back to the empty part of the field where Lucian and Galen stood watching them.

"Well done, both of you," Galen said as they drew nearer. He was grinning broadly. "I saw a few tricky moves there."

Matt and Arden grinned back, and Matt said, "I don't think those elves liked it all that much."

Galen shot the elves a look that made them hastily turn back to the sparring dummies.

"So…what's going on?" Arden asked.

Lucian smiled. "I have good news. It appears that your heroics with the fire yesterday have caused the elves to have a change of heart, Matthias. They have consented to give us whatever information they have about the locations of the Stones of the Elements."

Matt felt his heart leap as Emmon made a whooping sound.

"I knew you'd get it, Matt!" Emmon beamed.

Lucian smiled sadly. "Given that, though, it is time for us to leave Amaldan. We will meet up with Alem in the city of Gremonte. I received a letter from him this morning saying that he thinks it would be wise for us to return there as soon as we can. Besides, we have imposed ourselves upon the elves for long enough."

Matt opened his mouth, but did not speak. He would miss Emmon and Arden fiercely, and he would miss Amaldan which he found both energizing and calming, with its abundant plant and animal life.

But he was also weary of the prideful attitudes of the elves. Emmon, Arden, and some of the younger elves were not arrogant, but many of the older elves did not hide their annoyance at Matt's presence, and, more importantly, Matt guessed, at his possession of the Fire Stone. He knew that the elves' dislike for him was only a fraction of what they exhibited toward Galen, but it was exhausting to be disliked for reasons that were out of his control.

"Did you wish to say something, Matthias?" Lucian said.

Matt shook his head. "No, you're right. I…I need to start searching for the next Stone. I've put it off for too long."

Lucian nodded approvingly. "I will assist you in any way I can, Matthias. We will leave two days from now."

As they turned to leave, Galen patted Matt on the shoulder. "As will I."

Matt turned to Emmon and Arden, feeling sad about leaving them behind.

Emmon was smiling and his quiet green eyes gleamed with excitement.

"I'm coming with you, Matt. I've vowed not to consider my quest complete until all of the Stones of the Elements are found. I've been waiting for a week for you to say you were leaving. I can't wait to get back into the real world again."

"Really?" Matt said.

Based on Emmon's reaction when they first arrived in Amaldan, Matt was sure that Emmon would not have wanted to leave his home again. Maybe he found his fellow elves' attitudes oppressive after journeying outside of the forest.

Arden was also grinning. "The sooner we get out of here, the better. I swear, if I hear Lan say another word about me getting assigned a craft, I might scream. I'll never be allowed to be a scout if I stay here, and even if I did, I'd have to train under Lan for two to four years. No thank you. I'd much rather trek across Mundaria with all of you. You're a lot more fun than cranky, old Gramps."

Matt and Emmon laughed at her crinkled up face, prompting more threatening glares from the nearby group of elves.

CHAPTER EIGHT

"Come on, Matt. Wake up!" Emmon said, shaking his shoulder vigorously.

Matt groaned and opened his eyes. Emmon and Rankin stood over him, both looking impatient.

"What?" he asked irritably. The sun had not even risen yet.

"Grab your cloak, weapons, and pack," Emmon answered. "We already have provisions, so hurry."

"Why?" Matt said, confused. "Lucian said we're not leaving until the day after tomorrow."

"Lady Can asked me to show you something in the northeastern area of the forest. It's a long walk and we have to be back by tomorrow evening. So hurry up!"

Matt grabbed his pack, bow, and sword, leaving his knives on the bed, and swung his pack onto his back. When he joined Emmon and Rankin outside, Emmon shoved a parcel of food into his arms. Matt stowed it in his pack, and followed them down the ramp to the forest floor.

"Come on," Emmon said tensely. "It'll take us a while to get there."

Matt did not reply, but wondered why Emmon was so edgy. Matt had never seen him act so irritable before. Obviously, he was bothered by whatever Lady Can had asked of him. Rankin was also very quiet, and he avoided making eye contact with Matt.

"Are you going to tell me where we're going?" Matt asked, as they passed the Gathering Hall and turned into the tunnel of trees that led out of the Heart.

"To the Great Tree of Amaldan."

Matt's stomach jumped in excitement. He had heard many stories from Emmon and Arden about the Great Tree. It was said to be where the elves got their magic and was, therefore, revered above all else.

"Do you know why?"

Emmon shook his head, and Matt noticed that he looked very worried.

"I wasn't given that information."

They walked in silence as they reached a wall of intertwining branches on the far edge of the Heart.

"The Tree is in the forest miles outside of the Heart, and only those familiar with earth magic are able to find it. If we begin our journey to the Tree here at the Heart, though, a path to the Tree will appear, and we won't get lost," Emmon explained.

Matt followed Emmon and Rankin through the archway and stepped into the wild Amaldan Forest. A narrow, almost imperceptible, trail snaked through the trees. It was slightly warmer in the trees than that it was in the Heart, but Matt still felt the chill of the early morning air. Rankin took the lead, walking purposefully, and Emmon walked next to Matt, his face strained.

After a few minutes of tense silent, Matt reached into his pocket and fingered Samsire's feather. He squeezed it firmly, calling Sam to him. Another minute passed and the alorath came swooping into view through the tops of the dense trees. Rankin stopped in his tracks as he caught sight of Samsire and his mouth twitched. Sam dove clumsily through the trees, breaking several branches and landing heavily.

"Hello," he said gruffly, attempting to regain his dignity after the less than graceful entrance.

Matt grinned at him. Rankin, who had grown pale, tentatively followed the others to Sam's side. Sam turned his head and snorted at the timid elf, and Rankin stopped in his tracks.

"Ignore him, Rankin. He won't hurt you," Matt laughed. "Cut it out, Sam."

"Where are you off to?" Sam rumbled.

"Emmon is taking me to the Great Tree on Lady Can's orders," Matt answered.

"Would you like me to fly you there?" Samsire said, trying to nose the broken branches out of his feathers and pretending not to notice the terrified look that Rankin gave Emmon.

"Thanks, for the offer, Sam, but we won't be able to find the Tree unless we follow this trail," Emmon said.

"I'll trail you from above then, if you'd like."

"That would be great. I feel like you should be close by, in case we need you," Matt said.

The alorath nodded, tousled Matt's hair with his nose, snorted again, and pumped back into the air. Matt, Emmon, and Rankin watched him go.

"How exactly did you make friends with that creature?" Rankin breathed.

Matt laughed. "I found him as a baby, and we've been friends ever since. He just pretends to be ferocious because he wants to get a reaction from you. He likes attention."

"That sounds a bit crazy, if you ask me," Rankin muttered.

"Well, you already knew I was crazy," Emmon said. "And now I've have some friends who are just as crazy as I am."

Matt and Emmon grinned at each other as Rankin shook his head in disbelief. Matt was relieved to see that Emmon had relaxed a little.

As they trekked through the forest, Matt found that Rankin was very practical and cautious, but also very agreeable. He asked Matt where he came from and about his travels, and soon they were all laughing. Matt learned that Emmon and Rankin were childhood friends, and that Rankin was apprenticed as a scout a year after Emmon.

They walked until their stomachs grumbled, and finally they threw down their packs and pulled out the food. Matt opened the package that Emmon had given him and munched hungrily on an apple.

"How much farther do we have to go, do you think?" Matt asked between bites.

Emmon looked around at the trees before answering. "A few hours maybe. We'll spend the night in the forest near the Tree and return to the Heart tomorrow."

Matt nodded and shoved a piece of bread into his mouth. They ate until their stomachs were full and the sun had passed the highest point in the sky.

"We should get going. It's getting late," Rankin said nervously, glancing up.

They continued their trek, their conversation eventually dwindling to silence. Matt followed the elves, hanging back slightly as he looked around the forest. The trees and undergrowth were not as green or lush as they had been closer to the Heart. Also, Matt noticed that there seemed to be a decrease in animal life. No squirrels, or even insects, wandered across their path. The air was cooler here, too.

Matt was about to point this out to Emmon and Rankin, when he plowed into Emmon's back

"What-," Matt started to say, but stopped when he saw them both standing motionless and open-mouthed, staring in horror at the forest before them.

The ground was black. Few leaves remained on the bushes, but those that did were dark and wilted. The trees were leafless, and a strange darkness crawled up their trunks like the fingers of a deadly disease. Their boughs were droopy and limp, as if the life had been sucked from them. The strange blackness infected every inch of the forest around them.

Emmon fell to his knees, his green eyes fixed on the scene. His voice was hoarse with emotion and barely audible when he spoke, at last.

"What has happened?"

Matt shook his head. They remained there, unmoving and unspeaking until the beating of Samsire's wings broke the silence. The alorath landed with a thump behind them, and he craned his neck forward.

"What is this?" he said, his deep voice echoing through the blackened boughs.

"I don't know," Matt whispered.

He stepped forward slowly and felt the chill of the air against his skin. He pulled his cloak around his shoulders as he carefully picked his way through the undergrowth. Rankin, Emmon, and Sam followed him in stunned silence. Matt looked around in disbelief. It was as if the forest had been poisoned.

What could cause something like this?

They walked for several minutes until they spotted an enormous tree standing alone in the charred landscape. Its trunk was old and weathered, but it was untouched by the blackness that infected the other trees and plants. Its boughs were strong and thick, and they stretched high with fleshy green leaves. The sight of the tree filled Matt with comfort.

"The Great Tree of Amaldan," Emmon breathed in relief.

They followed Emmon up the small hill to the Great Tree. Emmon approached it reverently, placing his head against its trunk and breathing deeply. Matt felt a sudden urge to reach out to the tree, too, and when he placed his palm on its trunk he felt a rush of power and energy flow through him as magic seeped into his hand.

"The tree's magic is repelling the darkness," he said aloud. "The darkness can't affect it."

Emmon was frowning. A large lower branch was missing, making the tree appear lopsided. A flat, mangled nub was all that was left of the great bough. Matt looked at the ground, and leaning down, ran his fingers over the heavy branch that had been hewn from the tree's trunk. Veins of blackness were visible along the fallen branch. Matt looked at the place where the bough had been broken. A spiral of blackness swirled through the flat surface, and several small streaks of darkness spread down into the trunk of the tree.

Matt tried to understand what this meant. He had never seen anything like it. What was this strange darkness that had killed the forest? He suddenly remembered something Lucian had told him.

"I think this is what Lucian meant by Dark magic," Matt said softly.

Emmon turned to face Matt, his fear obvious.

"Malik did this," he whispered. "He's poisoned the forest, and his Dark magic is infecting the Great Tree."

"I wonder if Lucian can fight this. He told me that even the most powerful magic can only hold back the darkness. That the only thing that can defeat darkness is light. Only Light magic can stop Dark magic."

"I don't think that Lucian can fix this, Matt," Sam said quietly. "Light magic can only combat a direct attack of Dark magic. It can counter a spell or strengthen a defense. It can be used to change the darkness that dwells in people's hearts, but this Dark magic is something entirely different. I don't think that even Light magic is powerful enough to remove this evil."

"But what do we do?" Rankin said, on the verge of tears.

Emmon shook his head. "I don't know. I don't know."

They made camp just outside the infected area. Samsire lay down nearby, and Matt, Emmon, and Rankin sat on their blankets, staring silently at each other. After a while, Rankin started a small fire and put ingredients in a pot for a stew. Matt and Emmon watched him mutely, each lost in their thoughts.

Matt's head ached. He had no idea how to save the forest, and he could only hope that Lucian would know what to do.

"What will happen if the Great Tree is overcome by the darkness?" Matt asked Emmon.

Emmon shifted uneasily. "I'm not sure. We believe that the Tree is the source of magic in the forest and also the source of the elves' magic. I don't know what will happen if it dies, but I do know that it will be devastating to the forest and to the elves."

"The stew is ready," Rankin said dully.

They ate unenthusiastically and Samsire disappeared into the forest to hunt. He returned no long after, burping loudly, and then settled against the trees. After the sun had disappeared and the stars twinkled above the treetops, they unfurled their bedrolls and said subdued good-nights.

Matt lay awake for many hours. Eventually he fell asleep, but he had fitful dreams of swirling dark clouds and a cruel voice slicing through the darkness. He awoke early in the morning and found that Emmon and Rankin were still sleeping. Sam was gone, most likely looking for breakfast.

Matt got to his feet and rummaged through his pack. His stomach grumbled hungrily, and he quietly ate a handful of nuts as he watched the pink sunlight begin to filter through the trees. Tomorrow he would be leaving Amaldan forest, and it was possible that the forest would die before he returned. The thought filled him with a deep sadness.

He heard a slight rustling in the trees behind him. As Matt turned something large collided with him, and he cried out as he fell. A huge, dark creature had pinned him to the ground, its teeth barred and its white eyes glazed.

A garan.

CHAPTER NINE

Matt struggled ferociously to push the garan off of him, yelling wildly, but it sank its sharp claws deep into his chest and shoulders. Matt screamed as blood spilled from the wounds. Blind anger and fear flowed through him, and his mind focused on the deranged creature standing over him.

Without thinking, Matt felt tingling in his fingers and a shock of magical energy shot into the garan. The garan loosened its grip in surprise and pain, and Matt felt its weight disappear from his chest as Emmon hit it in the head with a tree branch.

Emmon pulled Matt to his feet as the garan rolled over and pulled itself into a crouch. It growled threateningly and paced around them. Matt glanced down and saw Doubtslayer's hilt protruding from the top of his pack. If he just had an instant, he could grab it. He took a step sideways and reached for the sword. The garan lunged. Matt dove to the ground and the garan leapt over him.

Matt fumbled for his sword, struggling to free it from the scabbard. The garan had turned and was rushing toward him again. It was inches away, when Rankin shot an arrow into its foot. The garan shrieked and yanked out the arrow, then fell back into a crouch and lunged at Matt. Matt threw up a magical shield around himself and the garan fell off of it limply, but the shield was rushed and was easily broken. Matt freed his sword, but the garan was now attacking Emmon.

Emmon had managed to grab a knife and was slashing at the garan's muzzle. Undeterred, the creature swiped at Emmon's throat with its claws. Emmon nimbly avoided the strike and dove to the side. Matt ran to him, swinging his sword and cutting a deep slash along the garan's side. It shrieked and lunged at him, but Matt quickly stepped aside.

Instead of turning around to face them, the garan placed its weight on its front legs and swung its back legs at Matt and Emmon. Its sharp claws cut through their tunics, and they tumbled backward as they tried to avoid the deadly weapons.

As the garan moved to strike at them again, Rankin hurtled into its side. The garan wavered and fell, but quickly regained its footing, leaping at Rankin and grabbing his right leg with its teeth. Rankin screamed in pain and fell to the ground as the garan dragged him across the forest floor.

Matt and Emmon scrambled to their feet. Matt ran after the garan and stabbed it at the base of its neck. The piercing shriek was abruptly silenced as Emmon shot an arrow into its chest. It fell, dead, black blood spilling from its wounds, its mouth still clamped around Rankin's leg.

Rankin moaned in pain. Carefully, Emmon extracted the dead garan from his leg and used his knife to open Rankin's pant leg. Deep slashes and gouges lined Rankin's leg all the way up to his thigh, and a bone in his calf was obviously broken. Rankin fainted.

"Get my pack, Matt. And a straight, three-foot long branch," Emmon ordered urgently.

Matt tossed the pack, gritting his teeth as the wounds on his shoulders pulled open with the effort. He picked up a branch and broke it into the size Emmon had asked for. Emmon opened a small leather package full of herbs and ointments.

Matt watched queasily as Emmon poured water down Rankin's leg and applied a thick ointment along the deep slashes. Matt handed him a spare tunic, and Emmon ripped it up into thick bandages, which he wrapped tightly around Rankin's leg with the branch behind it to immobilize it.

The makeshift splint appeared to slow and then stop the bleeding. Rankin moaned, but remained unconscious. When he was finished, Emmon turned a pale face toward Matt and handed him the remains of the tunic.

"Sam will have to carry him back," Emmon said.

Matt nodded and shoved his hand into his pocket, squeezing Sam's feather. As they waited for Sam to return, Matt wiped his sword on the grass, and stowed it back in its scabbard. He strapped it to his back, and strung his bow in case he had need of it. Samsire swooped down into the trees.

"What happened?" the alorath asked, catching sight of Rankin.

"A garan," Matt explained gesturing to the prone body of the garan. "Obviously this darkness affects more than just the trees."

"Will you carry him, Sam?" Emmon asked the alorath.

The alorath nodded and lowered his wing so that they could hoist Rankin onto his back.

"I'm sorry, Sam, but we'll have to put a rope around you both since Rankin isn't conscious," Matt said.

"Don't worry about it. I don't suppose there will be room for the two of you then, will there?"

Emmon shook his head and wrapped the rope around Sam, careful to place it so that it wouldn't impede his wings. Rankin regained consciousness just as Emmon finished. Without a word, he gripped Sam's neck tightly, his face a ghastly white. Matt couldn't tell whether his injured leg or the idea of flying on Sam's back was more painful to Rankin.

"Hey, Matt," Sam said kindly, just before he leapt into the air. "I think you should have Emmon do something about those shoulders of yours, okay?"

Matt looked down at his blood-soaked tunic and nodded. "I'll be fine, Sam. Don't worry."

Emmon went to work on Matt's wounds and when he was finished, they set off toward the Heart in silence, carrying their swords. Matt was filled with terrible sense of foreboding.

* * *

Hours later, Matt and Emmon sat with Lucian and Galen.

"What can we do about this Dark magic?" Matt asked.

Lucian rubbed his stubbly chin, concern etched on his face.

"Well, I agree with Samsire that it won't be easy to stop. It has spread too far. I do not believe that Light magic can defeat it. No, something stronger is needed. We need something that heals. I've been thinking about this ever since you returned this afternoon, and I think that what we need is Water magic. Its healing powers could combat the darkness and purge the forest of this poison."

"Well, we don't necessarily need the Water Stone then, do we? Sam has Water magic."

Lucian shook his head. "The Water Stone is raw elemental power. Samsire's power is different. He can create water and control it, but he can't use it as a healing force. He may be able to heal some things eventually, once his abilities have been fully awakened. Even then, healing of this magnitude will probably be beyond his capacity.

"The Water Stone is our only hope. We must find it. I am hopeful that the information given to us by the elves will help us in that quest. We will go to Gremonte as planned, and we will confer with Alem before we set off on our journey."

Matt's heart plummeted. He did not have any idea where the Water Stone could be, and by the time they found it, most of the forest might be covered by the darkness, including the Great Tree.

Lucian looked at Matt kindly, as if he understood his fears.

"It will be some time still before the darkness taints the Great Tree. It could be, months, years even, until the Tree is irrevocably damaged. This is, above all else, a warning to us that Malik's power and reach are growing."

"Lady Can sent me on the quest for the Fire Stone because the Great Tree was in danger," Emmon said. "She knew about the darkness, and maybe she knew that I would find you, Matt, since you are the one who can wield the Stones of the Elements. She knew that Malik was poisoning the forest and that you are the only one who can stop him. That's why she wanted you to see the Great Tree today, Matt. Because she knows you are the one who can prevent its death."

They fell into silence, each lost in their own thoughts.

"Matt, did you think that garan was different than any garan you've ever seen?" Emmon finally said.

Matt nodded. "I was just thinking about that. It seemed more intelligent than the garans we've run into before. I mean, it anticipated our attacks and it pulled the arrow from its leg."

"Hmm," Lucian said.

"That's odd," Galen said. "Garans are more intelligent when they are being controlled at close-quarters. It's not likely that Malik is anywhere near here, but someone else could be ordering the garans to attack you, Matt.

"It could just be a coincidence, couldn't it?" Matt said hopefully.

"There have already been two attacks since we arrived here, Matt. Both on you. And about a week after we arrived here, when I was alone in the forest, I heard something in the trees that I sensed was evil. Even though I was alone, it didn't attack me. I think it was a garan that had been sent to find you. It wasn't interested in me at all."

Arden walked into the room and Emmon brightened. "Arden! Have you found out anything about Rankin?"

Arden nodded gloomily. Emmon's face fell.

"Don't worry," Arden said. "Rankin's fine. His leg is broken, but he'll be fine. He came around a few hours ago, but he's asleep now."

"What's the matter then, Arden?" Galen asked.

"Lan won't let me leave with you tomorrow."

"What?" Matt cried in outrage.

Arden nodded. "I know. I told him it was ridiculous and that it was important that I go with you, but he says that I must complete my duties as an elf and train at the diplomacy center. What he really means is that he wants me to train to be a lady. The only lady I know well is your mother, Emmon, and no offense, but I don't really want to be like her."

Emmon grinned, but then quickly scowled.

"Didn't you tell him that you'll learn three times as much by coming with us? We've been traveling together for months. We can't go without you!"

Arden shook her head sadly. "You know how Lan is. There's no arguing with him! He even threatened to forbid me from leaving Amaldan again. Ever. He said that you only got permission to go because you were a proper elf since you've already completed your training. You should have seen his face when I told him that I want to be a scout. He was furious that I was sparring with Matt the other day."

"I'm sorry, Arden," Matt said after a moment. "Is there anything we can do?"

"No, I've already tried everything. You'll just have to go on without me."

"If it makes you feel any better, Arden," Galen said. "I'm not going either."

"What?" Matt cried again.

Galen grinned. "I've decided to start spying on Malik again. That's what I did before I met all of you troublemakers, and I think that now, more than ever, we need to keep an eye on our enemy."

Matt was silent for a moment. It would be strange traveling without Galen and Arden. They had scarcely been out of each other's company for the past few months.

"Cheer up, Matt," Galen said. "It's just for now, until things are a little…safer."

"Come now, I think some sleep is in order so that you can handle the trek tomorrow," Lucian said.

Before leaving the next day they went to the Gathering Hall to express their gratitude to Lady Can and Lord Balor. Matt was surprised to see their horses saddled and waiting, and a cluster of advisors, including Emmon's father and Counselor Lan, standing outside the great wooden doors of the hall.

"What's going on?" Emmon hissed in Matt's ear.

"I don't know. I guess they want to get this over with quickly."

Lord Balor stared at them coldly.

"Your horses have been fed and are ready to ride, Wizard of Light," Balor said. "We wish you a pleasant journey."

Lucian's eyes were shining dangerously. "We are very grateful for your hospitality Lord Balor. I would like to express my gratitude to Lady Can, as well. May we see her?"

Balor paused and turned his eyes to Matt. "She has fallen ill and is unable to see you off."

"I am sorry to hear that. Please tell her that we wish her well," Lucian said stiffly.

Lady Can had looked ill at the summer solstice, but she hadn't appeared ill enough to be bed-ridden.

An elf handed Lucian a scroll tied tightly with a strip of leather.

"As agreed, here is the information that you requested," Balor sais tersely. "I hope that it will aid you on your next journey."

Lucian accepted the scroll graciously, but his jaw was clenched tightly as he bowed good-bye.

Arden gave Matt and Emmon a hug. "Be careful, okay? I won't be around to get you out of trouble."

She glanced at Counselor Lan, who was watching her carefully.

"He won't let me out of his sight," she whispered to them in disgust.

"I wish you could come with us," Matt said sadly.

They mounted their horses and started down the tunnel that led out of the Heart. Arden stood alone, waving at them, until they could no longer see her. Galen, with Lucian's hawk, Raumer, on his shoulder said good-bye when they reached the end of the archway.

"Do try to stay out of trouble, you two," Galen said, grinning widely at Matt and Emmon. "Especially you, Matt. I know it will be difficult, but even the improbable is possible. Lucian, I hope to catch up with you before long. I'll send Raumer with news."

"May fortune go with you, my friend."

Emmon pulled his horse next to Matt's. Samsire joined them soon after, and he walked with them, talking more than usual in an attempt to lighten the mood. By lunchtime, Matt could no longer suppress his curiosity and he turned to Lucian.

"What does the scroll say, Lucian?"

Lucian smiled at him and drew out the scroll. Matt and Emmon watched eagerly as he unrolled it. Lucian scanned the parchment and his eyebrows arched in surprise. He chuckled slightly.

"What does it say?" Matt demanded.

"It appears that the elves of Amaldan may have discovered where the Water Stone is hidden," Lucian replied. "I doubt you've heard about the mythical dwarf city of Oberdine?"

"What's Oberdine?" Emmon asked.

"It is spoken of only in legend. It is a hidden dwarf city," Lucian said with a mysterious smile. "I can see why the elves did not wish to give this to you, Matthias, aside from the fact that they do not trust you. It must be a great embarrassment for them that the dwarves, their rivals, are guardians of one of the Stones of the Elements."

He chuckled again. "I will not say anything else about Oberdine. Alem is something of an expert on the matter, and given that we are traveling to Gremonte to see him, I will not rob him of the opportunity to explain it to you."

Both Matt and Emmon started to protest, but Lucian only smiled.

"Alem will likely have information for us on how to find it. If you want to know more, then you'd best get your horses moving so we can reach him sooner."

Matt and Emmon reluctantly mounted their horses, but they did not pass up the opportunity to pester Lucian with questions throughout the day. The wizard was unyielding, and eventually they gave up and settled back to enjoy the ride.

It was a seven day journey to Gremonte. On the second day, they left the sheltering boughs of Amaldan and rode into the unrelenting heat of the plains. Lucian entertained them with legends and stories about the first settlers of Amaldan and the magical creatures that roamed the land.

After five days, Matt felt considerably happier than he had when they'd left the Heart, and he began to feel excited about the days ahead. The absence of Galen and Arden was noticeable, and Matt missed them both, but he also enjoyed the small camps that he, Lucian, Emmon, and Sam made each night, and the quiet that settled on the plains as the sun approached the horizon.

On the morning of the seventh day Matt began to quiz Lucian about Gremonte.

"It is a marvel, that is certain," the wizard said. "Gremonte's designers were attempting to build an independent city. Obviously, they aren't completely isolated from the rest of Mundaria, but they are extremely self-sufficient and protected.

"One of the most important aspects of the city, since it is entirely underground, is the below-surface river that runs through it which is their water source. The architects of Gremonte found the cavern through a hole in the earth. Sunlight manages to shine into that hole many hours a day onto a field of grain. The grain is an important food source for the people of Gremonte, although most of their food is gathered from outside the cavern."

"Don't people find the hole and walk right into the city?" Matt asked.

"Ah, but it was a dwarven city once. The dwarves have magic of their own which they use to protect their mines from greedy souls or wayward travelers. Most inhabitants of Gremonte still have small amounts of dwarven blood, and they have also continued to practice some aspects of dwarven culture."

Matt smiled at the thought of seeing Alem again.

"Lucian, you said Alem sent you a letter telling you to come back. Do you think something is happening in Gremonte?"

Lucian did not answer at first. "I don't know, but I sense that something is amiss. We will find out shortly."

They arrived at the towering stone gates of the city early in the afternoon. The only thing visible from the surface was a huge mound of earth with a path cut through it that led to two enormous doors. On either side of the doors, green flags bearing the symbol of an axe and a shovel, snapped loudly in the wind

"It is I, Lucian the Wizard of Light," Lucian said as he banged loudly on the door.

The doors slowly groaned open until they were open wide enough to let Lucian through. Matt and Emmon followed him closely, and as soon as Striker's tail passed through the opening, the doors slammed closed. Lanterns, tucked into recesses in the walls, lit the descending tunnel. The horse's hoofs clopped noisily against the stone floor.

Eventually, the tunnel flattened out and widened. Before them was a massive cavern with hundreds of stone buildings with lanterns hanging from their walls which cast an unearthly yellow glow onto everything. In the center of the cavern two immense stones jutted out of the ground, reaching nearly to the roof of the cave.

The city was strangely quiet. The stone streets were empty except for a few people carrying buckets of water.

"Where is everybody?" Matt asked.

Lucian frowned. "That is a very good question."

A uniformed shoulder was running toward them.

"Wizard!" he exclaimed breathlessly. "Thank goodness you're here."

"What has happened?"

"A plague!" the soldier said. "More than half the city has fallen ill."

CHAPTER TEN

Lucian stared at the solider in disbelief.

"Take us to Chief Golson immediately," he finally said.

They hurried through the vacant streets. Many of the lanterns were not lit and the cavern glowed eerily. When they reached the city center they stopped in front of a doorway carved out of the giant protruding stones they had seen from afar. The two guards standing at the doors tensed when they saw Lucian approaching.

"I am here to see Chief Golson," Lucian said calmly.

"You're a wizard, aren't? Can you do anything about the sickness?" one of them said.

"I will do what I can," Lucain said.

The guards opened the heavy doors. The hall was tall and wide, constructed around the existing stone slabs and the natural slope of the cavern ceiling. In the center of the grand hall, was a throne-like chair where a stout man with a black goatee and thick arms sat. A girl about Matt and Emmon's age stood next to him.

"Lucian," the man greeted him grimly. "You have returned, at last. I trust you know of our crisis."

"Very little," Lucian replied. "You must tell us what happened, Chief."

"Of course, but first, introduce me to your companions, my friend."

"This is Emmon of the Amaldan Forest and Matthias of the Western Reaches."

"Ah, good," Golson said, smiling slightly. "And this lovely young lady is my daughter, Natalia."

She smiled. She looked very nice, but since she was the daughter of the city's ruler, Matt immediately wondered if she was as snobbish as Duke Rellin's daughter, Cadia, was.

"Now," Lucian said impatiently, "what of this sickness?"

Golson sighed heavily. "It came out of nowhere. A miner fell ill, and then more followed. There are hundreds now. No one has died yet, but we have found no cure."

"What are the symptoms?" Lucian asked.

Golson held up his hand. "Before you ask too many questions, Lucian, you should know something. Your friend Alem...he has fallen very ill."

Matt gasped. Alem, his teacher and mentor, his only friend for years, was seriously ill. Lucian looked stricken, the way that Matt felt.

"I'm terribly sorry," Golson muttered uncomfortably.

Natalia stepped forward. "I have become friends with Alem during his time here. I will take you to see him."

They nodded and Natalia led them quickly through the hall. As she stepped onto the street, she tripped and tumbled to the ground with a yelp. Emmon was the first to reach her, and gently helped her to her feet.

"Oh, I'm sorry," she muttered, blushing bright red. "I'm clumsy sometimes."

Emmon smiled at her, forgetting to let go of her arm. Natalia smiled self-consciously and ducked her head down. Matt glanced at Lucian. The corners of Lucian's mouth were twitching, but he managed not to smile.

Abruptly, Natalia took off again. They followed her through the streets, looking nervously down the empty streets. The air around them was heavy with anxiety.

"All of our healers have gathered to search for a cure," Natalia explained to them.

"What are the symptoms?" Lucian asked.

"They all have a fever and a terrible cough. And they're very weak. At first, it was just the elderly and the very young that were sick, but now it's happening to everyone."

Finally, Natalia led them into a small, stone building, where people were rushing from room to room with wet rags in their hands and worried expressions on their faces. Children were sitting against the walls along the hallways, looking pale and frightened.

Natalia forged a path through the sea of people. Matt glanced into the rooms as they went by and saw that dozens of cots had been placed in the rooms, many surrounded by people.

Upstairs, Natalia turned into a small room with a single bed occupied by a small, balding dwarf.

"Alem!" Matt cried as he entered the room.

Alem lifted his head feebly. The dwarf's usually rosy, round face was gaunt and frail. There were dark circles around his sunken eyes, and his skin looked even more wrinkled than before. Matt, Lucian, and Emmon circled his bed, but Natalia stayed by the door.

"I'll be with my father if you need me," she said.

Matt sat down next to the bed and looked into Alem's face. Alem had aged so much that it seemed like years since he had seen his tutor, rather than the few weeks that it had actually been.

"Hello, old friend," Lucian said gently. "How are you feeling?"

The dwarf glared at them and said in a hoarse voice, "What's the matter with you three? No cheery greetings for your friend? You look like you've been given a death sentence! I apologize that my face is ugly enough to make you all look so glum."

Despite themselves, they all laughed at their cranky friend.

"Where are Galen and Arden?" Alem said, his voice thick with disappointment.

Matt knew that the dwarf was fond of both of them, especially Arden.

"Galen is searching for Malik and Arden was forced to stay in Amaldan because her grandfather wants to turn her into a lady," Matt answered.

Alem looked highly affronted. "Humph. They need to leave that little one alone. She's perfect just the way she is. Never seen anyone that age with so much gumption. Staying there in Amaldan with those stuck-up elves is going to ruin her. Besides, who in their right mind would want to spend their days rotting away in a forest?"

Matt smiled. Alem had lived in the forest for as long as he had known him. They all sat in silence for several moments while Alem coughed violently.

"Why did you not tell me what was happening in your letter, Alem?" Lucian asked him, his voice pained.

Alem did not answer. Matt knew the dwarf hated being fussed over, but he wished that Alem had let them know that he was ill.

"I've seen this sickness before," Alem said at last, his voice scarcely above a whisper.

Lucian studied the dwarf's face. "What is it, Alem?"

"The old protections that were placed on the deserted mines have worn off. About a week ago, a worker went down to check on things in the old mines. He was the first to fall ill. Dust had collected on his clothing, and a strange white vapor emanated from the dust.

"Soon many more became ill and the mine was closed off with the proper magical precautions again. But it has spread. It's the very same illness that plagued the dwarves a hundred years ago. The very same illness that stopped the dwarves from going to the Battle of the Endless Fields to help the elves and men. It wiped out half our population back then, and the remaining dwarves went into hiding."

He began coughing violently again, but managed to croak, "I was just a child then, and the children and the elderly are the most vulnerable. I became sick, but I managed to cheat death. I'm not likely to do it again."

"Don't talk that way, Alem," Matt said, jumping to his feet.

Matt felt anger bubbling in his stomach. Alem seemed to have already given up, and if he didn't fight it he would die. Matt knew that Alem was too stubborn to give up this easily. Matt realized that they were all staring at him sympathetically, and he unclenched his fists and slowly sat back down.

Alem looked at him with mournful eyes, but nodded slowly.

"I'm sorry, Matt," he croaked. "You know I'm not a quitter. It's just that I've lived through it before, and I know what to expect…I'm just being realistic."

"Alem, I think the only sure way to save you, the good people of Gremonte, and Amaldan is by locating the Water Stone," Lucian said. "After a little pressure, the elves finally shared with us that they believe the stone is hidden in Oberdine. What do you say, old friend? Do you think you could help us with that?"

Alem stared at Lucian for a moment, and Matt saw a faint twinkle appear in his eye.

"Matt, could you hand me my bag."

Matt handed the bag to Alem, and the dwarf grasped it feebly, carefully withdrawing a small leather notebook.

"This holds all my secrets," Alem croaked reverently.

The pages crackled as Alem opened the book. They were worn with age and use, and the ink was barely legible. He shuffled through the book, muttering. They watched patiently as he turned each page of scribbled handwriting.

Finally, he squawked in triumph, withdrawing a folded piece of parchment covered in strange markings. He opened it with trembling fingers. Drawings of trees and mountains were scrawled all over the inside of the parchment, and towns were labeled with names.

"Ah…I found this years ago when I was traveling around Mundaria. This map was drawn by Dorn the Adventurer himself!"

"Dorn the Adventurer?" Matt asked.

"Don't tell me you've never heard of Dorn the Adventurer?" Alem wheezed.

Matt shook his head.

"I guess you never got around to teaching me about him."

"Dorn's adventures are not something you teach, boy! They are something that every self-respecting man should just know!"

Lucian placed a hand on Alem's shoulder.

"Forgive me, Alem," he said smiling. "But had you not taught me about Dorn, I would know nothing of the great adventurer. And I would still consider myself a self-respecting man."

Matt and Emmon grinned at each other as Alem glared at Lucian.

"Fine, fine. I will explain," Alem grunted. "Dorn was a dwarf adventurer. After Malik's demise a hundred years ago, Dorn set off to explore the world. He conquered many of the world's most dangerous landmarks, climbing insurmountable mountains and battling great, evil creatures. He went in search of the legends of Mundaria, to prove or disprove their existences, and then he laid hidden clues along the way so that others could find them.

"Dorn was a tricky dwarf. He escaped death's clutches many times, but he believed that he was meant to escape. According to Dorn, only twice should he have actually died, but he cheated death, instead. The first instance was before the Battle of the Endless Fields when Dorn, like many dwarves, became sick from the vapor in the mines. He was expected to die quickly, but he survived, the last dwarf to pull out of the sickness."

"The second instance was when Dorn was searching for the Land of the Forgotten. He was trapped in a cave along the Cliffs of Adern because the entrance had been blocked by a rockslide. He wandered through the cave for days with no food or water. When all hope was lost, he saw light seeping through a small hole in the wall of rock. Eventually, he dug himself out and found himself in a field of strawberries."

Alem sighed and stared, unseeing, at the map. They waited for him to continue, but he was lost in his memories.

"What about the map?" Emmon asked, finally.

"Hmmm? Oh, the map," Alem wheezed sleepily. "I found it when I was a young dwarf. It was quite a discovery, I must admit. You see there on the bottom? Those are clues. Clues to the fabled city of Oberdine."

Matt felt a rush of excitement at the mention of Oberdine. He and Emmon both leaned forward eagerly. Alem pushed the map toward them, and Matt could see loopy, elegant writing at the bottom of the page.

"What do you know about Oberdine, Alem?" Matt asked.

"It is a hidden city built by dwarves. The dwarves disappeared there to escape the rest of the world. The city is rumored to be entirely self-sustaining, and was likely the inspiration for Gremonte. But the reason that Oberdine became a legend is because of its healing waters. It is said they can heal any ailment.

"Lucian, if we could find the Water Stone and the healing waters of Oberdine, we should be able to save everyone, right?" Matt said, leaning forward in his seat.

Lucian nodded gravely. "I do hope so, Matthias. Don't forget that we aren't certain that Oberdine does exist. Up until now, it has been only a fable. If the elves believe that it exists, though, we can be relatively certain that it does."

A loud, gravelly sound beside him made Matt jump, until he realized that Alem was snoring. Smiling, Lucian quietly pushed back his chair. Matt grabbed the map off of Alem's bed, and they quietly made their way into the hallway.

"Come," Lucian said. "I must discuss this with Golson.

Chief Golson was fiddling absent-mindedly with his long, black goatee, and Natalia was sitting next to him, reading a book when they arrived back at the great hall. She stood up eagerly when she saw them.

"You spoke with your friend?" Golson inquired.

Lucian nodded. "Yes. Alem has given us valuable information."

Golson leaned forward in his seat. "Something that could cure this sickness?"

"Yes. The healing waters of Oberdine."

Golson sputtered as if he were choking on a large piece of food. His face turned bright red as he laughed loudly.

"Oberdine is simply a myth, nothing more. You cannot truly believe that a fabled city will save us!"

"It is no mere fable," Lucian said, his eyes flashing. "There is more proof of the city's existence than you realize. Alem has given us clues from Dorn the Adventurer himself. And we have other information that leads us to believe that it exists, as well."

Lucian held up the map and Golson's eyes widened in surprise.

"If we can determine the meaning of Dorn's words, I believe they will lead us to Oberdine."

Golson's face was unreadable as he twisted his goatee more rapidly around his thick finger.

"Do as you wish, my friend. Natalia will show you where you will be sleeping while you are staying with us."

Out in the street, Natalia's cheeks were very flushed as she turned to speak to them.

"He's so stubborn! I'm sorry if he offended you," she said. "I believe you'll find a way to cure all those people."

"Thanks, Natalia," Emmon said, smiling broadly.

Matt gave him a sideways glance, but Emmon ignored him.

This time, Natalia led them to a strange building that appeared to be hollowed out of the cavern wall. It had two large pillars on either side of the entrance that supported the overhanging stone of the cavern wall. Windows carved from the stone were scattered at different levels above the entrance.

"This is the library," Natalia explained. "We don't have room anywhere else since so many are ill, and nobody ever comes here anyway, so I thought you might like to stay here."

Lucian smiled. "It will work perfectly. Thank you very much, Natalia."

She smiled, glanced shyly at Emmon, and then hurried down the streets. Matt gave Emmon another look.

"What?" Emmon said. "I'm just being polite. And besides, she's really nice."

"And it doesn't hurt that she's very pretty, too, does it, my friend?" said Lucian with a smile.

Emmon elbowed Matt, and they followed Lucian through the entry. It was surprisingly light inside the library, and Matt realized that there was a very deep skylight in the ceiling of the tall room. There were stairs on either side of the doorway and many shelves of books, but only a fraction of what they had seen in the library at Hightop. The upper level was filled with comfortable armchairs and soft rugs.

"Excellent," Emmon sighed.

They dropped their packs and collapsed into the chairs. Although they had traveled from Amaldan at a leisurely pace, only occasionally trotting or galloping, Matt still felt the ache of the saddle. He yawned as he stretched in the chair. Lucian, however, began to pace around the room. His gray eyes narrowed as he concentrated on the map he held in his hands.

"What does it say, Lucian?" Matt asked.

"Have a look." The wizard handed him the worn piece of parchment.

Matt strained to read the strange handwriting:

Venture first to the city that lives in shade,
shielded by giants of stone, children of grass.
On the green, crowned hill, at the home of silent voices lays the next clue.
When the crown turns gold, look for the jewel,
an adornment for the crown.
It is there that you will find the next step for the city of Oberdine.

Matt frowned and handed it to Emmon.

"City that lives in shade? Where is that?"

"That, Emmon, is what we must puzzle over," Lucian said and resumed his pacing.

Matt yawned again. "I don't think I have the energy. Could we just rest for a while?"

After pacing for several minutes, Lucian relented. They found a cabinet of food in the corner, and raided its shelves. Matt and Emmon found a chessboard on the main floor of the library, and Emmon taught Matt the different moves of the pieces. They slowly played through several games. Matt lost miserably every time, but thought it quite enjoyable.

Natalia stopped by later in the afternoon when they were eager for a distraction after hours of discussing Dorn's clues. She took Matt and Emmon to the underground wheat field and the river that Lucian had described to them, and they dangled their feet over the ledge overhanging it. The wizard had been right. It was an amazing sight.

"Have you made a plan yet?" Natalia asked them hopefully.

"No," Mat replied grimly. "The clue isn't exactly clear."

"What does it say?"

Emmon handed her the copy they had written of the clue. She gave it back to him so quickly that Matt thought that she had not had enough time to read it, but then he saw her lips moving silently, as if reciting it from memory.

"City that lives in shade," she said out loud. "Hmm. I suppose that could be a nickname of a famous city. Let's see, Apetain was known as the Tower Ring, Karespurn as the Fortress, Ridegfell as the

Leaning City." She bit her lip. "I don't remember a city in shade, though. I could look back through my books. I might have come across a reference to a shaded town at some point…"

She trailed off when she realized that Matt and Emmon were both staring at her. She blushed and clapped her hand over her mouth, as if she hadn't realized that she had spoken aloud.

"Sorry," she said, embarrassed. "Well…I guess I don't really know what it could be. I wish I did. I know how important it is."

The hope in Natalia's face vanished, and Matt felt a profound sense of guilt and fear. They had been wasting away the afternoon while Alem's life and the lives of half of the population of Gremonte were depending on them. There was no time to waste. It was imperative that they decipher Dorn's clue as soon as possible.

CHAPTER ELEVEN

"Let's just try the first part, then," Matt suggested the following morning as they all paced around the upper room of the library. They had worked on the clue until late the night before and had begun again at daybreak.

Emmon clenched the map in his hand, staring at it as if his eyes could will it to reveal its secrets.

"'Venture first to the city that lives in shade, shielded by giants of stone,'" Emmon recited wearily.

Matt's brow furrowed in concentration. City that lives in shade...out of the sun...hidden... He shook his head. He did not know much about geography, or legends. Sighing, he turned to Lucian. The wizard was muttering under his breath, but did not seem to have any new ideas either.

"Anything?" Matt asked quietly.

The wizard shook his head.

The dull thump of Emmon repeatedly kicking the leg of an armchair was the only sound in the room. After several minutes of intense silence, Lucian sighed and sat down.

"I must say, I am amazed that Alem managed to keep the fact that he had possession of the map secret for as long as he did," Lucian remarked.

"Why?"

"He showed it to me a few years ago, but he told me at the time that the existence of the map was well known. Dorn, tricky as he was, was not a subtle dwarf. He boasted and bragged of his achievements. Alem was not exactly shy when he was a young dwarf.

"I have no doubt that Malik has also guessed that the healing waters of Oberdine are the location of the Water Stone. It is even possible that Malik has traced the map to Alem. I suspect that that was why he was pursued by garans when we were traveling to Hightop months ago. His dwarf aura made him easy to track."

Matt suddenly remembered how Lucian had rushed to Alem's aid when they were traveling to Hightop and found him cornered by garans in the Glade Forest.

A thought struck him.

"Lucian," he said uneasily.

Suddenly, Natalia burst up the stairs into the room. Her eyes were full of tears.

"Natalia! What is it?" Lucian asked, concerned.

"The worker who escaped the collapse…the one who fell sick first," Natalia said, tears now streaming down her face. "He just died."

Fear rippled through Matt. Soon, the rest of the city would follow suit. Including Alem.

"He died this morning. He was old, but…"

Matt grabbed the map from Emmon and said fiercely, "We have to figure this out!"

Emmon's face was now very pale. "We're trying."

Matt turned back to the clue, reading the lines feverishly with a sick feeling in his stomach.

Lucian cleared his throat. "Matt, you were saying something before Natalia arrived?"

Matt could hear the strain in Lucian's voice.

"I was just thinking," Matt said hesitantly. "Well...I was wondering if we can be sure that this plague was caused... naturally."

Lucian considered him for a moment. "Are you suggesting that it could have been caused intentionally? You think Malik could have had his hand in this?"

Matt nodded, and Lucian closed his eyes.

"Matthias," he said quietly. "You could be right."

Matt's heart skipped a beat as he turned to Natalia. "Do you remember anyone coming into Gremonte before the sickness began?"

Natalia thought for a moment. "Well, we always get visitors from the surface who barter with us for fresh fruit and other crops, but there is one man who I do remember. He wasn't one of the usual vendors. He had a meager crop of vegetables with him, but didn't even try to haggle with the officials. All he wanted was to see the city. I'm not sure how far into Gremonte he went, but I do know that he was allowed in after making quite a scene about it."

"Can you describe him?" Lucian asked, now listening keenly. "Was there anything unusual about him?"

Natalia nodded. "He was dark-haired and tall. I would say he was thick, muscular. A large man. And there was something unique about him. He had a long scar down the left side of his neck."

Matt met Lucian's gaze. He had known Natalia for only a day, but he knew not to doubt the accuracy of her memory.

"Rock Thompson," Emmon said. "That sounds like Rock Thompson."

Matt shivered at the memory of the cruel man, and their last encounter. The burn scar on Rock Thompson's neck was caused by Matt when he unintentionally used the Fire Stone to save Emmon from Kerwin's knife.

"If that was, indeed, Rock Thompson," Lucian said, "Then you are most likely correct, Matthias."

"Rock Thompson started the plague?" Emmon said. "Why?"

"Not Rock. Malik," Matt said. "Malik wanted to start the plague because…well, I don't know."

Then another thought struck him. "It's because he wanted me to search for the Water Stone, and he knew that's what I'd do when I found out about the plague. Malik doesn't know where the Water Stone is. He wants me to find it for him."

Lucian's face was grave. "If you are accurate, Matthias, and I think you might be, we must proceed with extreme caution. Malik will be waiting and watching our every move. And if we locate the Stone, you will be in more danger than ever."

They fell into silence. Matt's heart raced. He knew that Lucian was right, and he was afraid.

"Well, we can't do anything about that right now, but we can decipher this clue," Emmon declared, pulling the map toward him. "Come on, let's do this."

Matt stared at the page, focusing on the first two lines. Shielded by three giants of stone…giants of stone…boulders, maybe, but they had already tried that and they hadn't been able to think of a city surrounded by boulders.

"Giants of stone," Matt said thoughtfully. "Could they be mountains?"

They had already tried that, too. Lucian and Emmon both stared at the map.

"Where, though?" Matt asked. "There are mountains everywhere."

"What about Hightop?" Emmon suggested.

"No. It's here," Lucian said, pointing at the map. "Dornhelm. See the mountains in front of it? Dornhelm was named for Dorn, though most of the inhabitants don't know who he was. Yes, that would make sense. Not only is it shaded by the mountains, but by the seven hills surrounding it. The mountains' children. The children of grass."

"Is that it, then?" Matt asked, his chest filling with hope.

Lucian's brow furrowed. "We could be on the right path, but we won't be sure until we reach Dornhelm. I am guessing that we will not be able to decipher the next clue until we have correctly found the first. Now, Natalia, I think we should let your father know that we are leaving."

Lucian and Natalia left the library, and Matt and Emmon went to say their good-byes to Alem. The crowded halls were now shockingly silent in the small stone building. All that could be heard was the coughing and moaning of the infected. Matt and Emmon quietly crept up the stairs and found Alem lying in his bed with his leather notebook clutched in his hands. The wrinkles were deep in his sallow face, but his eyes brightened visibly when he spotted them.

"Do sit down, sit down," he croaked.

Matt and Emmon explained what they had discovered.

"Well done!" Alem said. "When will you leave?"

"Now," Matt said.

Alem nodded. "Good. You must hurry. Once one dies, others will follow."

* * *

They shouldered their packs, now laden with provisions, and walked quickly through the streets of the city to the stable near the exit tunnel. Though it was early, Matt could feel the sun's heat seeping into the cool cavern. It would be a scorching day. As they finished saddling their horses, Chief Golson stepped into the stable.

"I must ask a favor of you, Lucian," he said.

Natalia was standing next to him, wearing a tunic, loose pants, and an excited expression. She had a large pack on her back.

"Please take my daughter with you. If Oberdine does indeed exist, I want a representative of Gremonte to be there upon its discovery," he said, placing his hand on Natalia's head. "And I would also like for Natalia to be far from the dying and the dead."

Lucian sighed. "As you wish, Golson."

Natalia beamed, but stood by silently as Lucian quickly saddled a horse for her and gave her a boost into the saddle. Emmon handed her the reins, smiling happily.

The sunlight assaulted their eyes as they left the duskiness of the underground city and made their way up the hill.

Matt glanced around uneasily. If Malik had indeed unleashed the plague onto the city, his spies would be watching them. Lucian seemed to feel the same unease. He urged his horse into a trot and then a gallop. The teenagers followed close behind, until Matt and Emmon realized that Natalia was no longer on her horse, but yards behind them, on the ground.

CHAPTER TWELVE

The way to Dornhelm was not particularly treacherous, it was mostly plains and an occasional rolling hill, but they were traveled at a sluggish pace. Natalia lacked as much coordination on a horse as a toddler learning to walk. She only fell off her horse twice more, but she slipped from her saddle several times, dangling helplessly on the side until her horse slowed to a stop. Each time, Emmon cheerfully helped her back into the saddle. She tried to stay on, good-naturedly accepted advice, and never complained, but their pace was greatly slowed.

Samsire flew in wide circles above them, occasionally swooping down to talk. Matt smiled as he watched Sam flying lazily above. When the alorath first made himself known to Natalia, she had gone quite pale, but did not scream as Matt had expected. Her horse did not take kindly to the meeting, however, and promptly tossed her from its back.

"Why don't you go ahead with Sam?" Natalia asked Matt on their second day of traveling as she rode cautiously beside Emmon.

Matt had considered this option before but had decided against it. "It wouldn't really cut down the time at all. I would still need to wait for the rest of you in Dornhelm.

"I don't think Sam would mind, though," Emmon put in looking up at the sky. "He's looking rather mutinous."

At that moment, the alorath dove down at the horses and flew over them, his claws barely missing the tops of the riders' heads. Matt yelled at him, trying not to laugh, as the horses whinnied in fright. Samsire roared loudly, and the sound echoed across the fields and bounced off the hills. Lucian, who was riding slightly ahead, twisted in his saddle.

"That's enough fooling around, Samsire," Lucian yelled sternly. "Fly elsewhere if you cannot resist pestering."

Sam flashed the wizard a toothy grin and hurtled through the air just above Lucian head, and then past him, until he became a speck on the horizon within minutes. Matt shook his head and sighed, but couldn't help smiling.

"How much further to Dornhelm?" Matt asked when Lucian was riding beside him again.

Lucian looked into the distance. "Probably three more days at this pace."

Matt nodded, but he felt his stomach sink. Would the sick people in Gremonte survive long enough for them to bring back the cure? Who knew where Dorn would send them after Dornhelm? There was also the question of whether or not they were being followed. They had not seen a soul since leaving Gremonte, but Matt still felt anxious.

Lucian, noticing Matt's concern, added, "We have some time, Matthias. Most of the citizens of Gremonte were not exposed to as much of the vapor and dust as the miner who died. And he was quite old. They are a resilient people. We will return to them as quickly as we can. And so far, it seems that our location has not been detected. I have not seen anyone following us. At least that won't slow us down."

Matt tried to quell his anxiety as they rode slowly across the grassy plains by thinking about other things. Natalia seemed to have found a remedy for her nerves by relaying a stream of facts about the landscape, nearby towns, and eventually about Dornhelm.

"It's quite an interesting place, actually," she said as they made camp that evening. "Dorn founded it nearly fifty years ago, when he was quite a young dwarf. He liked to make his mark on the world and thought that a settlement in his name would be the best way to preserve his legacy. That way he could have a permanent presence in the world. He saw the hills that surround Dornhelm as an opportunity to protect the city and also to draw people there to trade because of the unique landscape."

She paused for air and Emmon broke in. "How do you know all this, Natalia? I thought that you had hardly ever left Gremonte."

"Oh, well, I read a lot, I guess," she said. "There's not much to do in Gremonte, so I always go to the library."

"I could read a mile of books and not remember things like that," Emmon said admiringly, and Natalia went pink again.

"Take that guy over there," he said, pointing at Matt. "For the life of me, I couldn't tell you what his name is. I only know that he likes to drag me on ridiculous journeys which usually involves almost certain death."

He looked at Matt forlornly and Matt threw a stick at him. Natalia giggled and Samsire snorted into Matt's hair, causing Emmon and Natalia to laugh even harder. Sam smiled down at Matt playfully.

"Well," Lucian said, casting Emmon and Natalia an amused look. "I hate to ruin the fun, but we might as well make good use of this time. It is time for you to try using the Fire Stone again, Matthias. You may have need of it soon. We will soon know if you are ready."

Matt's stomach clenched. He knew that Lucian was right, but he was still dreading the experience. He glanced at Emmon, who had stopped laughing and was watching him with a mixture of sympathy and curiosity. Matt climbed to his feet and walked away from Sam to where Lucian stood.

Matt faced Lucian in the dim light and reluctantly removed the pouch from around his neck. He slid the Fire Stone from the safety of the pouch into his hand and felt its familiar warmth seep through his fingers. He gripped it firmly and immediately felt a jolt of energy shoot up his arm.

"Now, remember what I told you before. Clear your mind and blend your magic with the Fire Stone. Slowly, this time. I think you may have forced it before."

Matt nodded nervously and shut his eyes. He breathed deeply, willing his rapidly beating heart to slow down. He focused on the magic inside him, letting it spread through his arms. Tentatively, he concentrated on the tingling power that radiated from the Fire Stone. He felt his own magic brushed up against the fire magic and he recoiled in sudden panic.

He looked up at Lucian and shook his head.

"I can't do it."

Lucian studied him with his steady gray gaze.

"I am confident that you can, Matthias. You cannot ignore the Fire Stone any longer. I took you to Amaldan so you could learn more about magic and the Fire Stone, and so you could have a respite from your quest to fine the other Stones. But now, with everything that has happened, time is running out, my friend. It is imperative to your safety and to the success of this quest that you know how to use the Fire Stone."

Matt sighed. "All right. I'll try again."

He fought to control his fear and focused his attention on the magic again. He tensed as he felt the warmth of the Fire Stone pushing against his own magic again. Slowly, he felt a peculiar sensation spread through his body. It was not like the wild dance that had claimed him the previous time.

This was different. It was like the tingling he felt whenever he used non-elemental magic, but this was more intense and it quickly spread through his body. It was like a rejuvenating drink that warmed him to his core. The air around him felt electrified.

He opened his eyes and was surprised that even when his focus wavered, his body was still energized with more magic than he had ever felt before, and strangely, he also felt like he could control it.

"Amazing," he whispered.

The energized feeling reminded him of when he learned the sight invocation to recognize magical auras. Only this was much stronger. Matt closed his eyes, gathering the magical energy. He thought the word 'sight' to himself and opened his eyes, blinking furiously.

Lucian was looking at him strangely. "Are you all right, Matt?"

In the darkness, he could see a slight, shimmering, light border around Lucian. When Lucian had unmasked his aura for Matt to see before, it had been much brighter.

"Is your aura unmasked, Lucian?" he asked.

The wizard looked shocked. "No! Can you see it?"

Matt nodded. "It's faint, but I can see it."

"Can you feel the magic of the Fire Stone?"

Matt nodded and Lucian smiled broadly. "Then, it is as I hoped. The Fire Stone has joined with you, and your magic has been intensified. Unmask your own aura."

Matt did so and Lucian's eyes widened. Matt looked down at his hands, and saw a blinding white light.

"Your aura is much stronger and brighter than before," Lucian marveled. "And your sight invocation is more sensitive. Now let's see if you can weild the Fire Stone's magic. Try to create fire and then control it."

Matt nodded, feeling more confident. He thought back to the night that he had unwittingly used the Fire Stone when they were fighting Kerwin and Rock. Emmon had later described it as a jet of flame erupting from Matt's palm.

He looked down at the small oval stone in his left hand. The dancing stripes of red, orange, and yellow that flicked across its black center were like live flames. He raised his right palm, looking at it curiously. Matt imagined a roaring fire in his mind. He closed his eyes and focused on the image, fueling the flames with magical energy. His limbs grew hot and intense tingling stabbed at his arms.

"Matt, open your eyes!"

Matt's eyes shot open, and he stared at his right hand in amazement. A small ball of flame rolled around in his palm, hovering slightly above his skin. It was real fire, an orb of swirling flames.

Matt breathed. "I did it."

Lucian chuckled, in wonder. "I would say so! Well done, Matthias!"

Matt lifted his hand to examine the orb. It was perfectly balanced above his palm, and he felt that he had total control over it. It would only leave his hand if he wanted it to.

Suddenly, the Fire Stone slid from his sweaty fingers and fell softly onto the grassy plain. The ball of fire disappeared in a sputter of sparks, leaving only a thin trail of smoke.

"So as soon as you dropped the Fire Stone, you lost control over the fire," Lucian explained. "Since the fireball was fueled by your energy melded with the stone, it could not thrive when the stone's magic was gone. Sit down, Matthias. You look like you're about to faint."

Matt was suddenly acutely aware of the exhaustion seeping through his body, yet he also felt strangely energized. He lowered himself onto the ground and returned the Fire Stone to the black pouch dangling from his neck.

"I am guessing that now that you can control the Fire Stone, you will be able to use the stone just as effectively by wearing it around your neck as by holding it in your hand. Physical contact, even through the fabric of the pouch, is the key component,

"I feel tired, but I also feel like I could do any invocation that I want," Matt marveled.

"Now that you have unlocked the Fire Stone's power, your full magical potential has been awakened. You must continue to train in all aspects of magic, using both the Fire Stone and non-elemental invocations. If you are to find the other Stones of the Elements, your skills must be finely tuned.

"You have accomplished a great task, Matthias. I commend you. An ordinary wizard could not do what you have just done without years, perhaps decades, of dedicated work, and even then they might not succeed."

Matt felt a swell of pride build in his chest. Lucian did not give out compliments readily, especially when it came to magic. Matt climbed to his feet and followed Lucian back toward the fire. Emmon, Natalia, and even Sam, were staring at him in awe. Matt sat down, embarrassed by the attention.

"You'd think none of you had ever seen fire before," he joked, but felt immensely satisfied with what he had just accomplished.

Natalia laughed, but her eyes were still wide. Matt realized how strange it must be for her to be thrust into a world of magic and danger after living in the sheltered realm of Gremonte.

As Matt laid on his bedroll that night, he felt a sense of personal satisfaction. He felt, for the first time, that he might someday be able to handle the task assigned to him in the prophecy that declared him equal to Malik. He knew that he was young and inexperienced and that he had still a lot of work to do, but for the first time he felt like his quest to find the Stones of the Elements and the Immortality Scroll, was more than just an improbable dream.

CHAPTER THIRTEEN

The feeling sustained him during the next few days. The task at hand felt more manageable. They were able to increase their pace as Natalia became more adept at riding. The weather stayed tranquil.

Still, their mission felt more urgent as they went, and they all became more and more anxious to reach Dornhelm.

On the fifth morning Lucian pointed to a cluster of large hills with a group of mountains immediately behind them.

"Dornhelm is in the middle of those seven hills," Lucian explained.

"One of them must be the 'crowned hill'," Matt said excitedly.

Lucian's eyes twinkled. "Most likely. The hills are a famous landmark, and it would be typical of Dorn to hide something in a well-known, much traveled area. He liked to trick the world into thinking they knew something and then throw a surprise at them."

Matt yelled out to Emmon and Natalia, who were riding several hundred feet behind them.

"Dornhelm is within those hills."

They all sped up, and as they drew closer, Matt realized the benefits of the wall of hills surrounding the city. The hills were tall and steep, and they overlapped each other, leaving only narrow gaps between them. It would be difficult to penetrate the city's defenses with a large army since they would have to file in one or two soldiers at a time. Matt was nervous and excited as Lucian led them through a gap between the hills. He glanced up at the sky, but there was no sign of Samsire.

The hills created a sort of enormous, grass bowl. In the center was a town, very unlike the other towns they had seen. The buildings were all made of wood with thick, wooden slats lining the slanted roofs, and all built on the undulating grass in the center. There were no streets running between the buildings, only rough, worn-down grass corridors.

They followed Lucian up the main passageway. Most of the buildings had signs dangling over their porches, and at the back of each shop was an elongated structure that appeared to be the shopkeepers' homes. Matt was enthralled by the names of the shops. He could not decide exactly what they sold at *The Essential, Indispensable, Requisite Shop of Absolutely Everything.*

"'ey! Who're you?" an angry voice shouted

A grubby, stocky man blocked Lucian's path, his hands positioned indignantly on his hips

"We are just visitors," Lucian answered calmly. "Is that a problem?"

The man's mouth twisted into an ugly sneer that revealed a scattered set of broken, yellow teeth. "What's your business 'ere?"

"Who, may I ask, are you?" Lucian inquired, and Matt noted that the wizard's normally serene face was tense.

The man laughed hysterically, swaying slightly as he did. Before he could answer, a large man with enormous hands gently pushed him, and the surly man crumpled to the ground.

"Don't mind Bruce," the large man said. "He's an old fool. Might I interest you in some lodging?"

Lucian nodded briskly, unclenching his fingers from around his staff.

"That would be much appreciated."

"I'm Carver," the man replied. "I own an inn just over there. I have stables where you can keep your horses."

Lucian dismounted and shook Carver's enormous hand. As they followed Carver through the street, people stared at them curiously, and Matt could hear them whispering as they passed.

"The stable's there if you'd like to tend to your horses. I'll meet you inside."

Matt led Striker into the stable and tethered him next to Innar. He glanced at Lucian, who appeared to be deep in thought.

"Is something wrong, Lucian?" Matt asked.

"I was just thinking back to the last time I was here and I am worried it might cause problems for us," Lucian replied. "A few years ago I traveled here with Galen, and we stayed here for a while.

"Galen managed to get in a fight with one of the locals. Although we had been careful not to use magic while we were here so as not to draw attention to ourselves, I was forced to enlarge Galen's opponent's nose to prevent the fight from going too far. For the other man's safety, not for Galen's. We left right after it happened, so there is the possibility that I may be recognized."

"What did he do to make Galen angry?" Matt asked.

Lucian smiled slightly, but did not answer. He patted Innar fondly, and they all walked under dark clouds to the inn. They filed inside and found that more than half of the tables were filled. Carver was talking animatedly with his large hands to a small bald man in the corner. He turned around at the sound of the door and made his way over to them.

"All set, then? How many rooms would you like?" he asked, grinning broadly.

Lucian pulled a small drawstring bag from his pack. "Three rooms, please. For a day or two."

He counted out several golden coins from the bag and dropped them into Carver's hand.

"Right, then," Carver said, happily clutching his gold. "I'll have my wife show you to your rooms."

A plump woman bustled over to them and led them up the stairs to their three rooms. Lucian and Natalia each had their own room, and Matt and Emmon had the third. There was only one bed, but Matt was pleased to see that unlike most inns, there was a fat stack of pillows and blankets piled in the corner of the room.

"I'll flip you for the bed," Emmon said with a grin as he pulled out a small wooden disc with a tree on one side and a bow on the other.

Emmon won the bed, but Matt was content with the mound of goose down pillows. They did not linger in the room for long, but stowed their belongings and met Lucian and Natalia on the main floor. They stepped outside only to be met with the roar of thunder and the clatter of rain against the thick wooden roofs. They retreated back into the noisy inn and sat down at a vacant table.

"Do you have the map with you, Matthias?" Lucian asked, glancing around to ensure that they weren't being watched. "Since we cannot explore the city right now, we might as well spend the time deciphering Dorn's clue."

Matt nodded and flattened the map out on the table. The hills and mountains that shadowed Dornhelm were now obvious on the map.

"Read the clue again," Emmon suggested.

Matt recited Dorn's clue once more and they all listened intently.

"Well," Matt said slowly. "What about the word 'crown'? What could be a crown on a hill?"

"What about a ring of rocks?" Natalia suggested.

Lucian shook his head. "No. Dorn would want something more permanent that would not be likely to change over time. He liked leaving his mark."

"Besides, we have to think about what could 'turn gold'," Emmon said.

They fell into silence, thinking again about the words. Matt searched for a metaphor or a secret meaning but could find none. The pounding of the rain and raucous noise of the crowd around them were distracting.

"Lucian? Is that you?" a disbelieving voice behind them suddenly asked.

Matt looked up and saw the small bald man who Carver had been speaking with. Lucian's his face brightened considerably.

"Beagan?"

The man laughed joyfully and clapped Lucian on the back. "It is good to see you Lucian! It's been at least two years!"

Lucian got to his feet and shook the little man's hand, smiling broadly. "It's been too long, Beagan. How are you?"

Beagan shrugged. "Same as always. It's been quiet. This is the biggest crowd we've had in months."

Lucian sat down and pulled back a chair for Beagan to sit in. The small man sat down and looked around the table.

"This is Natalia of Gremonte, Emmon of Amaldan, and Matthias of the Western Reaches," Lucian said, introducing each of them.

Beagan nodded at them, smiling, but then turned back eagerly to Lucian. "Traveling again? Is Galen with you?"

Lucian shook his head. "No, he is off on an adventure of his own."

They spoke for several minutes until Lucian excused himself to get drinks for everyone. Beagan watched Lucian leave, and then he turned to Matt, Emmon, and Natalia.

"So you know Galen?" Matt asked curiously.

"Ah, yes! He traveled here with Lucian a few years ago. 'Course I knew Lucian from when we were both in Karespurn years ago," Beagan said wistfully. "I'm a barman here at the inn. Lucian and Galen stayed here for a month a few years back. I got to know Galen pretty well. I was sad to see them go."

He chuckled slightly. "They left in quite a hurry, actually. Rather amusing story."

"What happened?" Matt pressed, wanting to know the details that Lucian had failed to elaborate upon.

Beagan smiled. "Well, unlike the Western Reaches, the Middle Realm is ruled by the-"

"Middle Realm?"

Beagan looked surprised that Matt hadn't heard of it, but Natalia beat him to the answer.

"Middle Realm is the region from Dornhelm to Karespurn," she said pointing to Dorn's map. "It also stretches from Perth to Borden and Lopane."

Matt suddenly remembered one of Alem's lessons, and his description of the five regions, the Western Reaches, the Middle Realm, the Southern Province, the Lower Region, and the Eastern Edge.

"I remember now," Matt said quickly. "But what does it have to do with Galen?"

"Well...oh, yes. The Middle Realm contains the city of Karespurn, the stronghold of military power and also the city of the Commanding General. All of the other cities of the Middle Realm are ruled by active or retired officers, and they all report to the Commanding General. Dornhelm is ruled by Captain Grallam.

"Grallam is rather a young man, though not as young as Galen. Well, anyway, Grallam was in here having drinks, and he'd had a few too many," Beagan continued. "Soon he started to act like a fool. He staggered around the room yelling at people, and started accusing old Bruce of being a dirty thief. Bruce may not be the sharpest tool in shed, but he's no thief.

"Everyone knew this, even Lucian and Galen, who were visitors. Galen got to his feet and tried to calm Grallam from the other end of the bar. But the captain wouldn't have it. He yelled at Galen, telling him he was a weak man and a coward and other things of that nature. Galen pulled a knife off the counter and flung it across the room at Grallam, pinning him to the wall by his sleeve. You can still see the mark over there.

"Well, Grallam ripped away from the wall, and he became a mad man! He grabbed old Bruce in a headlock and yelled at Galen to show his strength. I've never seen anyone move as fast as Galen did. He punched Grallam in the stomach and twisted him around, forcing him to release Bruce. And then, Galen backed off, but Grallam ran at him."

Beagan's eyes began to shine with amusement. "Lucian stopped the fight by using magic to enlarge Grallam's nose to the size of a peach. Afraid that Grallam, as head of the city, would try to evoke revenge, Lucian and Galen left Dornhelm within the hour. That's the last time I saw either of them."

Matt and Emmon were grinning. It was typical of Galen to stand up to an injustice, whatever the consequences, and to do it with flair.

Beagan noted their smiles and said, "I take it you know Galen well."

They both nodded vigorously.

"Ah, here's Lucian!" Beagan said.

Matt had the distinct impression that Lucian had left just so he didn't have to suffer through the story of their rapid departure from Dornhelm.

* * *

Galen closed his eyes, trying to focus his senses on his surroundings. In the silence of his mind, he could hear the faint pounding of feet, against the earth. He opened his eyes and peered into the darkness. They were out there, somewhere, but they were camouflaged by the darkness.

"What are you?" Galen muttered.

His horse whinnied nervously and Galen stroked her neck, resting his hand on his sword hilt. His horse whinnied again, louder this time and Galen tensed. He knew that whatever was out there was nearby.

"Easy," he soothed softly, quietly sliding his sword from the scabbard.

The horse became even more agitated, its ears flattened against its skull. It let out a shriek of fright as a large, shadowy creature emerged from the darkness, glinting claws outstretched. The horse reared up in terror and Galen was thrown from the saddle. The force of the collision knocked the air from his body, and in that moment the garan leapt on him and pinned him to the ground.

Galen quickly freed his arm and swung his sword, catching the garan in the back before it could strike. It fell to the ground, unmoving. Galen got to his feet, staring at the hideous creature. He moved toward his nervous horse, stroking her face to calm her.

"Where did it come from, girl?" he said, more to himself than to the horse.

It had been two weeks since he had left Amaldan searching for clues of Malik whereabouts. He had begun by riding across the northern plains, taking a roundabout path toward Marlope and

Northwood Forest, hoping for signs of activity along the way. Now, he had certainly found some. He knew well that the presence of one garan meant that there were likely others nearby.

He looked around, trying to decide which direction the garan had come from. He held his sword out in front of him, and he unhooked the strap that held his throwing knife at his thigh. The light was dim since there was only a sliver of a moon, but the terrain was relatively flat. He led his horse quietly through the grass, peering doggedly into the darkness. A sudden shriek to his left made him freeze in his tracks.

Letting go of the horse, he crawled along the ground toward the sound. The ground dropped off several feet ahead. He moved quietly to the edge of a small valley.

There were hundreds of twisted creatures prowling in the grass. Garans. An army of garans.

"Shut up!" a voice barked. "Can't you get these things to quiet down?"

Galen froze. He knew that voice all too well. His eyes found the large, muscular man overseeing the garans. Galen's heart skipped a beat. Rock Thompson. Anger rushed through him and he fought the urge to attack him.

"The scouts have not reported back yet, sir," one of the few men reported.

"I don't have time for scouts! The creatures are mindless, anyway. Now move! Night is the only time we can travel and we're losing time right now. I only have the power to disguise the garans when they aren't moving. We must continue to travel under cover of night, and we must hurry. The boy is miles and miles ahead of us. Do you want to be responsible for losing him? Do you want to tell the Commander that it's your fault?"

The garans began to move, and Galen realized he was in their path. As swiftly and silently as he had arrived, he sidled away and jogged back to where his horse was waiting. He sheathed his sword and pulled himself into the saddle. The boy they referred to could only be Matt, and that meant Matt had an army of garans on his trail. Galen had to warn his friends.

"Come on, girl," he said, patting the horse's side. "We went looking for trouble and we found it. We've got work to do."

He yanked the reins and galloped into the night, knowing how lucky he was to have discovered the army of mindless killers. In the distance, he could still hear their wailing and the angry shouts of the men barking orders.

CHAPTER FOURTEEN

"Arden? Arden, are you paying attention, at all?"

Arden reluctantly looked away from the window where she had been watching the archery range and tried to focus on the instructor, a very refined elf in an elegant dress who was glaring at her in frustration.

"No," Arden answered honestly. "I'm sorry, but I just don't find any of this interesting. History is interesting, but not the history of leading ladies of elven society. And especially not their dresses."

"But you, too, could grown up to be an influential lady," her instructor said patiently.

"By selecting the best gown for evening wear?" Arden retorted. "I don't think so."

The instructor did not reply, but gracefully glided to the window.

"Arden, if you ever wish to achieve prominence in elven society, you must learn to pay better attention."

Still standing at the window, her instructor began speaking again about the history of dress fabrics and colors. But Arden was not listening. She was ready for just such a moment. She reached into her pack beside her chair and pulled out a small pouch. Sal, one of the apprentice food growers, was the best boysenberry grower in Amaldan and could grow them to three times the normal size. He had given her these berries three days ago, and she had kept them in her pack ever since so they would get nice and soft. Quickly, while the instructor's back was still turned, Arden pulled out four giant boysenberries. Then Arden pulled out her small slingshot and fitted one of the mushy berries into the strap.

The instructor was still lecturing, her back turned to Arden. Taking careful aim, Arden let the first one fly. It splattered against the instructor's backside, sticking for a moment and then falling limply to the floor. It left a particularly lovely stain, purple and blue, with hints of red. Arden fired another, and another, until the back of the dress was splattered with a swirl of colors. Arden examined it appreciatively. The design blended nicely with the pale yellow fabric.

"Now, Arden," the instructor said, turning away from the window and stepping unknowingly onto the fallen berries. "I'm glad that we had this discussion."

"Yes, ma'am," Arden agreed, smiling brightly.

"Good," her instructor replied. "You may go for the day, but I expect better of you next time. Please take this letter to your grandfather to inform him about your attention problem."

Arden grabbed her pack, jumped to her feet, and made for the doorway, grateful to finally leave the hut. She stopped at the door to call back, "Oh, and that's a lovely dress you're wearing today!"

Giggling to herself, she trotted across the Heart. She breathed in the fresh air outside. Even though the Lady Lessons hut was part of the forest like everything else, it always felt so stuffy in there. The whole forest was starting to feel stuffy.

If only she could have gone with Matt, Emmon, and Lucian and not be trapped enduring Lady Lessons every day. She hitched up the skirt of her dress and hurried across the ramps until she came to the hut where she lived with her grandfather.

She peeked cautiously inside but saw no sign of Lan. Sighing in relief, she crept to her room and began rummaging around for her other clothes. Anything to get out of the dress.

"Arden. Why are you here?"

Arden's heart plummeted to her stomach. She slowly turned around to see Lan standing in the doorway, his bow slung over her back. Grudgingly, she handed him the letter that the instructor had given her to deliver to him. He took the letter, still staring at Arden as he opened it. She waited uncomfortably as he read. She knew what it would say, the usual rant about her lack of respect and poor behavior.

Lan finished reading and threw the letter to the floor. Arden braced herself.

"Arden, I will no longer stand for this!" he said angrily. "You have spent too much time wandering the forest and traipsing across Mundaria. It is time that you learn some real skills and some manners! And if you do not cooperate, I will make you cooperate!"

"I try to cooperate, really I do, but think how you would feel if you had to listen to someone talk about dresses for six hours!" Arden snapped back. "I want to do something more important with my time!"

"Arden, I have always made my decisions with your best interests in mind," Lan said. "Your parents would want you to comply with my wishes."

"My parents?" Arden said incredulously. "Do you think they would want me to do something that I hate and go through each day wishing I was somewhere else, just as long as I comply with your plans for my life?" She shook her head. "They would never want that for me."

"Arden!" Lan snapped, his face growing red. "How dare you suggest that I would do something against your parents' wishes! I have taken care of you and raised you so that you can become the elf that you are truly capable of being!"

"Oh, and sending me to lady classes is going to make me the best elf I can be?" Arden retorted. "Let me be a scout! Or better yet, let me go with Emmon and Matt and actually do something worthwhile in the world!"

She pushed past him and ran out the door.

"Arden!" Lan yelled after her.

Arden ran across the ramps, ignoring the dress. Despite her frustration, she knew that Lan really believed that he was doing the right thing. She knew that he was afraid of something happening to her, that he was afraid that he would lose her the way he'd lost her parents. Sighing, she leaned against the balcony.

She was so absorbed in her thoughts, that she barely noticed the flutter of wings beside her. An Amaldan falcon had landed on the balcony beside and was waiting patiently for her to take the letter it carried.

Glancing around, Arden read the letter swiftly. It was from Galen. She was desperate for news about her friends. As she read, Arden began to realize something else. She couldn't defy her grandfather, but maybe there was another way to handle it. She began to formulate a plan.

Making up her mind, she tucked the letter into the shoulder of her dress and ran back to the hut, hoping that her grandfather was still there. She caught him just as he was walking out of the hut.

"Wait, Grandfather!" she cried.

He looked at her without emotion. "What is it, Arden?"

"I...I wanted to apologize," she said swiftly. "I'm sorry. I acted poorly and I was wrong. I'll work very hard at my lessons and maybe I'll even be able to use what I've learned out in the real world."

Lan looked surprised but pleased. "I'm glad that you came to your senses, Arden. I will be sure to watch your training closely and perhaps you will get the opportunity to practice your new skills."

Arden waited until he had walked away and then ran back into the hut. She found pen and ink in her room, and she hastily scribbled a reply on the back of Galen's letter. She watched the hawk disappear into the trees, hoping that her plan would work and that maybe she could finally leave the dresses and Lady Lessons behind.

* * *

Matt tried to ignore the angry protests from his legs as he climbed up the steep, slick hill. The rain had stopped that morning, and he and Emmon were exploring the four eastern and northern hills that surrounded Dornhelm.

"I don't see anything on this one," Emmon called to Matt.

Matt reached the top and looked down the sides. He could see no sign of a 'crown' as Dorn's clue suggested.

"No, I don't see anything, either," he declared resignedly.

From the top Matt could see the undulating ground beneath Dornhelm, even in the dusky light of the evening. Beyond the city he could see the hills that Lucian was checking. Natalia was somewhere in town trying to gather information from people in the streets.

"We might as well head back. There's nothing here and I'm starving," Emmon said.

Matt agreed. They nearly rolled down the slippery slopes, and they plodded along the muddy pathway that led into the city. The dead grass had been torn away in the rain, and the paths were now troughs of puddles and muck.

By the time they reached the inn, their boots were heavy with mud. Matt tried to wipe them on the doorstep, but it did little good. The floor of the inn was already mud-streaked, but Matt felt remorseful when he noticed the face of a girl who was futilely trying to mop the floor. He grinned at her apologetically, but she glared at him.

Matt and Emmon quickly retreated to a table where Lucian and Natalia sat, looking grim.

"Did either of you have any luck?" Matt asked hopefully.

They both shook their heads and Natalia said, "There's nothing unique about the hills, according to the townspeople. And I've tried to think of everything I know about geology and about Dorn's history, but I can't think of anything."

Her face was flushed with frustration. "What are we going to do?"

"We're going to keep searching," Emmon said. "If there's anything that I've learned from our crazy adventures, it's that you'll never even have a chance to get anything done, if you don't try. If we keep searching, I guarantee that we'll find Dorn's clues, and we'll follow them all the way to Oberdine. Even if it takes us months, we have to keep trying so we can save as many lives as we can."

Emmon's impassioned speech filled Matt with new determination. Natalia was looking at Emmon with admiration.

"Well said, Emmon. That is exactly what we have to do," Lucian agreed approvingly. "But for now, let us eat."

Beagan came by their table and merrily ladled a thick stew into four bowls. They all ate hungrily, listening to the quiet music played by a group of musicians in the corner. Several couples danced nearby.

Twenty minutes later, the chatter died as the door was thrown open by a tall, neatly dressed man with frenzied eyes. His most striking feature was his nose. It was so large that it almost obstructed his vision and the bulbous tip stuck out further than any nose Matt had ever seen.

Matt glanced over at Lucian, but Lucian had disappeared, and Emmon and Natalia were absorbed in conversation.

Matt followed the man to the bar and stood against the nearby wall so that he could hear what he was saying.

"I heard that the magic man has been here," the man growled.

Beagan cowered slightly. "I don't know, Captain Grallam."

Grallam slammed a fist on the table. "I know he's here, Began. Where is he?"

"I-I don't know," Beagan whimpered. "You should ask Carver."

"Carver!" Grallam yelled. "Carver doesn't know him. You do. I watched you when he and that scarred fellow were here before. You know them both. Where is he?"

Beagan cowered again but did not respond. Grallam raised a hand to strike him. Matt conjured a shield around Beagan without thinking. Grallam's fist violently bounced backwards and he lost his balance. He fell hard against a rack of cloaks and then to the floor. The cloaks fell in a heap on top of him.

Grallam struggled to his feet, angrily flinging off the cloaks, and he looked around frantically around the room. His eyes, crazy with anger, finally landed on Matt. Grallam stared at Matt for a moment, and then he rushed at him. Matt's fingers tingled fiercely. He raised a hand and the cloaks began to tie themselves around Grallam's face and arms, binding him tightly. Grallam shouted furiously.

Eventually, a few people made their way over to untie him, but Matt, Emmon, and Natalia did not wait to see what Grallam would do next. Within seconds, they had climbed the stairs, where they slammed into Lucian, standing on the top step, struggling to suppress a smile.

CHAPTER FIFTEEN

"Well, Matthias, obviously your next lesson needs to be about being more discreet," Lucian reprimanded Matt the next morning.

Matt shrugged. "Beagan was the only one who saw, except that idiot, Grallam."

Lucian gave him a stern glance. "Even so, do you understand that now you are in even more danger than you were before? You might as well have stood at the top of one of those hills out there and shouted your presence. Magic always leaves its mark. Especially in places where there are many people.

"Now that you have made your magical abilities apparent, you will most likely attract the attention of those who are already looking for you. When was the last time you practiced your sight invocation?"

Matt hesitated. "In the plains, when I used the Fire Stone."

Lucian's glare became even more severe. Matt shifted uneasily. He felt guilt burn in his stomach. He knew Lucian was trying to keep him safe

"You need to practice every morning. Detecting magical auras should become automatic for you. And it is essential that your aura be masked at all times."

"Won't my enemies mask their auras, too?" Matt asked.

Lucian smiled. "Yes, but you might find a careless one here and there, and there is also a good chance that your enhanced abilities with the Fire Stone will allow you to see through other masks."

Matt nodded and immediately closed his eyes to practice. He let his magical power fill his body until he could feel his sight invocation working. He opened his eyes, but Lucian's aura was masked.

He followed Lucian out the room and down the hall. Emmon and Natalia were waiting for them at the top of the stairs where they were talking animatedly. Matt was surprised to see a haze of bright white light surrounding Emmon. He realized that since all elves had magical abilities, they must have auras, but he had never seen Emmon's aura before.

"Emmon," Matt said. "Shouldn't you be masking that aura of yours?"

Emmon was startled.

"Since when did you start checking auras?" Emmon said, grinning. "You're right, though, I haven't masked it, yet. Maybe if you did a little less snoring during the night, I could sleep better, and have the energy I need to hide myself."

Natalia laughed and Matt punched Emmon on the arm.

After breakfast, they walked outside the city to examine the surrounding hills again. The morning quickly transformed into afternoon, and the shadows of the enormous mountains disappeared as gray clouds covered the sun. Weary and unsuccessful, they retreated back to the inn.

Lucian conversed quietly with Beagan as Matt, Emmon, and Natalia sat at a table, hovering over Dorn's map. They struggled to make sense of the clue, searching desperately for a hint about the location of the crowned hill.

"Aye. Things are festering along the Eastern Edge," they could hear a man at the bar saying to Lucian. "It's only a matter of time before-"

The rest of the man's words were drowned out by a loud gasp from Natalia.

"Silent voices…what about the dead?" she said.

Matt nodded. "That would make sense. So, where would they be, a cemetery? That could be it! Hey, Lucian!"

The wizard walked to the table, and Matt quietly told him about Natalia's idea.

"Maybe there's a cemetery around here somewhere," he said.

Lucian grabbed the sheet of parchment and read the clue again.

He walked quickly back to Beagan, and they heard Beagan say, "It's past the church, of course. You can see it from the road."

Lucian strode to the door with the teenagers close on his heels. Sure enough, just over the roof of the nearest building, tall stones were visible on the peak of a small hill near the church. The gravestones circled the hill and looked exactly like a spiky crown.

"That's it!" Matt said triumphantly. "It's not one of the seven hills. We weren't looking low enough!"

"But, what about 'turning the crown gold'?" Natalia asked.

Lucian answered without hesitation. "The sun. When the sun reaches a certain point in the sky it should make the stones look gold. It is too cloudy, today, and too late for the sun to shine in that direction. We'll wait until tomorrow to look for the jewel, and then we'll finally get to the bottom of Dorn's mystery."

The remainder of the afternoon and evening seemed to drag on for ages. Matt could not quell his anxiety and excitement. He felt a strong sense of urgency. Every day that past was a day closer to death for many of the people in Gremonte. He knew that the others felt that urgency, too, especially Natalia, since her friends and neighbors were ill.

Just before sunrise, Matt shook Emmon awake and slipped on his boots.

"Come on, Emmon," Matt urged as the elf groggily pulled on his dirt encrusted boots. "We don't know when the sun will hit the hill. Let's go!"

"I'm coming, I'm coming," Emmon protested as he stumbled through the door after Matt.

Lucian and Natalia were already standing in the hall. They crept quietly down the stairs. They found Carver shifting chairs around to different tables, and Beagan was sleepily rubbing down the counter with a wet rag.

Carver looked up. "Beagan tells me you were looking for a ladder. You're not planning on doing any damage to my roof, are you?"

Lucian shook his head and held up his hands. "No, good man, we are not. We only need access to your roof for a short time."

Carver did not look reassured, but gestured to the side door with his giant thumb. "It's just outside the door there. Don't do anything costly."

"We wouldn't even consider it. Thank you, Carver," Lucian said, smiling.

He gratefully accepted a loaf of warm bread from Carver's wife, and they walked into the muddy alleyway which was crowded with wooden crates, barrels, and a rickety ladder leaning against the side of the building. Tucking the loaf of bread under his arm, Lucian climbed carefully to the top rung where he disappeared onto the roof. The others followed close behind.

The roof was steep, and it was difficult, at first, to avoid sliding, but eventually they were all seated. They chewed quietly on the warm bread. The sun was barely visible, but the hills still cast a shadow over the inn. Matt shivered. As they waited, Matt and Emmon began discussing whether swords or arrows were better weapons.

"Look!" Natalia interrupted, standing up and beginning to slide down the roof.

Matt and Emmon both caught her arms and held on to her as she pointed. The circle of gravestones had a faint yellow glow with the sun shining on it.

"Look for the 'jewel' of the crown," Lucian reminded them.

Within minutes there was a flash of blue light from a tombstone in the center of the cemetery. Matt and Emmon immediately moved to the ladder and ran wildly toward the hill. It was essential that they get there before the light shifted off the stone.

Matt got there first and found a gate to right of the church that led to the graveyard. It was locked, so he placed a foot on the latch and heaved himself over it. Breathing heavily, he ran up the small hill to a flat ledge of earth that encircled it upon which many of the graves were situated. He hurried to the center of the graveyard, where they had seen the blue glow. The light died just as he reached the tombstone.

He bent down in front of it and wiped off the dirt that covered the writing as Emmon caught up with him. It read:

This shall be my final resting place, but Death, mark my words:
Twice I have cheated you, though thrice I may not. But I am Dorn the
Adventurer, and no other has had adventures more fortunate than
mine.
Here lies Dorn the Adventurer
"May your adventures lead you to good fortune"

"May your adventures lead you to good fortune," Matt read out loud.

"That doesn't exactly tell us much, does it?" Emmon said.

"That was Dorn's most famous line. It is still sometimes used as a farewell greeting," Lucian said as he and Natalia joined them.

"Dorn prepared his own grave before he died?" Matt asked curiously.

"Yes, it was rather strange. He did not want to be buried anywhere except for the place where he was most famous," Lucian said. "Perhaps now we know the reason for that."

"Is that all it says?" Emmon asked, disappointed.

Matt got to his feet and examined the face of the stone. At the very top, there was a tiny hole where a small sapphire had been placed. Matt walked around to the back of the stone and ran his hand down its smooth surface. He spotted a small scribble of writing carved at the bottom of the stone.

"Wait!" he shouted and bent down, reading it out loud:

The lair of the wild pig is the place to look.
At the very top of the highest point is
where the secret will be revealed, at the point where light pierces darkness.
Now read this once more.
Look carefully at the words above, and delve into their meanings,
for they will provide the answer.

Lucian frowned and bent down next to Matt to read it. "Another clue. It doesn't sound like this is the last one either."

"The lair of the wild pig?" Emmon said incredulously. "We're supposed to find a pig's nest?"

"No, wait," Natalia said calmly. "Look there at the end. It says to 'delve into their meanings'. Those words could be saying something different, or maybe telling you to look for different words."

"Well, a lair could be...a...," Matt tried, trying to come up with an idea.

"A den, of course," Lucian supplied. "And a wild pig would be a boar. Matt, hand me that map. A boar's den..."

"...isn't any different than a pig's nest," Emmon muttered.

Matt tried to suppress his laughter and it came out as a strangled snort.

"Something to add to the conversation, Matthias?" Lucian asked.

Emmon grinned as Matt pulled Dorn's map out of his pocket. Lucian took it and scoured over its contents.

"Ah!" Lucian said at last. "Yes, that would make sense."

"What would?" Mat said eagerly.

"Boar's den is the city of Borden. It's southwest of Dornhelm and has one of the tallest towers in Mundaria, aside from the tower at Apetain, of course. That would be the highest point that Dorn is referring to. We must go to Borden."

CHAPTER SIXTEEN

An hour later, they stood at the door of the inn with Beagan, who looked dismayed.

"Do not worry, Beagan," Lucian assured him. "This will not be our last meeting."

Beagan nodded. "Be careful out there, Lucian. Things are changing."

"I will, old friend," Lucian replied, patting the little man on his shoulder.

Matt shook Beagan's hand and followed Lucian out the door. As they were saddling their horses, Raumer swooped into the stable, screeching loudly. He landed on Lucian shoulder. Matt suddenly realized that both Raumer and Samsire had been absent during their stay in Dornhelm. He felt guilty that he had been so preoccupied with their search that he hadn't even thought about Sam during the past few days. He wondered where he was.

About thirty minutes into their ride, Samsire swooped down beside them. Natalia was nearly thrown from her horse again, but this time managed to hang on.

"Sam!" Matt yelled. "Where have you been?"

"Around," the alorath said. "Did you figure out the clue?"

"Yes, no thanks to you."

Samsire growled. "What did you expect me to do? Fly into the city? Burn down a few buildings?"

"Peace, Samsire," Lucian said. "We are headed to Borden. That is where the next clue lies."

Sam glared at Matt and Matt glared back at him.

"I'll fly ahead."

Without another word, the alorath jumped into the air and flew toward the mountains. Lucian turned to Matt and gave him a stern look.

"You would do well not to anger him, Matthias."

Matt nodded. He was angry with himself for being grumpy with Sam when he'd been so happy to see him, but Sam had been irritable, too. Matt knew that Sam was probably feeling lonely and bored, and that's why he had been flying off for long periods of time, but his absences bothered Matt.

He shrugged off the thought, and tried to focus on their hunt for the Water Stone. Lucian had decided to go around the mountains rather than cutting through them, and they were riding hard now that Natalia was finally comfortable riding.

Though he was tired when they stopped to rest that evening, Matt did not protest when Lucian suggested that they have a magic lesson.

"Why don't you show me what you can do with the Fire Stone?" Lucian suggested. "I know you've been practicing."

He had been practicing often over the past week. He had become much more adept at wielding the magic of the Fire Stone, and he could quickly delve into its power to create fire or manipulate it in a variety of ways. He could create flame, reduce it, increase it, and dismiss it, as long as the stone had contact with his body, either inside or outside the pouch. Without the Fire Stone around his neck, though, he had no control over fire.

Matt spent ten minutes demonstrating his abilities with the Fire Stone to Lucian. Samsire watched with interest. When the fire flared up in Matt's face at the end of the lesson, Samsire leaned forward and blew on it with an overly large spray of water, quickly soaking the fire and Matt.

Matt wiped the water from his eyes and tried to glare at Sam, but Sam was innocently licking his feathers. Matt knew that Sam was punishing him for snapping at him earlier. He began to laugh. Sam's eyes twinkled as he nudged Matt affectionately with his nose. All was forgiven.

"Now that you have that settled," Lucian said, "perhaps you would be willing to learn something new, Matthias?"

Matt felt a stab of excitement.

"When we were in Amaldan, I told you about my knowledge of Light magic and what it can do. I think it is time for you to know more about it.

"When I was a young man, I received formal magical training in Karespurn by the members of the wizard council. They not only trained me in magical aspects, they also taught me of Malik's darkness and evil. I began to notice the lasting effect of Malik's magic. I wondered what made him so powerful and what could combat his power. I explored all types of magic, and eventually, after tireless work, I discovered Light magic."

"Malik discovered the magic of Dark, but I discovered the magic of Light. Light magic is neither elemental nor non-elemental. It is in a category of its own. Both elemental and non-elemental magic exist in nature, but Light and Dark magic are created and fueled by living objects. They reflect the traits of the magician wielding the magic. They are essentially good magic versus evil magic."

"How do you use it?" Matt asked eagerly.

"I will show you," Lucian said, his eyes twinkling. "Light magic is not controlling like elemental magic, nor is it obedient to your will. Light magic comes from the calmness and serenity in your mind. Harness that natural energy. Imagine yourself creating light. Use the magic to make it so, as you have done with the Fire Stone and with non-elemental invocations. Magic is essentially the power of will."

Matt smiled. This was typical of Lucian. He always gave him just enough information to get started, but he always compelled Matt to work it on his own.

"Try it, Matthias. Use the experience that you had with the Fire Stone to create light. And use the experiences from performing non-elemental magic to help initiate it."

"It doesn't really seem any different than anything else that we've done," Matt muttered.

He closed his eyes and immediately felt the familiar tingling in his fingertips as his energy focused into magical electricity. He burrowed deeper into his mind where it was peaceful, trying to push past the constant worries and doubts that plagued him. Gradually, his thoughts began to relax. After what seemed like hours, but was probability only moments, Matt realized that he felt no anxiety, only serenity.

He opened his eyes and concentrated on the air above his palm. Like when he used the Fire Stone, a small spark appeared and swelled into a shining orb, but it was made of light rather than fire. It was a perfectly contained white ball that pulsated slightly.

Unlike when he was controlling fire, Matt could not feel the weight or presence of the light. It was almost as if it didn't exist. Matt tilted his hand and passed the orb into his other hand. Briefly, he wondered if he was imagining the light and felt a pang of self-doubt.

The light disappeared instantly.

"If you stop focusing on the feelings which summoned the light, you will not have enough power to fuel it," Lucian explained. "Another interesting trait that I forgot to mention is that Light magic can be applied to another object, such as a stone. It is a temporary condition that will cause the object to glow like a lantern. "

"That's useful, I suppose," Matt said, still not fully comprehending the use of Light magic or what it meant.

Lucian gave him a knowing smile. "Light magic is strange, isn't? I don't even fully understand it, so don't worry if you don't. Just remember that Malik is the master of Dark magic. I feel that in some way, Light magic will be vital in your attempt to defeat him. Light is the only thing that can truly conquer the Dark. Just as the only thing that can truly defeat evil is goodness. Powerful magic can keep the Dark at bay, but only Light can defeat it."

Lucian's gray eyes studied Matt thoughtfully. "And, Matthias, I want you to listen to me carefully. Though your future seems like it has already been decreed, remember that we all choose our own destinies in the choices that we make. Only you can decide which path you will take."

Lucian put his hand on Matt's shoulder, and they walked back to the fire where Emmon and Natalia were sitting. Matt leaned against Samsire, thinking about what Lucian had said until he drifted off to sleep.

The next day, they rode even harder, pushing the horses faster and faster. They stopped to eat around midday, but they did not stop again until they could scarcely see the ground ahead of them in the dusky light.

"We'll camp here," Lucian finally declared.

They all groaned in relief, nearly falling out of their saddles. Matt unfastened his pack from Striker's saddled and spread his bedroll on the ground, wincing at his sore legs. He collapsed in a heap as Lucian started a fire and prepared a stew. Every muscle in Matt's body ached. He barely noticed when Sam landed in their camp and curled up behind him.

Hours later, Matt was startled awake by the loud whinnying of horses and Raumer's angry squawking. The horses were pulling desperately against the rock they were tethered to. Matt yelled, as Innar broke free.

"Lucian!" Matt shouted as he jumped to his feet and ran toward the horses, but it was too late. The four horses took off in a mad gallop in the direction of Dornhelm.

"We will never catch them," Lucian said in exasperation. "Where is Raumer?"

Raumer flew to Lucian's shoulder. The wizard rummaged around in his back and quickly scribbled a note. "Take this note to Beagan so that he will take care of the horses," Lucian said and then added, "And then find Galen and see if he needs you."

The hawk squawked obediently and took flight.

"What happened?" Emmon asked.

"Something spooked the horses. Sam, did you do anything to frighten them?"

The alorath, who was curled up in a tight ball, poked his head out from under a wing, yawning and shaking his head fiercely.

"Hmm," Lucian said, peering off into the night. "Then it was something else. That is unfortunate. My staff was attached to Innar's saddle. Well, we must travel by foot now and with all haste. Morning is on its way, so we'll take advantage of this early morning temperature and leave soon."

Matt turned to gather his things, but sensed movement in the darkness behind him. Fear trickled down his spine, but he could see nothing in the dim light. He clutched the pouch around his neck and focused his magical energy, remembering what Lucian had taught him. After a moment, an orb of white light sputtered above his palm. He thrust his hand forward, straining to see.

Natalia screamed and Matt jumped backward as a black shape leapt out at him.

"Matt!" Samsire roared.

The alorath jumped into the air, wings outstretched as he lifted into the air, barely clearing Matt's head. He hit the ground with a thunderous crash, snatching the creature in his claws and throwing it ferociously. Matt heard it land with a piteous yelp and then stagger off into the distance.

"Garan!" Sam growled.

Emmon pulled Matt to his feet, holding his bow at the ready. "Did you see any more?"

"I don't think so," Matt said, breathing heavily. "That was obviously what spooked the horses." He looked at Lucian. "They must be following us, Lucian."

Lucian nodded gravely. "Yes, Matthias. We need to be careful not to lead our pursuers directly to Oberdine. And we must hurry."

They quickly cleaned up their small camp and gathered their things. Within minutes, they were walking, heavy packs on their backs. The sun was not yet visible on the horizon, but the darkness was fading. Sam decided to stay closer now, circling back frequently, while watching the surrounding landscape for anything that looked threatening. They were all edgy and much more watchful than they had previously been.

The traveling was slow without horses, and before long Matt's back, shoulders, and legs were aching. The sun grew hotter and their packs grew heavier with every step. It was a relief when Lucian told them to stop for lunch at midday.

Matt hungrily fished an apple from his pack and settled down on the side of the hill. Emmon and Natalia joined him as Lucian stared into the distance.

"Do you think there are more garans behind us?" Natalia said quietly.

Matt could tell that she was afraid.

"I wouldn't worry," Emmon reassured her, putting his arm around her protectively. "If there are, I don't think they will attack us. They want us to lead them to the Water Stone. The garan that we saw earlier was probably a rogue."

Natalia shivered despite the heat. "I guess you're right. It's just that…I've read about the Commander of Shadows and the old war. I thought I knew what it was like…but this morning when that garan came out of the darkness…"

"It's okay to be afraid, Natalia. Nothing can prepare you for what it's really like to see a creature like that."

Natalia nodded, looking at Emmon gratefully. Matt glanced at Sam, who was trying to hide a grin. Matt shifted his gaze to Lucian and concentrated on keeping a straight face.

"How long until we get to Borden, do you think?" Matt asked, changing the subject.

"Probably three or four days now without the horses."

Matt's hand slipped as he was cutting a bruise out of his apple and he cut a small gash in his finger.

"Four days?" Emmon groaned. "How many will die while we are walking?"

Lucian nodded. "Come along then, my friend. The fewer breaks we take, the more quickly we will get there."

They all pulled on their packs and started off again. Matt jogged to catch up with Lucian, sucking on his cut finger. Lucian glanced down at him.

"You have a question, Matthias?"

Matt grinned. "Lucian, didn't you say once that there is a non-elemental magic form of healing?"

"Yes, but it can only be used for minor injuries. It feeds on your own strength to heal the ailment, and it takes a good deal of strength to heal even a very minor injury. All you have to do is channel your magical energy to the afflicted area. Unlike most non-elemental invocations, you must use the word 'heal' to control your power, and then slowly heal each layer of the injury.

"It's a tedious and exhausting process but it can be used to relieve pain. Even the most advanced wizards can do no more than heal a broken bone. That is why the Water Stone and the healing waters of Oberdine are so important."

"Why does the Water Stone have the ability to heal? What makes water so special?"

"Ah," Lucian said. "You ask an interesting question. Water is the element that feeds all life. We could not survive without it. That is the greatest wonder of the Water Stone. Its power to heal comes from the connection it has as the source of our existence. We cannot live without water.

"But even the magic of the Water Stone has limitations. My understanding is that, although the Water Stone is able to heal the injury or illness completely, weakness lingers, and strength must be regained."

That night they camped against an outcropping of rock that shielded them on three sides, and Sam placed his massive body between the four travelers and the vast open space. The nearly full moon created an unnatural glow on the plains. After a light dinner, without a fire to draw attention, they collapsed wearily onto their bedrolls.

Long after the others fell asleep, Matt lay awake. Sam's muffled, rhythmic breathing was comforting against his back as he listened to the many strange noises in the tall grass beyond him. He was not thinking about garans, though, but about the Water Stone. He examined the partially healed cut on his finger, and then casting a glance toward Lucian's sleeping form, he placed his other hand over his finger and tried to focus his energy. He muttered the word 'heal' under his breath, but nothing happened.

Remembering that Lucian said that each layer of the wound must be healed, Matt examined it more carefully. He focused on the layer that had begun to grow over the cut and muttered 'heal' again. This time, Matt immediately felt his energy seep away. He sat riveted, as a very thin layer of skin began to form over the cut. He felt himself unconsciously reach into the wild magic of the Fire Stone for strength, and his energy increased immediately. The layer of skin continued to grow until it covered the open cut.

He began to feel lightheaded, and he was forced to withdraw himself from the fire magic that was threatening to overtake him. He sat still for several moments as he regained control. He looked back down at the cut and poked at the thin membrane of skin, understanding now what Lucian had meant by different layers. It was an exhausting, and potentially dangerous, process to heal a wound with non-elemental magic.

Matt's last thought before he fell asleep was how urgent it was that they find the Water Stone.

CHAPTER SEVENTEEN

Late in the afternoon of the seventh day since leaving Dornhelm, Lucian spotted the tower of Borden through the trees. The day before, the landscape had changed dramatically as they left the rolling green fields and entered a forest similar to the Glade Forest where Matt grew up. He was glad to breathe in the sharp scent of pine that was so familiar to him. Soon, he spotted the tower above the treetops.

"I see it!" Natalia said. "We're almost there!"

Matt could hear the relief in her voice. He, too, felt the aching in his legs and back, and he had several blisters on his feet, though he didn't dare try to heal them since he was so exhausted already. It would be nice to have a comfortable bed and warm, fresh food.

The sun was falling below the trees as they drew close to the forest edge, and Lucian walked with increased urgency

"We must be at the tower 'where light pierces darkness, when night falls or we will have to wait until tomorrow's sunset,'" Lucian said.

The trees began to thin around them, and a dirt path appeared that stretched from the forest into the city. The buildings were made of wood and stone, all of different sizes and shapes with a variety of flat and slanted roofs. An enormous tower loomed above them. In the fading light, Matt could make out the coned roof of the tower and the room beneath it with a single window.

They hurried down the dirt path as it transformed into a stone. Wagons and carts clattered around them, and vendors loudly hawked their wares. Lucian led them through the street, narrowly avoiding the maze of carts. They were repeatedly jostled by the swell of people. Finally, they found themselves at the foot of the tower in the center of the city.

"Come," Lucian commanded, opening the large, wooden door of the tower.

They entered a small, circular room with a large table in the center. A small bespectacled woman sat behind it. She peered up at them through thick lenses, her lips puckered into a sour grimace.

"May I help you?"

"We need to go to the top of the tower. Will you kindly direct us to the stairs?" Lucian asked, barely hiding his impatience.

Darkness was almost upon them.

"This tower is used for astronomical and historical purposes. Borden was built around it, you know."

"Yes," Lucian said more forcefully. "We are amazed by it and wish to look upon the city. There must be an enjoyable nighttime view."

The woman's puckered lips unfurled at the corners. "I'm afraid I can't let you up."

Lucian sighed and pulled out his heavy bag of coins. He poured a healthy amount into his palm and dropped them one by one onto the woman's desk. Her eyes followed each dropping coin, and her surly grimace transformed into a strained smile.

"I'll have Tridard show you up," she said without blinking. "Tridard!"

A boy with greasy hair emerged from a door behind her, and she said loudly, "Tridard! Take these people to the top of the tower!"

The boy nodded wearily, beckoning to them as he disappeared back through the doorway. They followed him without a word as he plodded dutifully up the narrow, winding stone staircase.

"Ya sum of doz stargazers or sumpthin'?"

Lucian smiled mysteriously. "Of a sort."

"A heap of 'um come t' this ole tower 'cause 'o what it do."

"What does it do?" Matt asked, more to distract from the burning in his legs than to satisfy his curiosity.

"Turns. Ya hold onta some ol' handle an' da 'hole top o' da tower turns. Crazy," Tridard said, shaking his head in bewilderment.

"Would you mind picking up the pace a bit, Tridard? It's important that we reach the top as soon as possible," Lucian said.

They began to climb faster, but the stairs seemed to stretch on endlessly, and their legs silently screamed in protest the whole way up.

"'ere 'tis," Tridard said.

He pushed open a heavy trap door above their heads with great effort until it clanged loudly against the stone floor above. He heaved himself into the room and reached down to help them through the hole in the stone floor, one at a time.

Setting his pack on the ground, Matt looked around the room. There was a small table covered in tools in the center of the room and a heavy spool of chain with a turning handle. The room was a strange hexagonal shape and a single window was carved out of one of the walls.

"Aye's headin' down now. Dats da handle ta turn't," Tridard said as he jumped through the hole onto the steps.

Lucian closed the trap door after him and quickly walked around the room before stopping at the window. A small shaft of moonlight shone through the window onto the far corner of the room.

"This is perfect," Lucian said. "I'm guessing that we must turn the room until the moonlight shines through the window onto a certain point on the wall."

Matt and Emmon both grabbed the handle of the giant spool with the chain wound around it. It was difficult to turn and they were both panting by the time they had moved it a notch. As the chain slipped out a small distance, the entire room shifted with a great deal of groaning and creaking. Matt and Emmon were both thrown backward, nearly knocking Natalia off her feet.

"Look," Lucian said, pointing to the slashes of moonlight on the wall and then pointed at the window. "You see that design in the center of the window? It focuses the moonlight onto a certain spot. Let's try two more turns."

Matt and Emmon reluctantly returned to the handle and threw all of their weight against it until the chain groaned and more links slipped off the spool. Again, they were thrown back violently, this time into the small table, causing a hammer to fall and hit Matt on the head.

"One more turn!" Lucian prodded them.

The third turn was easier, but the jolt threw Matt into Lucian's stomach and a whoosh of air escaped the wizard's mouth.

"Er...sorry, Lucian," Matt muttered hastily, though he was grateful for the soft landing.

"That's quite all right, Matthias. You have done what we needed you to do."

Matt followed the wizard's gaze and saw that a beam of moonlight came through the window into a fine point on the opposite wall. Lucian groped at the wall and muttered 'reveal,' but nothing happened.

"Hmm."

"Maybe we should try using this," Natalia said, picking up the hammer.

Lucian backed away and Natalia hit the wall hard on the spot marked by the light. They shielded their eyes as pieces of the wall flew everywhere. Lucian reached his hand into the large hole, and he withdrew a small stone tablet. He dusted it off and Matt read the writing on the tablet out loud:

If you are one who has been following my clues, then I commend you. If you are merely a curious mind, I would advise you to return this tablet to the place you found it for a more informed adventurer to find.

If you are a Faithful Adventurer, it pleases me that you have followed in my footsteps. I know that you are anxious to learn my secret, so, I will waste no more words. Look south of this tower where you will see a mountain looming above the rest. That is where the secret lies.

Never forget that you have followed in my footsteps.
May your adventures lead you to good fortune,
Dorn the Adventurer

They crowded around the window, squinting out into the darkness. Beneath the glowing moon, several large, shadowy shapes were discernable. One mountain, however, stood above the rest, slightly southwest of Borden.

"Those are the Crane Mountains," Lucian said. "There is only one mountain, though, that deserves a visit. Come, now. We have found what we needed."

They shouldered their packs, Lucian dropped a few coins on the table for damages, and they flung open the trapdoor. One by one they lowered themselves onto the staircase below, and they hurried down the steps. Natalia and Matt both tripped several times, nearly tumbling down the endless spiral. They were all tired and disoriented from the long journey from Dornhelm. Matt forced himself to focus on the thought of a warm bed that awaited him at a nearby inn.

When they finally reached the bottom of the stairs and opened the door to the main room of the tower, the woman glowered at them from behind her spectacles.

"You certainly took your time up there," she said disapprovingly.

"Thank you for your kindness," Lucian said courteously, and then added under his breath, "and I hope we shall never meet again."

Matt, Emmon, and Natalia scurried out of the tower behind Lucian before the woman could register the last comment, and as soon as the door had safely slammed shut, they burst into laughter.

"I don't know what you young people find so funny," Lucian said, his face a mask of innocence. "Come, let us find a place to eat and sleep."

They grinned at each other and followed the wizard to an inn nestled in the shadow of the tower. It was small, but the quiet atmosphere of the bar was comfortable and cozy with puffy armchairs that engulfed them like hungry bears when they sat in them. They ate a hearty meal of venison and fleshy potatoes, and Matt soon found himself dozing in front of the hot fire.

"Go to your bed and sleep," Lucian told them. "Tomorrow we shall decide on our next action."

They each gave Lucian a grateful look and within minutes they were asleep in soft beds.

* * *

When Matt woke the following morning, he felt more relaxed than he had in weeks. They were only a step away from solving Dorn's mystery. He stretched leisurely and glanced out the window. The sun was already shining brightly, and Matt could hear the yells of vendors and people in the street. Yawning, he pulled himself out of bed and glanced over at Emmon, whose unruly golden hair was sticking up in every direction was bobbing energetically as he pulled on his boots.

"Hey," he mumbled sleepily.

"Hey," Matt replied. "Want to get some breakfast?"

Emmon gave a groggy, noncommittal jerk of his head, but followed Matt downstairs where Lucian was sitting in one of the overstuffed armchairs, reading a book. There was a plate of warm toasted bread sitting on the table, and Matt and Emmon grabbed several pieces.

"Hi, Lucian," Matt mumbled through a mouthful of bread and sat in the chair next to him.

Lucian looked up from his book and smiled. "Good morning, Matthias."

"What are you reading?"

Lucian flipped the book closed. "*Chronicles of Fortune*. It's written by Dorn the Adventurer. Alem gave it to me a few years ago, and I thought it would be helpful to see if he mentions anything about the Crane Mountains. I have already checked for mention of Oberdine, but he speaks of it only as his most famous discovery."

Matt swallowed his toast. "Did you learn anything else that we should know?"

Lucian gave him a wry smile. "Dorn was very careful not to reveal anything except to the most stalwart explorer. You know, Alem spent half his life searching for Dorn's secret. He idolized him, and after traveling across Mundaria, he finally found Dorn's map buried in a never-used book about the creation of rivers in the library at Dornhelm. Alem lived there in his younger days."

"Alem lived in Dornhelm?" Matt asked.

"Yes. He relocated to his quiet home in Sunfield many years later, when his adventuring days were over."

Matt tried to picture Alem as a fearless adventurer, but the only image that came to him was of the squat little dwarf standing with his arms crossed grumpily over his chest with a little wisp of hair sticking up on the top of his head.

Matt finished eating his toast as Natalia walked down the stairs. She was wearing a blue dress instead of the grubby traveling pants that she had worn for the past two weeks. Matt turned to see Emmon's reaction, and he wasn't disappointed. Emmon was wide awake now. He was smiling broadly and he managed to reach the bottom of the stairs before Natalia did. Natalia went pink.

"I have asked around the inn and the town for information about the mountain south of Borden," Lucian said, ignoring Emmon's sprint across the room. "No one in Borden seems interested in the land to south of them, but many have suggested that we go to Lopane which is just west of the mountain we intend to search."

"Lucian, look!" Natalia interrupted.

Outside of the window, Raumer the hawk was preening his feathers on the windowsill. Glancing furtively around the room to ensure that the innkeeper was not watching, Lucian opened the window, and Raumer flew onto his shoulder.

"Who's the letter from, Lucian?" Matt asked curiously. "What does it say?"

Lucian smiled at him. "Give me a moment to read it, Matthias."

They all watched Lucian eagerly as he read.

"It is from Galen," Lucian said sounding surprised and concerned. "He says to stay in Borden. He will be arriving here by late afternoon."

"You don't look happy. What's the matter, Lucian?" Matt said.

"Galen would not abandon his work to join us unless something important had happened," Lucian replied gravely.

Matt felt a knot of foreboding building in his chest, but he tried to ignore it and focused on the thought of Galen rejoining them. The next few hours passed slowly as they waited impatiently for Galen to arrive. Matt was eager to hear what Galen had learned, no matter how dark or ominous it may be.

To pass the time, Matt and Emmon convinced Natalia to teach them to knit just to see if it really was as tedious as it looked, but they failed miserably, and eventually they took to sword fighting with the knitting needles, instead. In the end, Matt accidentally kicked over the chessboard on the table and pieces flew in every direction.

"So this is how you amuse yourselves when I'm not around."

Matt jumped to his feet.

"Galen!"

Galen's tall frame filled the doorway. He was smiling broadly, but his face was pale and travel weary, and the long, jagged scar that ran down his face was prominent. Behind Galen was a tall, sharp-chinned elf whose dark eyes glared at Matt judgmentally, and behind him was a much smaller figure with long, brown hair and brown eyes, wearing a pale green dress on her slender frame.

"Arden?" Matt said incredulously, his jaw dropping.

She smiled serenely and followed the other elf to an armchair where she sat down, gracefully crossing her ankles and placing her hands in her lap. Matt looked at Emmon, who was staring at Arden like she was an unknown species. Galen's smile grew even bigger as he watched their reactions. He dropped his pack to the ground and collapsed into the armchair next to Matt.

"I sent a letter to Amaldan telling the elves that I would not be returning, and I received a letter back requesting that I return temporarily so that Miss Arden and an escort could accompany me to Borden," Galen explained. "Isn't that right, Miss Arden?"

She smiled sweetly. "Yes, it is, Galen. It is a pleasure to see you all again."

Emmon's eye twitched involuntarily. Natalia shifted uncomfortably, glancing at each of them uncertainly. They had told her all about Arden, and she was most certainly wondering who this girl could be.

"So, er...Galen," Matt said awkwardly, trying to ignore Emmon's expression. "What have you been up to?"

Galen smiled secretively. "Oh, I've been traveling around."

Matt sensed that Arden's escort was listening closely, and Matt knew that Galen did not trust the elves with certain information.

"It is quite a mess in here," Arden said suddenly, looking at the chess-piece scattered floor, speaking in a high-pitched voice that was not her own. "I am surprised that you do not take better care of your surroundings."

They fell silent as Arden tilted her head inquisitively at Matt and Emmon. Hesitantly, they dropped to the floor and gathered up the chess pieces.

"I trust you read my letter," Lucian said to Galen, breaking the silence.

"Yes, Gremonte," Galen said, nodding gravely. "Fortunately, it will be difficult for the illness to spread to cities above ground if precautions are taken, but we must do everything we can to save Gremonte. I was very sad to hear that Alem is one of the ill."

Lucian and Galen continued to converse for several minutes, and Matt listened closely, but heard nothing that he didn't already know. Natalia resumed her knitting, the clinking of her needles ticking like a clock in Matt's brain. Eventually, the conversation dwindled to silence. A few locals drifted into the inn for a drink, but their quiet murmurings were not enough to alter the awkward hush in the room.

It was a relief when dinner was finally served, and they could stuff their mouths full of food to save them from the need to speak. Arden would occasionally comment on the meal with phrases like, 'I think the potatoes could use a bit more spice.' Eventually their plates were clean, and they fell back into silence. Even Galen didn't seem to know what to say.

"Have you heard from Hal?" Matt ventured uneasily.

Galen nodded. "About a week ago. He wishes you all well. He says that his training is going quite well, though he often has to hide because Barrum sends envoys of his own soldiers from Hightop to check on the goings on in Ridgefell."

"Well, it's getting quite late," Arden said, stifling a yawn. "I think I shall retire."

"It's barely dark," Emmon protested weakly.

Arden got to her feet and gave Emmon a disdainful look. "I am very delicate. I must get my rest."

"I will get us some rooms," her escort said, speaking for the first time.

"You don't need to get one for Arden," Natalia said graciously, also getting to her feet. "She can share with me."

Arden did not smile, but nodded in satisfaction. Her escort gave the innkeeper a few coins before following Arden and Natalia up the stairs. Matt and Emmon were left alone with Lucian and Galen. Galen laughed heartily at their shell-shocked expressions.

"Don't worry about Arden," he said. "I sent her the letter letting her know I was going to come find you and she managed to convince Balor that it would be an excellent diplomatic mission for her to travel here. I think Balor thought it would be an ideal opportunity to spy on you, Matt."

"Spy on me? Why?"

"Lady Can has grown sicker still. Balor thinks it is your doing. He is not pleased that a human is the One foretold by the Prophecy of the Elements. He thinks that your magic may be Dark."

Matt started to utter a protest but Galen stopped him, smiling. "Don't kill the messenger, Matt. That's what many of the elves think. I'd get used to it. That's the way they've acted toward me, too, since they feel the same way about merglings. Don't blame Arden for it either, she was really excited to see everyone."

Matt fell silent, but Emmon said sarcastically, "She's got a strange way of showing it."

"Now, Galen," Lucian said. "What have you really been up to?"

Galen's blue eyes shone. "After you left, I traveled east to see if I could glean any information about Malik's doings. It wasn't long before I found something."

"What?" Matt asked excitedly, forgetting about Arden for a moment.

"I saw a group of garans, hundreds of them, moving together. I came across a few of them accidently and assumed there were more, but I thought that they were trailing me since I am a known opponent of Malik. I traveled southwest until I was west of Dornhelm and southeast of Gremonte, and I waited.

"I did not spot the garans again until about twelve nights ago, when I saw them moving like a massive shadow across the plains. I overheard two of the men talking and I realized that they were following you. I had already sent Raumer back to you so I could not warn you, and I didn't know you were in Dornhelm.

"I had been given one of the Amaldan falcons and since they only know the way back home, I sent word to Arden that I was traveling to find you. I went to Dornhelm and spoke with Beagan the afternoon after you had left, and he told me you were heading to Borden. Arden wrote me back, telling me that she and an escort were traveling southwest to meet me. We met outside the city, and here I am. In other words, you are being trailed."

"We suspected as much," Lucian said quietly. "Though, we had no idea that there were so many. Our horses were spooked a few nights after we left Dornhelm, but we saw only one garan. They must be keeping a safe distance around the cities and traveling only at night." Lucian paused. "The question is how are the garans being controlled so masterfully from such a great distance? Without careful guidance, they are nothing but wild, vicious animals."

Galen looked grim. "That's the other part that isn't very reassuring. The garans are being led by Rock Thompson."

"Rock Thompson," Matt said hollowly.

Rock was the only man Matt disliked more than Kerwin.

"Ah, you know who he is," Galen said. "But do you know his story?"

Matt and Emmon shook their heads.

"Thompson was his name originally. He was a poor, but cruel man, living in a small village. Not content to live his meager lifestyle, but unwilling to work his way to a higher status, Thompson turned to thievery. His first venture was a small farm. His goal was to steal the pig and sell the meat. He snuck into the barn just before dawn and killed the pig. One of the farmer's sons, however, walked into the barn to fill the troughs, and Thompson pulled out the knife he had used to kill the pig and he attacked the boy, leaving his arm maimed and useless.

"Thompson continued with his thievery. Whenever his victim stumbled upon him as he was robbing them, he would maim them. Eventually, Thompson sought an encounter any chance he could, and began to injure his victims badly enough that they would suffer and die days later, but never badly enough that they would die immediately.

He moved around and was merciless to his victims. He was no longer for money alone, but because he was evil. Rock's notoriety spread and it was not long before Kerwin approached him and took him as his lieutenant."

Galen paused, staring into the flames of the roaring fire, his scar pale in the dim light of the fire.

"I told you, Matt, that when I left Amaldan at the age of sixteen I thought I could conquer any foe. Well, I soon met an expert swordsman in the forest. He wounded me badly and cut my face as a mark of his work. It was Rock Thompson who left me in the forest to bleed to death."

CHAPTER EIGHTEEN

"Wake up, Matt!"

Matt groggily opened his eyes and realized that Emmon was kicking his bed.

"Come on. Galen said that we have to leave while it's dark so we won't be noticed."

Matt groaned and grudgingly rolled out of bed. He had gotten very little sleep, thinking about garans and Rock Thompson and Kerwin. Everyone was waiting for them near the door. Standing uneasily beside Galen was Arden, dressed in simple traveling pants with her hair pulled back into a long braid. She looked slightly pale.

"Arden?" Emmon said, bewildered.

Galen stuck a finger to his lips, silencing him, and walked outside into the pre-dawn blackness. The streets were eerily quiet. Their shadows bounced threateningly off the walls in the lantern light. Galen silently led the way to the opposite side of the city, with Matt bringing up the rear. They wove between the buildings, staying in the narrow, less-used passageways.

Just as the others disappeared around the corner of one building, a hunched woman carrying a broom appeared in Matt's path.

"Whoa, sorry," Matt said, placing one hand on her shoulder and one hand on the building to avoid slamming into her.

In the dim light of a nearby lantern, Matt saw her studying him with dark eyes. Wrinkles creased the corners of her eyes and forehead as she squinted at him. Her voice was low and raspy.

"Mmm...I can tell that it burns within you. It must be strong in your parents. Oh, yes, you and your parents are strong. I can feel it. But you are different. Perhaps one of your parents is...ahh, yes."

A chill traveled down Matt's spine.

"Hey, Matt! Come on!" Emmon whispered as he came back around the building corner.

"What?" Matt called back distracted.

"Come on!"

Matt hastily looked back at the woman but she had disappeared.

Shaken, he followed Emmon to where they were all waiting. They all stared at him quizzically.

"What's up with you?" Galen asked. "You look like you've seen a ghost.

"There was an old woman back there in the street who said that 'she could tell that it burns within me'. Lucian, is my aura masked?"

The wizard nodded. "Yes, there's not a sign of it."

"She mentioned my parents."

Matt hastily repeated her words and they all looked puzzled.

"I have no idea what she was talking about, Matthias. She probably wasn't right in the head," Lucian said. "Don't dwell on it. We have a long walk ahead of us today. And please do not permit yourself to be left alone like that again. I'll walk behind you for now."

Galen led them out of the city at a rapid pace, as they all watched for signs of garans. Matt tried to focus on the darkness surrounding them, but his mind kept drifting to the old woman. Her words played over and over in his head, and he wished desperately he could understand what she had been saying to him. He was sure that she wasn't crazy. There had been something about her eyes that made him know that she had been telling him the truth and that she could see something that he could not.

They were far from the city by the time the darkness began to fade. They paused briefly to catch their breath.

"Ugh...finally!" Arden said laughing. "I can't tell you how nice it is to be able to speak like someone who has more than half a brain in her head!"

Matt and Emmon stared at her, exchanging puzzled looks. She suddenly flung her arms around both of them and laughed again.

"Honestly, did you really think that was me back there?" she said. "I had to promise to act 'proper' on this 'diplomatic training mission'. But now, seeing as I don't have an escort anymore, I consider myself free to be me again!"

"I would have said something to you," Natalia said to Matt and Emmon apologetically. "But Arden made me promise not to tell."

Arden hugged Natalia and the two of them trotted cheerfully after Galen and Lucian like they had been friends for years, leaving Matt and Emmon to stare at them dazedly.

"Are you two going to stand there all day?" Galen called back.

Matt and Emmon hurried to catch up, ignoring Galen's mischievous smile. Matt was content to spend the morning listening to Arden and Natalia talk happily. Samsire joined them a few miles into their journey for an enthusiastic hello to the newcomers, and after soaking up the attention for a few minutes, he flew ahead to check for anything out of the ordinary.

At midday, they stopped to eat for the first time. Matt sat down on a rock next to Arden as she devoured her bread.

"So, what's 'diplomacy training' like?" he asked as her as he broke off his own piece of bread.

Arden rolled her eyes in disgust. "Misery. You sit there in a dress all day long doing nothing except learning a few courteous phrases, how to sit properly, and what color dress to wear. The elves don't even use diplomatic envoys anymore. None of the elves do. Not Amaldan or Southwood or Northwood. Basically it's just a well-disguised ploy to teach 'rebellious' girls like me how to be ladylike. Lan wouldn't have it any other way."

"I take it you were good and didn't get into any trouble?"

Arden flashed him an impish grin. "You know me. I did everything I was asked... and then some. One day we were helping out the cooks, I suppose I wasn't technically supposed to throw the bread dough, but when they said 'toss the dough' I couldn't resist. And then there was the boysenberry incident. My instructor wanted me to learn about fabric colors and patterns, so I did. Personally, I think purple and blue look lovely with yellow."

Matt grinned, but Arden sighed. "It wasn't all fun and games, though. In order to get here, I had to convince the rest of the elves that it would be good training for me to go and that it would allow them to spy on you through me. Balor really doesn't like you, Matt."

Matt shifted uncomfortably. "Yeah, that's what Galen said."

"I couldn't stand it any longer, though, and I knew that you wouldn't say anything dumb in front of my escort, so I kept pretending to be a proper lady diplomat, hoping that I could somehow get away from him."

Her voice trailed off as they watched Natalia tease Emmon about his especially unruly hair.

"It's good to be with all of you again."

Matt felt a strange feeling when she smiled at him.

"Let's get moving again," Lucian called.

Despite the rapid pace that Galen set, the remainder of the day was enjoyable. Matt felt like the empty pit in his stomach had been filled now that Galen and Arden were back.

But he couldn't stop thinking about the woman he'd met in the street that morning. Her words kept replaying over and over in his head. He wanted desperately to know what she had been trying to say to him, and he was certain that it was important.

Late in the afternoon, Samsire flew down to meet them.

"Hello, Sam!" Arden said cheerfully. "See anything good up there?"

"Nothing but the slow progress of you two-legged beings," the alorath replied, nudging Matt forcefully in the shoulder and nearly knocking him over.

"Hey! Maybe you need to find something to do instead of making yourself a nuisance all the time," Matt replied, smiling.

Sam grabbed the neck of Matt's tunic in his mouth, lifted him in the air, and threw him up onto his back.

Grinning, Sam said, "I think you need to have a little fun. I'll be in charge of that."

The alorath leapt into the air as Matt gripped his neck tightly. As Samsire leveled and began to pump his wings in a soothing rhythmic motion, Matt no longer felt the unyielding heat and the tension of their quest. He felt only the wind against his cheeks and Sam's sleek feathers beneath his fingers. He peered around Samsire's leathery head and saw his friends staring up at them.

He tried to lift a hand to wave, but Samsire suddenly pulled up, and Matt slid backwards against his wings. Matt struggled to hold on, laughing as he regained his balance. He loved flying with Samsire more than anything else, and he experienced the usual disappointment when they gently landed back on the ground. He slid off the alorath's back and patted him on the side.

"Thanks, Sam," Matt said, smiling. "Now I know what to say to get a ride from you."

Samsire grinned and nudged him before lunging back into the air.

Later that afternoon, Matt was walking beside Galen, and noticed how unusually quiet he had been since rejoining them.

"Is something wrong, Galen?" Matt asked.

Galen forced his eyes away from the distant horizon and smiled slightly. "Not at all."

"You know, I met someone really unusual when we were in Dornhelm," Matt said. "A man with the largest nose I've ever seen."

Galen grinned broadly and his eyes twinkled as Matt continued.

"Beagan told us about your...uh...encounter."

Galen cast a glance in Lucian's direction, who was talking with Emmon, before turning to Matt and saying, "So you know how his nose got so big then?"

Matt nodded. "Lucian-"

"Well, Lucian may have started the enlarging invocation but he merely wanted to distract Grallam, hoping to prevent a fight. He only created a peculiar feeling in his nose. I was the one who, accidentally, of course, grew the old fool's nose to the size of a large peach. How's my handiwork holding up?"

"Now it just looks like a small apple."

"Hmm," Galen said, chuckling and rumpling Matt's hair. "I think I might need to pay a visit to old Grallam one of these days and remedy that shrinkage."

That evening, as they set up camp, Matt faced the circle of stones they had laid for the fire and carefully focused on the warm stone against his chest. Eventually, he managed to conjure a small flame at the tip of his finger to light the pyramid of wood Galen had constructed.

"Handy," Galen said and blew on the fire to make it grow.

It was much merrier around the fire than it had been in days, and despite his exhaustion from the early start and hours of rapid walking, Matt felt more hopeful and energetic than he had in days.

They weren't too far from Lopane and the mountain that might hide the fabled city and healing waters of Oberdine. There was a general feeling of optimism around the camp, even though they were uncertain about Gremonte's fate. It was that feeling that lulled Matt into a pleasant sleep and allowed him to forget the words of the woman from Borden.

The following morning, after a quick breakfast, they started to walk again. As they traveled, they spotted several very large hares wandering across the fields in front of them, unaware of the intruders. Their ears suddenly twitched in alarm, and they turned their faces to the side so their wide eyes could see the visitors.

"You see that hare, there?" Galen said, pointing to one on the left. "I'll bet you I can catch it."

"Without using magic?" Matt looked at him skeptically. "I think it's probably too fast for you."

Galen winked at him. "Watch and learn, my friend."

They all stopped to watch as Galen handed his pack to Matt and moved stealthily through the field so that he was behind the hare. The animal's ear twitched slightly, but it showed no sign of noticing Galen.

Galen bent down low and held his hands out at the ready. When he was three feet away, he leapt at the hare. As the hare jumped into the air, it kicked a foot back and hit Galen hard in the face. Galen was thrown backward with such force, that it looked like he had been leveled by a small horse.

"Galen!" Arden yelled, and she and Matt ran over to the his prone figure.

Galen's body was twitching strangely, and Matt thought that he was having some sort of convulsion. When they reached him though, they saw that he was shuddering with laughter. He sat up, holding his stomach as he laughed. His left cheek had a very red paw print across it, with shades of purple already creeping in.

"Are you all right, Galen?" Arden asked.

Galen didn't answer because his laughter left no room for speech. Matt started to chuckle at the absurdity of the situation.

"Hey, look!" Emmon cried, pointing to the crest of the small hill behind them.

Matt and Galen looked up and saw the hare Galen had tried to catch sprinting back over the small hill toward them, accompanied by two other fierce-looking hares. The hares were running straight at Galen, a strange glint in their large black eyes. Galen's laughter caught in his throat and he let out a strangled croak.

"Let's go!" Galen shouted, scrambling to his feet.

They ran back toward the others, with Galen stumbling behind them. Matt glanced over his shoulder and saw that the hares were close on Galen's heels. Galen, realizing he couldn't outrun them, abruptly stopped running, ready to jump out of the way.

"Can I use magic, yet, Matt?" Galen yelled.

It was too late though, as the hares barreled at him at full speed. He jumped high into the air as the hares reached him. They ran past him, and Galen fell hard onto his back. The hares, seeming to lose interest in their pursuit, hopped off in the opposite direction, stopping to chew on the grass as they went.

As Galen slowly got to his feet, they all burst into uncontrolled laughter. Even Lucian was chuckling.

"I'll get the next one," Galen muttered.

"Yeah, if I were a hare," Emmon said, grinning. "I'd be trembling with fear."

Galen was slightly irritable for the remainder of the day, but no one brought up the hare escapade until that night when they were sitting around the fire.

"I'll take first watch," Galen suggested after finishing their dinner.

"Sure," Matt said with a grin. "Just keep a look out for hares."

CHAPTER NINETEEN

The next day, in the middle of the afternoon, Matt spotted a cluster of buildings in the distance.

"That's Lopane," Lucian declared. "It is a rather small, poor settlement. The people in Lopane are farmers mostly. It is definitely one of the quieter towns."

They reached the northern edge of Lopane just before nightfall. There were crude dirt streets running through town, and the buildings were disorderly and old. There were very few people walking in the streets and the few that were stared at them mistrustfully. Matt felt very unwelcome.

Lucian found a small, shabby inn on the outskirts of town. A few locals were sitting quietly at the bar, but like the rest of the town, the inn had a lonely, forlorn feeling to it.

The teenagers sat down at a table as Lucian and Galen took a seat at the bar.

"So," Galen said conversationally to a man whose head was resting on the bar. "Know anything about that mountain to the east?"

"Uhhhhhh…"

"Apparently not," Lucian said.

"You folks looking to climb that mountain?" the man to Lucian's left asked.

"We have a certain interest in exploring it."

The man nodded. "It's famous for its hidden caverns and crevices. Some think it's a treacherous mountain."

"And is it?" Galen prompted.

The man thought for a moment. "It does seem to attract some adventurous men. But if you bring a few ropes for emergencies and don't rush your way up, it's as easy as climbing a ladder."

"Any of those men mention Dorn the Adventurer?" Lucian asked.

The man shook his head. "No. They all claimed to be climbing for bragging rights. Said it was no mean feat to climb the mountain. All crazy if you ask me. What's it got to do with Dorn? Wasn't he that mad, old man who ran around the world searching for legends?"

Galen nodded with a small smile. "That would be the one. Anything else special about that mountain?"

"It's tall, I suppose, so you'll want spare food and water, and like I said, you'll need ropes and things to get back down. It's about a day and half to the foot of the mountain. Why is it that you're so interested?"

"We're searching Mundaria for interesting landmarks," Galen said easily. "Excuse me, if you will, we've had a long day of traveling."

"Hey, wait," the man said. "What'd you do to get that bruise?"

Galen put his fingers up to the enormous purple bruise on his cheek. "I got in a fight."

They stepped away from the bar toward the stairs, and the teenagers followed, struggling not to laugh. Arden covered her mouth, but her muffled snort made Galen turn to look at them.

"Arden," he said slowly, "you need to have a little respect for the great hare hunter."

* * *

Matt woke early the following morning, and though he tried to fall back asleep again, his mind wouldn't allow it. He lay on his bedroll on the dusty floor thinking about Oberdine and about the woman in Borden who had spoken the strange words to him. It seemed everything in his life was a puzzle - Dorn's clues, his parents, his past, and most of all his future.

Finally, he gave up trying to sleep, slipped on his boots, and stole past a sleeping Emmon.

Galen was at the base of the stairs.

"Good, you're awake," he said quietly. "Would you like to come with us to get a few supplies?"

Matt nodded. Lucian was waiting outside the door.

"Good morning, Matthias," he said cheerfully. "Up bright and early?"

Matt stifled a yawn. "Unfortunately."

"Come on," Galen said, punching him playfully on the arm. "Time's a wasting!"

Matt grinned and followed them into the dusty streets of Lopane. The fresh morning air was crisp. There were more people walking through the streets than there had been the night before.

"They're off to the fields," Galen said. "The earlier the better, before the heat begins its assault."

Matt nodded, understanding well. Back in Sunfield, he often worked in the fields through the day. It was long, tiring work, and the cool mornings were much preferred to the hot afternoons. He watched the people pass, dressed in their worn and dirty work clothes. Lopane was much larger than his village, but he recognized the same simplicity of existence.

They went into several stores where they bought as much food as they could carry up the mountainside - dried meat, bread, apples, seasoning for stews, and other rations. They also bought two ropes and several spare waterskins. When they left the last shop Lucian's bag of coins was considerably lighter.

"Where did you get all that money, Lucian?" Matt asked as they walked back to the inn.

"I was granted a sum of money when I achieved a seat on the wizard council in Karespurn. I only sat with the council for a short while since the council and I had...ah...different ideas about certain things," Lucian said with a smile.

"I went away in search of you, Matt, the one of the prophecy, supposedly under their orders. But the council and I knew both that it was better that I leave. So, I kept the money, as it had been rightfully given to me."

He opened the door of the inn and they stepped inside. Galen turned to Matt with a grin.

"So to summarize, Lucian was given their money, argued a bit, and then left to go chasing around after mythical people and places," Galen said.

Lucian glared at him. "Sometimes I still puzzle over why I consented to travel with you for so long, Galen."

"Pure guilt, I suppose," Galen answered as they climbed the stairs.

"Yes, that must be it. Otherwise, I would certainly be a senile old fool."

"That could be true, as well," Galen quipped.

Matt shook his head, smiling, and slipped through the doorway into his room where Emmon was putting his pack together.

"Here," Matt said, tossing Emmon one of the parcels of food. "You might want to make room for that."

Matt rolled up his bedroll and stuffed his own package of food into his pack

"If the mountain's been visited so often," Emmon said as he loaded, "how is it that no one has found Oberdine before?

"I was wondering the same thing," Matt said. "Maybe there's another clue, even though Dorn's clue in the tower made it sound like the mountain was the final stop."

"The city is obviously very well hidden. I don't think it's going to be easy to find."

Matt nodded. If Dorn was the only one to have found the mythical city, it must be well concealed. According to the legend, it was entirely closed-off from the outside world. Matt could not imagine that it would be easy to find even if they knew what to look for.

"Well, difficult is nothing new," Matt grumbled.

"That's for sure."

They shouldered their packs and left the drab room. Arden and Natalia were in the hallway putting their share of the supplies in their packs.

"Come, now," Lucian said. "Let's make our way to the mountain."

"Does making our way involve breakfast?" Arden muttered under her breath, but Lucian did not hear. She turned to Matt.

"What are you smiling about?"

"Nothing," Matt said and followed Lucian down the hall.

Lucian seemed incredibly eager to reach the mountain, and he set off at a ferocious pace. They all struggled to keep up. They did not stop to eat until they were far outside the borders of Lopane, and Arden finally persuaded Lucian to take a break.

"You'd think he'd want to eat, too," Arden said as they reluctantly pulled on their packs once more.

* * *

"In addition to Oberdine, Dorn also claimed to have found many strange, unimaginable creatures," Lucian said as they walked. "He said that mythical creatures actually existed and that he had seen them him-"

"Well, he was getting old, reaching an advanced age when dreams start to be confused with reality," Galen finished. "Actually, I think that with Dorn, dreams were the norm."

Matt and Emmon laughed.

"We can only hope that Dorn was not delusional about the existence of Oberdine," Lucian said gravely.

Galen became serious. "You're right. A great deal depends on that."

The mood was more somber throughout the remainder of the day. They walked mostly in silence, only occasionally exchanging a few words, which left nothing to distract them from the aching in their legs or the ferocious intensity of the sun's heat. Matt forced himself to focus on the words in Dorn's note in the tower, turning them into a kind of mantra to keep him moving forward. Samsire checked in with them periodically.

Just before darkness claimed the earth again, Dorn's mysterious mountain was looming above them. Its nearness revitalized them, but its massiveness was disconcerting. It would be easy to miss a clue to Oberdine's location on the mountain's immense slope. They were silent as they unrolled their bedrolls to sleep.

Matt felt like he had just fallen asleep when Galen shook him awake the next morning. He only had time to eat a dry piece of bread and pull on his pack before Lucian told them that it was time to leave.

"I have a feeling that today will be prosperous," Lucian said brightly.

"You're beginning to sound like Dorn," Galen said, and then spoke in a very deep and pompous voice, "Yes, good fortune. I am the most prosperous adventurer of all time." He pointed a finger at Emmon and put his hand on his hip. "You, young man, may your adventures lead you to good fortune...like mine."

Matt, Emmon, Arden, and Natalia snorted in laughter and Lucian smiled. "Yes, I do feel a bit like Dorn. Only, hopefully, a bit taller."

"Lead the way then, Oh Mighty Adventurer," Galen said with a mock bow.

Lucian returned the bow and took the lead, venturing fearlessly into the dense forest of pine trees that covered the lower half of the mountain. After carefully positioning their packs, the others followed. Galen joined Lucian at the lead. Eventually, Natalia fell behind, and Emmon dropped back to help her up a particularly treacherous cluster of rocks.

"What do you think we're supposed to be looking for?" Arden asked between breaths.

"I have no idea," Matt said.

Their conversation dwindled as the climb grew steeper. Breaks were few and brief. Finally, though it was still light, Lucian stopped on a wide, flat ridge of land.

"The climb gets steeper after this. We'll stop here tonight."

Gasping in exhaustion and relief, they collapsed on the ground at Lucian's feet. Matt helped Galen by conjuring a small flicker of flame on his fingertip to light a fire. Galen mixed a warm stew as they wearily watched the sunset.

Matt stared out over the treetops hoping that they had not missed a clue along the way which would reveal the location of Oberdine. Exhaustion plagued not only his body, but his mind as well, as he wondered once again if anyone had died in Gremonte during their long absence. How much time did they have left?

* * *

They continued up the mountain the next day, this time staying very alert for any signs of the city. Samsire was assigned the task of circling the mountain repeatedly to look for anything out of the ordinary or anything that could be considered a clue.

"Go ahead and take your sword out of your pack," Galen told Matt as the slope grew steeper. "If for some reason you lose your pack, you'll still want to have your sword with you."

Matt fastened Doubtslayer across his back, tightened the straps of his pack, and followed Galen up the slope.

"Even the tiniest oddity could be a clue," Lucian said again, a hint of desperation in his voice.

"I think that it would be at the hardest place to reach," Matt said. "Which means up. I don't think Dorm would choose a place for a clue where someone could accidentally stumble upon it."

"Hey, Matt," Emmon called from behind him. "Sam's up there."

Matt looked up, and because the trees had thinned considerably, he had a clear view of the sky. Samsire's large shadowy shape was circling above them. Matt shoved his hand into this pocket and gripped Sam's blue and green feather. The alorath paused in midair and changed course, plunging downward toward Matt. After a moment, he landed heavily on the slope beside him.

"Did you see anything?" Matt asked eagerly.

"I've circled the entire mountain many times," Sam replied. "There's a lake up ahead, but that's all."

"A lake?" Lucian said with interest. "Hmm. Let's keep going."

"I'll stay with you," Samsire told Matt. "I've had enough flying for a while."

Matt patted the alorath fondly on his massive leg and walked beside him. Lucian and Galen pulled ahead again, and Natalia stumbled through the maze of rocks with Emmon hovering nearby to help if needed. Eventually, Samsire fell back away from Matt, and when Matt turned around to see where he was, he saw Natalia warily climbing onto his wing. A grinning Sam lumbered over to Matt with a grateful Natalia on his back.

An hour later they climbed over a ridge onto a plateau where there was a large lake. The water was a very clear, iridescent blue, and Matt felt a surge of hope building in his chest. Lucian bent down to the water and swirled it around with his fingers.

"I wonder," he said quietly. "Could this be the famous water of a city long lost?"

"No," Galen said. "It's like Matt said. It's too obvious. Even if there was a city here, it's too easy to access. Besides, I think we'd know if these were the healing waters."

"You're right," Lucian sighed, getting to his feet. "It was just a hope."

Matt glanced around the area surrounding the lake. It was a solid rock plateau with a steep slope behind it. On the far side it dropped off steeply.

"Matt," Galen said. "What exactly did Dorn's note in the tower say?"

Seeing the strange glint in Galen's eyes, Matt quickly pulled off his pack and withdrew his journal. He read Dorn's message aloud while Galen listened thoughtfully. Matt looked at him expectantly when he finished and saw that Galen was pacing back and forth along the lake edge.

"'Faithful adventurer, it pleases me so that you have followed in my footsteps,' and 'never forget that you have followed in my footsteps,'" Galen said, looking up. "He mentions footsteps twice."

"That may be the clue, Galen!" Arden yelled and everyone turned to look at her. Her eyes were wide with excitement and discovery. "Look for footprints! Footprints in the stone!"

Matt understood the sense in her conclusion. Dorn would leave some sort of trail for them to follow, but it would likely be well hidden and not easy to recognize. They split up, each going in a different direction to search for anything that might look like footprints.

Matt and Sam walked toward the cliff at the far edge of the plateau, studying the ground. The brown-gray rock was uneven, but flat and unordinary. Matt thought he spotted a footprint carved into the stone, but it was nothing but a dip. They wandered closer to the edge, their gazes riveted to the rocks. Suddenly, Matt saw a crescent-shaped indent in the stone. He moved closer and saw a trail of crudely carved footprints leading off the edge.

"Hey!" he yelled. "I found something!"

Within seconds they were all crowded around.

"Those are definitely footprints!" Emmon said excitedly.

"But they lead off the edge," Natalia said in confusion.

"Maybe," Galen said slowly, "they lead *under* the edge."

Matt had an idea and looked at Samsire, but Sam had already dropped a wing for Matt to climb on his back. Matt scrambled on, and slowly, Sam pumped his wings until they rose into the air.

Abruptly, he dove over the edge and they streaked downward. Matt yelled silently as his voice was ripped from his mouth. Sam stopped abruptly, much farther down the mountain than had been necessary, and began flapping his wings so that they rose upward. Matt examined the rock face carefully as they moved alongside it.

He didn't see anything until they were just below the cliff edge where their friends stood. The edge of the plateau extended many feet beyond the cliff wall, creating an enormous overhang. Beneath the overhang, in the rock face, was a huge hole, nearly twenty feet wide. Beneath the hole, another ledge protruded from the cliff wall. Sam drew level with the opening.

It was a cave. Or a tunnel.

Samsire moved upward and landed back on top of the plateau and Matt slid off his back.

"What did you see?" Lucian asked.

"There's a hole just beneath this plateau. It might be a tunnel into the mountain beyond it. And there's a ledge beneath the hole that we could stand on."

"Can you fly us down, Samsire?"

The alorath nodded. "It'll be a little tricky to get close enough to the ledge for you to step onto it, but I think I can manage it. It's definitely too dangerous for you to try to reach it by rope since the plateau overhang is at least fifteen feet away from the cliff."

They divided into groups of two for Sam to take down, Lucian and Natalia, Galen and Arden, and Matt and Emmon. Matt waited impatiently as Lucian and Natalia climbed onto Sam's back and they disappeared over the edge. Sam returned a few minutes later and disappeared again with Arden and Galen.

Finally, the alorath returned for Matt and Emmon, and they dropped over the ledge. Sam positioned himself under the overhang next to the cave opening. He placed a front and back foot on the ledge and pumped only the outside wing so that Matt and Emmon could climb onto the ledge with the others and he could stay aloft.

They all moved inside the cave so that there was room for Sam to climb onto the ledge completely. He had to crouch down to fit into the opening. They all knew it would be uncomfortable for Sam to walk that way for any length of time, but no one suggested that he stay behind.

The air inside the cave was damp and musty and smelled like toadstools on the forest floor after days of rain. It was also very dark as they moved away from the opening.

"Come, let us see what awaits us," Lucian said as he picked up a stone. "Light the way."

Instantly it glowed with white light. Galen and Matt did the same. Sam's heavy footfalls echoed through the passageway. An uneasy feeling spread through the group. As they moved farther into the mountain, the temperature began to drop, and Matt pulled his cloak closer around his shoulders. The tunnel began to decline and the air became heavier still. Matt felt like they had been in the passageway for hours.

"How much farther do you think it goes?" Natalia finally asked. "Look!"

They could see light glowing ahead, and they lowered their light stones as the light grew brighter still. Suddenly, the light was so bright that it felt like they were outside again. Unlike outside, though, the temperature did not rise as it grew lighter. Suddenly the tunnel ended and they stopped abruptly at the edge of a drop-off.

They all stared in amazement. Before them was a brightly-lit, underground world, teeming with life.

CHAPTER TWENTY

The sight before them was more incredible than anything Matt could have imagined. It was a vast cavern, many times bigger than Gremonte, and within the walls was an enormous city of artfully crafted stone buildings zigzagging up a long, rock slope to a grand palace. Scattered around the city were several emerald green fields. The most striking aspect of the cavern was that it appeared to be in full sunlight, but they could see no source of light. There were no holes in the ceiling, no torches on the wall.

"The fabled city of Oberdine," Emmon whispered.

"This isn't a city," Galen breathed. "It's a civilization."

People were working the fields and bustling through the streets of the city.

"Look," Arden said faintly, pointing to their left.

Matt followed her finger and saw that to the left, on a cliff high above the palace was a small lake and waterfall, sparkling as if the water was filled with sapphires.

"The healing waters," Lucian said softly.

Lucian stepped forward out of the tunnel and onto a narrow ledge that snaked its way down the wall of the cavern until it met up with the cavern floor.

"Let us make ourselves known to the dwarves of Oberdine as quickly as we can so that we do not appear to be thieves," he said as he began to navigate his way down the path.

They all followed him down, unable to stop looking around in awe. The ledge was too narrow for Sam, so he extended his wings and floated down.

"Where's the light coming from?" Matt asked Lucian. "There aren't any torches or lanterns, and I can't see any holes for sunlight to shine through."

"I believe that that is part of the mystery of this magical world. It is an entirely autonomous settlement powered by some of the most advanced magic I have ever seen."

"So, it's Light magic then?"

"No," Lucian shook his head. "There are some forms of magic, Matt, that I do not understand and cannot explain. It is probably a kind of dwarf magic. They have amazing skills for mining and living underground."

The existence of the cavern and the city were so overwhelming that it was almost too much to take in. Matt had to remind himself that even more important than the existence of this city was the incredible water that was here, water that might be able to save the people of Gremonte.

As they made their way down the path, they could see many dwarves with their stocky physiques and heaps of hair. They did not seem to have noticed Matt and his companions slowly approaching their home.

"Lucian," Matt said, suddenly uneasy. "I don't think they're used to having visitors. Do you think they'll...er...welcome us?"

Lucian looked at Matt and said, "We will do everything in our control not to cause any animosity. And then, all that we can hope is that the dwarves will be hospitable."

Matt nodded, his excitement twisting into anxiety. From what he knew, only Dorn had ever visited the city of Oberdine and that was many years ago. The dwarves would probably not be very welcoming to uninvited visitors. It was obvious that they preferred to remain hidden. Matt uneasily adjusted the position of his pack and his sword.

The path finally ended between two fields, where Sam stood waiting for them. Between the two empty fields was another path, this one ending at the edge of the city. Lucian stepped confidently onto it. For the first time, Matt noticed the absence of the wizard's staff, which had been lost when Innar and the other horses had fled. It had been oddly reassuring in strange new circumstances.

When they reached the edge of the city Matt peered into the street and saw a few bearded dwarves walking away from them. They did not appear to have seen Matt and his friends behind them.

"Come," Lucian encouraged.

They followed the street as it stretched up the steep hill toward the palace at the top. They did not see any dwarves at first, and then, two stout dwarves appeared from an open doorway. One was male and the other was female, and they were engaged in lively conversation.

"I don't want you to sell that vase!" the woman said. "It's been in my family for fifty years!"

"But I already told Egbert that I'd sell it to him," the man argued. "He says he's going to pay us well."

"Well, you can tell Egbert-" the woman started, but stopped suddenly as she spotted Matt and his companions. "Ohh...."

"Hello," Lucian said with a small smile.

The dwarves stared at them in shock. Several other dwarves wandered down the street and within seconds they were surrounded by a crowd. Matt heard a symphony of gasps.

"Outsiders!" someone finally said.

"What do we do?"

Matt looked around at the shocked, scared faces of the dwarves. He felt the ground tremble as Samsire pounded up behind them and the gasping grew louder. Sensing the dwarves' alarm, Matt quickly moved over to Sam, and Sam lowered his head so that Matt could pat his nose to show that he was friendly.

"Hello," Lucian said serenely again.

The dwarves looked even more bewildered. Matt saw a fat dwarf grin and nudge his neighbor.

"We should keep them hidden," said a taller dwarf with a red, bushy beard. "They mean no harm."

"No!" a short black haired dwarf next to him said. "We should tell the king that they are here."

"They must be kept safe," the first dwarf argued. "We should hide them!"

"No," the second dwarf spat. "Where's the tower guard?"

He sprinted up the street in search of a guard.

"You should hide, or get away," the red-bearded dwarf told them urgently. "I don't know who you are, or what you're doing here, but the king won't take kindly to your presence. Why, we haven't had a visitor in two decades – and he was the first and only."

"Quickly! Leave!" another dwarf yelled.

"We mean no harm," Lucian argued. "We wish only to-"

"Are you deaf? The king won't want you here!"

"Lucian," Arden said tentatively. "Maybe we should do what they say."

"Yes, listen to the girl! She knows what she's saying."

Galen stepped forward and put a hand on Lucian's shoulder. "It might be a good idea, Lucian. They obviously know something that we don't."

A flicker of worry crossed Lucian's face. "Fine. Let us do as they say."

"That's a wise choice. Come with me," the red-bearded dwarf offered, beckoning them to follow him back down the street.

They followed the dwarf uneasily, distinctly aware of the watchful gaze of the other dwarves around them.

"You'll find that Oberdine is very divided," the dwarf spoke softly. "There are those who support our tyrannical, self-absorbed king, and those who don't. My name is Borgik, by the way. I support the resistance against King Agram. That's why I'm helping you hide."

"We appreciate your help," Lucian said. "We did not understand the trouble that we were stepping into."

Borgik stopped suddenly and eyed Lucian suspiciously. "How did you get here anyway?"

"You said that you had a visitor twenty years ago, correct? That was the dwarf, Dorn the Adventurer, correct?" Lucian said, and Borgik nodded in confirmation. "He left behind a series of clues to this city. It is a well known fable in the world outside."

"Fable?" Borgik said outraged. "Oberdine is more valuable than half of the outside world! You don't think it exists?"

"Well, seeing that we're here," Galen said calmly. "We obviously thought it existed. That's why we came looking for it."

"Oh," Borgik said, stroking his beard. "So you came here to prove its existence? We don't like being known to the outside."

"No," Lucian consoled him. "There is another city of underground people called Gremonte, and its citizens are very ill, including a dear friend of ours. We heard stories about the healing waters, so we came here in search of them."

Matt noticed that Lucian had avoided mentioning the Water Stone.

Borgik nodded in approval. "That's better. I-"

"Sorry to interrupt, but aren't we supposed to be hiding?" Galen said pointedly.

"Er…right. Come this way."

They were about to follow the dwarf, when loud shouts and a great clattering reached their ears.

"Oh, no," Borgik said, his face going pale. "It's the tower guard. I can't be seen with you! Our leader has already been taken captive by the king, and I can't jeopardize our resistance movement by being captured. Quickly! Go to the storage house over that way and hide in there!"

Borgik motioned in panic for them to go and with a hurried nudge from Samsire, they started to run toward a large building at the end of the street. The shouts behind them grew closer, and when Matt glanced behind them he saw twenty dwarves in armor with axes and spears descending upon them.

"Stop there! Stop in the name of the king!"

To Matt's surprise, Lucian skidded to a halt and held up his hands, gesturing for the others to do the same. Staying close to Sam, Matt slowly turned around to face the guards.

"Don't move!" the closest guard ordered. "Your presence is a direct violation of the law of King Agram."

"That's unfortunate. Seeing as we're outsiders, we had no idea that our presence was a violation of law," Galen said in a sarcastic voice.

"Be quiet, Galen," Lucian told him sternly. "Do you not remember the last time you offended the ruler of a city?"

"All of you, be quiet!" the guard shouted. "You will be taken to the king's palace!"

The guards swarmed around them. A guard took each of their arms and pulled them gruffly. Reluctantly following Lucian's lead, Matt allowed himself to be pulled forward up the street. He walked quietly until he heard scuffling behind him.

Matt turned around and saw that at least ten guards were attempting to push Samsire up the road. They prodded Sam's colorful feathers with their sharp, pointed spears. The alorath growled at them threateningly, but stepped forward. One of the dwarfs seemed to panic and stabbed Sam forcefully in the foot. Sam bellowed in pain, rearing up onto his hind legs. The dwarves yelled in panic, their spears up and ready to throw.

"No! Sam!" Matt screamed.

Anger burned in his stomach as he wriggled in the dwarves' strong grips. Wrenching from their grasps, he stumbled forward. He yanked the spear out of the hands of the first dwarf in his path.

"Matt, stop!"

"Matthias!"

The blood pounded in Matt's ears, muting his friends' pleas. Fearful for Sam's safety, he pushed the dwarf to the ground with a magical attack field and ran furiously at a dwarf who had just thrown a spear at Sam's chest.

CHAPTER TWENTY-ONE

Reaching over his shoulder, Matt clasped the hilt of his sword, but before he could pull it free, two strong hands grabbed Matt's wrists. Matt struggled to wrench away, ready to use magic again, when he realized it was Galen who held his arms.

"No, Galen," he yelled. "They are throwing spears at Sam…"

Samsire was not fighting back or attempting to fly away. He merely stood there as spear after spear hit him in the chest. Matt closed his eyes as an anguished moan escaped him.

"It's all right, Matt," Galen said quietly.

Matt opened his eyes and saw a haze surrounding Samsire like a bubble. The spears had fallen uselessly to the ground.

"Leave the alorath alone," Lucian said in a low tone that made Matt's blood turn cold. "He has done nothing to harm you."

Matt glanced at Lucian and saw that though the guards' were still holding his arms, his palms and fingers were turned toward Sam, creating the protective shield.

"He will come quietly, won't you Samsire?" Lucian asked.

The alorath looked around at the stunned dwarves and said in his deep, booming voice. "I will come quietly. But don't try to attack me again, dwarves. I could have hurt you badly, but I chose not to."

Sam's curved claws, sharp teeth, and angry eyes were enough to make the guards back off. They moved behind him and allowed him to follow his friends up the street, unrestrained. Galen released Matt's arms, and Matt walked alongside Samsire. The two guards who had been holding on to Matt still lay in the street rubbing their heads.

Dwarves gathered along the street, and Matt could feel their stares, some curious, some sympathetic, some triumphant, others afraid. Matt noticed Borgik's red beard in the crowd. He looked angry and crestfallen.

The palace towered above the city, a simple, but daunting, rectangular hulk of a building. The doorway was a detailed archway decorated with golden trim. Three sets of golden axes crossed above the arch. There were three guards standing at attention on either side of the door. Two stepped forward to face the head guardsmen.

"These…intruders were reported in the city street," the guard said. "We must present them to King Agram."

The palace guards nodded and permitted him to pass. Their eyes widened, however, when they saw Sam.

"Sir! What about this creature?"

"Make sure it stays here so that the king can decide what to do with it," the guardsmen ordered, leading Lucian into the palace.

Matt cast a glance back at Sam and saw the alorath's eyes gleaming dangerously.

"Keep moving," the guards said gruffly.

The spear pushed against his back convinced Matt to follow his friends into the large hall. There were huge pillars decorated with paintings of Oberdine. At the end of the hall, was the fattest dwarf

Matt had ever seen. He wore long red robes and was slouched in his throne, his small golden crown lying crookedly atop his head. His cheeks drooped in long jowls, and his stomach billowed into rolls. The only thing orderly about his appearance was his short brown goatee, slicked to a sharp point.

"King Agram, your majesty," the head guard said, bowing hurriedly. "These outsiders were found trespassing in the city."

"Bow before his majesty," the other dwarves hissed and pushed them into awkward bows.

"Outsiders?" Agram yelled, his face turning purple. "Humans, no less…and…elves! How dare you enter my realm?"

"My lord," the guard said weakly. "They brought a ferocious, winged beast with them, as well. He was terrorizing the guards."

Matt opened his mouth to protest, but Emmon kicked him sharply in the shin and he remained silent.

"This must be a new plot to unseat me. The resistance must be squashed!" the king bellowed. "They sent in these outsiders to overthrow me and take over my throne! I have a counterstrike for that! Submit the entire city to questioning! They cannot have my throne."

"If I may be so bold as to counter your statement, your majesty," Lucian said calmly, but Matt saw the glint of danger in his gray eyes. "We have only come to Oberdine in search of your healing waters."

"Thieves! That's what you are!" the king screamed, leaning forward over his swollen stomach.

"We will pay you generously for a small amount of water -"

"You are traitorous, murderous thieves! I'll have you sent to the fields and used as slaves. Yes! How would you like that? Slaves!"

A protruding vein on his forehead pulsated violently.

"Good king-," Lucian began again, attempting to calm the king's rage.

"Servant!" the king screamed and a terrified dwarf ran over to the throne. "Fetch me some wine and some….cheese, I think."

The servant scurried away as the king aimed a kick at his behind. The servant squealed and ran all the way to the door.

"What was I saying? Oh, yes," the king said muttered, and then he screamed again. "To the fields! You'll be slaves! But first, you'll be imprisoned until you tell the truth about your ties with the resistance. All but you, there." The king pointed a pudgy finger at Natalia. "You have a bit of dwarven blood in you, correct? You shall stay with me. You could be valuable. And you're a pretty little thing, aren't you?"

It was Matt's turn to kick Emmon who looked ready to leap at the king. Emmon struggled against the guards, but then stopped moving, his green eyes boring holes through the king's corpulent body.

"Now, then, guards take all but this one to the prison!" the king ordered. "And cage the winged beast!"

"You're making a mistake!" Lucian yelled as the dwarf guards dragged them out of the hall.

The king merely laughed, and Matt felt anger burning inside as he glanced back at a terrified-looking Natalia. Emmon's face was filled with rage.

The doors thundered closed behind them.

* * *

Rock Thompson stepped onto the smooth rock plateau and stared at the clear blue lake. The boy and his companions had to be around here somewhere. Angrily, he kicked a stone and watched it skip across the rock face and into the water. He turned around and faced the horde of eager, bloodthirsty garans. They stared at him with blank, white eyes and crouched threateningly on their four disproportioned limbs, their long snouts curled up to reveal their pointed teeth.

"Find their trail," he commanded angrily to his two men.

They sent three garans scampering mindlessly across the rock surface, sniffing feverishly.

Rock watched them move around chaotically. They had to find the boy. Involuntarily, Rock touched the tender scar that marred the left side of his neck. The boy had given it to him when he escaped the cavern with the Fire Stone.

And then, of course, Kerwin had failed to kill him. Kerwin had been trying to kill the elf when the boy had intervened, and Kerwin had failed to even kill the elf. Rock sneered at Kerwin's incompetence. He did not deserve to be the Commander's right hand man.

Rock knew that Kerwin thought of the hunt for the Water Stone as an opportunity to regain his authority and restore his reputation with the Commander, but Rock intended to use this opportunity to achieve glory for himself. He would be the one to succeed and present his master with his prize. And he would be the one to kill the boy. He would triumph where Kerwin had failed.

The garans wandered over to the left edge of the plateau and gathered in a circle. One of the garans raised its head and let out a blood-curdling shriek. Rock ran to them.

"What have you found?"

The garans ran closer to the edge, their noses still sniffing at the ground. Rock followed them and spotted several strange oval marks carved into the stone. He followed their path with his eyes and saw that the marks disappeared over the edge. It was the same path the mindless garans were now tracking with their noses.

"Halt!" Rock ordered.

The garans stopped in their tracks, forced to follow orders. One, however, was too close to the edge, and though it scratched frantically at the stone, it tumbled over the edge. Rock sidled to the edge and looked down, watching the garan fall. He could barely see it by the time it made contact with land, thousands of feet below.

He rubbed his scarred neck and considered the possibilities. The boy would not have foolishly followed the strange trail of carvings to his death. No. There had to be something else.

If the Commander was correct, which he always was, the boy was searching for the second Stone of the Elements, rumored to be in the mythical dwarf city of Oberdine. A hidden kingdom, Kerwin had said.

Rock considered this and concluded that the city had to be hidden within the mountain. Kerwin had also said that the kingdom had never been seen by anyone except for a hapless dwarf wanderer.

They obviously did not want visitors. Rock smiled cruelly. He could definitely use this to his advantage.

He turned to the agitated force of garans behind him with their sharp claws and teeth. His smile grew larger. Yes, it could work, if the boy had indeed reached the city. Rock turned away from the garans and focused on the wickedness of his plan, letting it fuel him.

Soon, he held up his hands and watched, his eyes glowing, as black mist flowed from his fingers. The Commander had given Rock a gift, instructing him in the use of Dark magic. Rock watched, satisfied, as the mist hardened into a hazy black shadow as tall as Rock. It had no features and floated slightly above the ground.

"Go under the ledge and into the city. Show yourself only to the ruler of the city. Tell him this: I am a shadow, a messenger. I bear a message from my master. It is this: I, a great general, send you greetings and warnings that I am pursuing a group of felons who have entered your city. They cannot be trusted, but are difficult to contain and only my great army will be able to do so. Allow my army to enter the city, and we will perform whatever deed you may desire. Open a way into the city, and we shall be at your disposal. Give your response to my shadow, and I will do your bidding."

Rock pointed to the edge of the plateau. "Go now, shadow. Deliver the message, accept a reply, and return to me."

The shadow moved, appearing to be only a slight flicker of movement in air, and then it disappeared. The shadow was unseeing and unhearing, capable only of replaying the poisonous message.

Rock waited impatiently for the return message, pacing in front of the assembled garans. The shadow did not return for many minutes. Rock threw a rock into the lake. Suddenly, he felt a shiver of cold air next to his left shoulder, and he turned to see the foggy shadow floating beside him.

"Do you have an answer?" he asked.

The shadow spoke, a whisper on the wind, an echo of the message-giver.

"I, King Agram of Oberdine, will open a way into the city under two conditions. You destroy the visitors and eliminate the rebellion against my reign. Make haste, General. Enter Oberdine."

CHAPTER TWENTY-TWO

The guards pushed them forcefully away from the palace, and Matt fell hard against the stone street. He grimly noted how strong the dwarves were despite their short stature. They pulled him roughly to his feet. Samsire stood in front of them, casting menacing looks at the guards.

"The king orders that these intruders be imprisoned until they speak the truth about their involvement in the rebellion," the head guardsman told them. "The beast must be caged."

Samsire growled as the dwarves brandished their spears. When he refused to move, some of the guards prodded him with their spears, and Sam roared so loudly that several of them dropped the spears and cowered behind their hands.

"Just go with them, Sam!" Matt yelled in desperation. "If you try to fly, their spears will bring you down. We'll come for you! I promise!"

The head guard growled. "Not likely. You won't escape our prison. Now, move the creature!"

Matt watched unhappily as the guards converged on Sam and dragged him away. The other prisoners were taken past the palace to a small street. It led them down a slope and curved behind the stone hill where the palace was perched. The palace loomed above them, and

Matt realized that it sat on the edge of a several hundred foot high cliff which dropped off precipitously. Beneath the palace, an archway was carved into the sheer rock cliff. Two armed dwarves guarded the doorway.

"Take them to cell four," the head guard commanded.

One of the dwarves saluted smartly, grabbed a torch off the wall, and beckoned for them to follow him. Matt followed Emmon into the narrow tunnel. He could scarcely see in the dim glow of the torchlight. On either side of them were cage-like rooms with bars reaching from the ceiling to the floor. Dozens of dwarves cowered in the corners of the cells, their dark eyes filled with hatred as they watched the guards.

They stopped in front of a cell, and a prison guard unlocked the door, gesturing for them to go in.

"Wait," one of the guards said. "Take away their packs and weapons first."

Reluctantly, Matt pulled his arms out of his pack straps and dropped it in the hands of a guard. He unbuckled the strap around his chest and pulled his sword and scabbard from his back. The others did the same. Emmon stared sadly at his bow as it was pried from his hands. Once they had given up their belongings, the guards pushed them into the cell.

"Hello," said a voice behind them after the guards had disappeared. "What did they get you for?"

They turned and saw three dwarves sitting together in the shadows in the corner. Their beards were long and scraggy and their clothing dirty. Unlike the other prisoners, however, their eyes were bright and curious.

"We simply entered the city and were attacked by the tower guard for being outsiders," Lucian answered.

"Oh, well, I should have guessed," the dwarf in the middle said. "Agram finds anything new a threat to his throne. Name's Ragnar. What are yours?"

"I am Lucian, Wizard of Light, and this is Galen, Matt, Emmon, and Arden."

"What brought you to Oberdine? It is quite a feat to find this city and then to be able enter it. Our last visitor was over two decades ago," Ragnar said. "That was under a different king, of course."

"We seek your healing waters for an underground city whose inhabitants are dying, including a dear friend of ours, who is also a dwarf. I offered to pay the king for our need, but he wouldn't even listen."

Ragnar chuckled. "Nay. Agram's so blinded by his own large nose he can't see the sense of anything."

The dwarf on his right let out a sort of hysterical squeak.

"So," Galen said conversationally, leaning against the wall. "What did you do to end up in this beautiful place?"

Ragnar grinned. "This is the cell for dangerous criminals. I am the leader of the resistance against King Agram. And this is my second-in-command, Harbin, here," he said gesturing to the dwarf on his left. "We were captured about a week ago. Myron," he pointed to the dwarf on his left who cowered slightly, "was the king's head chef.

He directly defied the king. A bold move. I wish he had joined us before he was captured."

Myron whimpered and said quietly, "It wasn't an act of defiance. I only put too much pepper in his majesty's soup!"

A giggle escaped Arden, but she quickly covered it up with a cough. Galen patted her firmly on the back, only to cause her to giggle again.

"Yes," Galen said. "We met a dwarf named Borgik when we first entered the city. He attempted to help us in the name of the resistance."

"Borgik! He is my brother. I am glad that he is carrying out our cause, even with Harbin and I imprisoned."

Lucian nodded briskly and said tensely, "I know your rebellion is important, but it is essential that we get to the healing lake. Thousands of people will die. We don't have much time!"

He jumped to his feet, pacing in front of the bars. His gray eyes flickered dangerously as he examined the bars. He grabbed them tightly.

"Lucian, what are you doing?" Matt asked. "Can you get us out? Why didn't you try to escape before?"

"There was a chance we could have been overpowered by the king's guards before. Now we have the upper hand."

"But-"

Lucian held his hands up and extended them slowly toward the bars. His brow furrowed in concentration and he grimaced as he pushed his hands apart, slowly as if pushing a great weight. The metal groaned loudly, echoing through the cell and down the hallway. The bars vibrated slightly and then the thick metal buckled, bending with the motion of Lucian's hands. After several moments, the bars had bent far enough apart that a man could pass through. Lucian stepped away, breathing heavily. No one spoke for a moment.

"I guess you really are a wizard," Ragnar said mildly.

Galen stepped forward as if this was the most normal thing to ever happen. He stuck his head through the gap, but then ducked quickly back into the cell.

"Stand back," he whispered. "Guards are coming."

Galen shuffled to the side of the cell and leaned casually against bars. Two guards came running over to the cell, confusion apparent on their faces.

"What was that noise? Hey, what's going on in here?"

They stopped in front of the cell, dumbstruck as they stared at the bent bars.

"Hello," Galen said cheerfully before diving at the surprised guards.

He knocked the first one off his feet and whirled around to whack the other one in the chin with his fist. The first guard had regained his footing, and began jumping from foot to foot with his raised hands balled into fists. Galen considered him for a moment before swiftly bringing his leg around the back of the dwarf's knees, and sweeping his legs out from under him. The guard fell, hitting his head on the cell bars and collapsing, unconscious.

The second guard was not to be as easily defeated. He charged at Galen, burrowing his head hard in his stomach. A gasp escaped

Galen's lips, but he managed to get his hands around the dwarf and push him hard into the wall. The guard dropped like a stone.

"Shall we?" Galen said, dusting off his hands.

"I wish you were a member of the rebellion!" Ragnar said in delight. "You could be quite useful!"

"You should see what he can do with hares," Arden said with a straight face.

"Well, we must be going. Unfortunately, we have a tight schedule," Lucian said to the confused dwarves, a smile hovering on his mouth as he ducked through the hole.

They all followed Lucian into the dark hall. Without the guards, there were only the watchful eyes of the amazed prisoners who had gathered at the bars of their cells. Ragnar, Harbin, and Myron crept out of the cell too, keeping a safe distance between themselves and the group of outsiders.

Lucian and Galen hurried to the pile of packs and weapons which had been taken by the guards. They quickly withdrew the weapons and passed them around. Galen handed Matt his sword and sword belt, but left the rest.

"We can return for the rest of our things later," Lucian said. "For now we must-"

A guard came rushing into the prison corridor, his face panicked and yelling to no one in particular, "It's the king!"

"What? Has something happened to him?" Ragnar asked hopefully.

The guard shook his head, gasping for breath. He seemed to be too upset to care that the prisoners had escaped from their cell.

"No, he's opened the way into the city!"

Ragnar gasped.

Lucian looked at him sharply. "Is there's another way into the city besides the one beneath the rock plateau?"

Ragnar nodded. "Yes. But only the king can open it. Only he has the key for the lever that opens it. There's a passage at the very farthest point of the cavern. I believe that on the surface it is at the far end of a lake, up against the mountain."

"But that's not all," the guard said fearfully. "There are hideous creatures coming along the passage. We could barely see them through the telescope, but they are horrible." The guard shuddered. "Dark and disfigured. One after the other. There are hundreds of them."

"Garans," Lucian whispered. "Rock must have followed us. Is there a man with them?"

"Yes, a couple of men, but there is one who appears to be the leader. I didn't like the look of him either. How could the king do this?"

"I think, your king is so concerned with his own power that he cannot see what is really happening," Lucian said calmly. "Those creatures will destroy the city!"

"The king is mad!" the guard said. "What should we do?"

"Release the prisoners," Galen said. "I'm sure they'll help you out with your king problem. Now, tell us, where is the alorath who came with us into the city?"

"Under the west wall of the palace, next to the cliff face."

"Right, then," Galen said quickly, addressing his companions. "We have to free Sam and he can fly us up to Oberdine's lake before Rock can reach it. No doubt Rock's after the Water Stone."

Lucian nodded. "Yes. Let's go quickly-"

"Wait!" Arden yelled before he could move. "I don't think that will work."

"Sure it will, Arden," Emmon said exasperatedly. "It doesn't get any simpler than that! We have to go."

"Well, we aren't going to get very far unless we do something about the king and the garans," Arden argued. "The rebellion can't do much without the help of the king's guards. Someone needs to unite them. And what about Natalia? When were you planning on freeing her?"

She waited impatiently for them to respond, annoyed at their expressions. "Well?"

"You're the only one who might be able to hold off the garans, Lucian," Galen said.

Galen turned to the guard and Ragnar. "You must persuade the guards to join with the rebellion to fight against these new intruders, and then you must help Lucian hold them back. Arden, you can help Lucian free Natalia and organize the men. Matt, Emmon, and I will free Sam and fly up to the lake to retrieve the Water Stone before Rock can get there."

"Yes! Yes!" Ragnar cried. "Stir the rebellion!"

Lucian nodded. "All right. We don't have much time. Rock and the garans will be here in minutes."

CHAPTER TWENTY-THREE

Lucian buckled his sword around his waist, and he and Arden helped Ragnar and Harbin free the other prisoners. The reluctant Myron and the guard followed. They rushed down the winding passage together to free Natalia and rally the king's guard

Stopping only to grab a torch, Galen led Matt and Emmon through a nearby passage going west. They wound through the underground tunnel for several minutes before they finally reached the entrance. They ran along the cliff wall until they found the entrance to another passageway that split in two directions.

"Which way?" Matt asked Galen, his heart beating rapidly against his throat.

Galen stopped for a moment to think. "West is this way, I think."

The passage was a narrow path sandwiched between two sheer rock faces, the wall of the cavern on one side and the cliff wall on the other. There would be nowhere to hide if someone came toward them on the path. Galen stopped suddenly and put a finger to his lips. He pointed silently forward.

The passage opened up into a large cave that was open at the top. A group of guards were looking into what appeared to be a large pit.

Galen quietly withdrew his sword and crept up behind the guards, holding his sword high above their heads. Silently, he brought it down, hilt first, onto one of the dwarves' heads, knocking him out. The dwarf slumped into the one of the other guards.

"Hey, what are you doing?" the guard asked the unconscious dwarf.

"He's taking a nap," Galen said from behind, causing the dwarves to jump.

"You! You're supposed to be in prison," the guard cried, and then turned to his fellow dwarves. "Get them!"

The crowd of dwarves stumbled over each other as they drew their weapons and ran wildly at Galen. He easily sidestepped them, sending several of them falling.

Before they could do anything else Galen grabbed three dwarves and put his sword threateningly to their necks.

"I would like to let your friends go so they don't have to endure a gruesome death," Galen said calmly to the other guards. "But that would only be possible if you allow us to free the alorath without a fight. And there is a very good reason why you might want to take me up on that offer."

"Why that's a terrible…what?"

"As we speak, a legion of foul creatures is invading your city. Your crazed king has let them in. I will give you a chance to do one of three things. You may get yourself to safety, stay and fight the invaders, or do whatever you choose, as long as you leave us alone."

The guard mulled this over for a moment. "All right. We'll go to the palace."

"Good," Galen said smiling and released the dwarves.

"Ha!" the dwarf yelled, running toward the palace. "I have the keys. You'll never free that beast!"

Matt's heart sank and he ran to the edge of the pit. A narrow ledge snaked down the side of the pit to the bottom where there was a large cage with Samsire in it. It was barely large enough for him. His wings were folded awkwardly and pressed against his sides.

"Sam!" Matt called and the alorath moved his great head to look up at him. He roared happily.

Matt jumped onto the narrow ledge and ran down it to the bottom of the pit. Galen and Emmon followed close behind.

"Just in time. My muscles are getting a bit cramped."

Instead of going to the cage, Galen went to the wall and began to move his long fingers along the enormous wooden corner beam. Emmon looked at Matt and raised an eyebrow. Matt shrugged.

"Aha!" Galen cried triumphantly.

"What?" Emmon and Matt asked simultaneously.

The mergling held up a bent nail that he had pulled from the beam with magic. Matt could not help feeling skeptical.

"That's supposed to help us get Sam out?"

Galen grinned. "Watch and learn, my young friends."

Matt stepped out of the way as Galen walked to the lock that held Samsire's cage shut. Holding it between his forefinger and thumb, Galen inserted the nail in keyhole and then let go.

"Just needs a little guiding force," Galen whispered.

Matt noticed that Galen's breathing deepened as he extending his fingers toward the nail. After a moment, his fingers began to move, and the nail bent into strange contortions as if it were made of cloth.

His fingers stopped moving abruptly and the nail stood still. With a satisfied smile on his face, Galen pushed gently on the head of the nail. There was a loud click and the lock opened. Galen lifted the heavy latch and swung open the enormous door to Samsire's cage.

"Ah…that's better," Samsire growled as he climbed stiffly out of the cage and stretched out his wings. "What next?"

Matt quickly explained to him that the king had allowed Rock and a legion of garans to enter the city, and that they had to reach the lake before Rock did.

"Right, then. I can carry all of you. Climb aboard."

Sam dropped a wing and they climbed onto his back. He pumped his wings and slowly rose into the air. They rose above the palace roof until they could see out over the city. An icy coldness spread through Matt. A plague of black, spindly creatures was swelling through the fields and into the city streets.

"Quickly, Samsire!" Galen yelled.

The alorath pumped his wings faster and faster, soaring high in the cavern, aiming for the tall cliff that towered high above the palace. They watched the garans swarming beneath them and panic clutched at their hearts. Matt hoped that Lucian and Arden had managed to rouse the dwarves to defend themselves against the mob of garans.

Samsire reached the top of the cliff quickly, landing beside the lake. The lake glittered even more brightly up close, and the gentle waterfall trickled down beside it, forming another small body of water. The lake was much larger than Matt had first thought, taking up nearly half of the plateau. The trees growing on the plateau were a vivid green and exceedingly healthy.

There was nothing indicating where the Water Stone might be hidden. When Samsire landed, they each went in a different direction to search. Carefully, Matt climbed down the rocky slope toward the shore. The strange, glittering water drew him near, hypnotizing him. It sparkled reassuringly, rippling gently. Watching it filled Matt with an overwhelming peace, as if the rest of the world had disappeared and all his worries with it. Suddenly, he had an idea.

"Emmon! Galen!" he called.

"What? Did you find something?" Galen asked.

"What if the Water Stone is in the lake?" Matt said. "That way it would be close to the healing waters and it would stay hidden from the dwarves."

Galen nodded slowly but before he could respond, Samsire roared loudly. Matt felt a rush of air as Sam flew directly over their heads. His long leathery tail wrapped tightly around Matt's chest, and then he threw Matt onto his back.

"Sam, what are-"

Samsire dove into the lake. The last thing Matt saw before his head went under the clear water were the shocked expressions on his friends' faces.

* * *

By the time Lucian and Arden reached the palace they had left the rebellion leaders far behind, and there were more than a dozen guards running after them. No guards stood in front of the elaborately decorated archway into the palace. Lucian opened the massive door, and they slid inside. Within seconds, dozens of guards converged on them.

"Move right!" Lucian said to Arden moments before the guards reached them, and he threw up a shield in front of himself.

The guards bounced off of it violently, falling against each other and against the floor and pillars. Lucian and Arden ran toward the throne, where the king was still lounging languidly on his pillows and looking down disdainfully upon the activity in the hall. Natalia sat beside him, her face now bright with hope.

"Guards! Seize them!" the king said, waving his hand.

Lucian whirled around as guards began to attack him. Lucian conjured another shield between the charging dwarves and he and Arden. Keeping one hand extended to hold the shield, Lucian turned to the king.

"We do not seek conflict with you, king," Lucian said, choosing his words carefully. "I only wonder what possessed you to allow those foul beasts to enter your city."

"Beasts? What beasts? The king would never allow intruders into the kingdom," a guard said in outrage.

Lucian ignored him, his attention focused on the king.

"I am protecting my rule! The great general who leads those creatures has promised to quiet the rebellion against my reign in exchange for your deaths! A good choice, if I do say so myself!"

Lucian remained calm. "Quiet the rebellion? The man and those creatures he leads, the garans, will not quiet the city of Oberdine! They will destroy your city. No one is safe from them."

The king's guffaws echoed through the now silent hall.

"You are a fool," Lucian said quietly.

The king jumped to his feet. "A fool, am I? We'll see about that!"

Before Lucian could respond, Arden darted forward and stood defiantly in front of the king, just feet from his throne. He smirked at her. An impish smile grew on Arden's mouth and she uttered an invocation under her breath. With a strangled gurgle, the king crumbled, falling forward and landing on his bulbous belly.

"Yes," Arden said matter-of-factly. "You are a fool."

The king whimpered piteously and Arden stepped over him to Natalia. They hugged and Arden quickly explained what had happened. Lucian turned away from the king and faced the guards. They looked stunned and confused, but none appeared to be concerned with the fate of their king. Lucian dropped his shield and addressed the dwarves.

"Your king has allowed foul, unnatural creatures into your sacred city. The creatures take orders from leaders who are even fouler than they are. It is time for you to perform your jobs as soldiers and serve your city. It is time for you to join the forces of the rebellion and defend your home. It is time for King Agram's reign to end."

As he spoke the last words, Lucian placed a glow of light around himself. A loud cheer erupted from the dwarves.

"Nicely done," Arden said with a smile.

Lucian allowed the light to dim, smiled, and said, "Arden and Natalia, I suggest we now join the rebels."

As if on cue, Ragnar burst through the door followed by Harbin who was dragging Myron, the cook.

"The creatures have reached the city edge, wizard!" Ragnar cried. "The rebels have evacuated the homes and are organizing outside the palace. We are at your command."

"As are we," a king's soldier said.

"Call up the rest of the tower guard," Lucian ordered.

Two dwarves scurried off to do his bidding and the remaining dwarves followed Lucian, Arden, and Natalia out of the palace. Thousands of dwarves armed with everything from swords and axes, to pitchforks and shovels, stood at the base of the hill. Looking past them, Lucian saw a dark shadow of garans overtaking the streets of the city.

"Now," Lucian said grimly. "We must fight."

CHAPTER TWENTY-FOUR

"Why did Sam do that?" Emmon asked Galen as Matt and Sam disappeared into the water.

Galen shrugged, annoyed. "Probably just wanted a little fun, as always. Great timing, I must say."

"What was Matt saying before Sam grabbed him?"

"He said that he thought that the stone was in the lake," Galen said.

He stared at the clear, sapphire-colored water. Matt was right, it would make the most sense for the Water Stone to be hidden in the depths of the healing waters of Oberdine. But it was unfortunate for them, as they had very little time to retrieve it.

"Let's look around some more," Galen said. "He may be wrong."

Galen loped up the small slope. He wanted to find the stone and leave this city. He glanced down. The black mass of garans had been confronted by the dwarves, visibly battling through their lines. Galen felt a flicker of hope.

Rock Thompson was down there somewhere. Unconsciously, his hand gravitated over his shoulder to the hilt of his sword. He grasped the worn leather wrapped around its handle, comforted by the contact.

"Galen!" Emmon yelled.

Galen reeled around, running down the small sloped to Emmon's side.

"What is it?"

"They're not coming back up! Matt and Sam are still in the water!"

Galen scanned the clear water, but could see nothing. There was no sign of them. He felt a growing dread. Something was not right.

"They're not coming back up!" Emmon said hollowly.

"That is unfortunate, isn't it?" said a voice behind them.

Galen's blood turned to ice. He did not need to turn to know that voice. It was a voice had hoped he would never hear again.

* * *

The impact of the cold water forced the air from Matt's body, but he clung tightly to Sam's neck as they swam deeper and deeper. He held his breath, waiting for the alorath to swim back up to the surface. Samsire showed no sign of changing direction. He continued to spiral downward through the water. Matt kicked furiously at Samsire's back, but he paid no attention.

Panic began to overtake Matt as he became more desperate to breathe. He kicked again, but still Sam did not pull up. Matt pushed off of his back and began to kick for the surface. He didn't know how to swim, but he knew he needed air, and he knew the only way to get to it was to go up. The crystal clear water was becoming foggy to him and he doubled his efforts to get to the surface.

The more frantically he kicked, the further away the light from the surface seemed to be. His limbs grew heavy and it was difficult to move. Panic and despair curdled into a heavy ball in his chest.

Suddenly, something wrapped around his waist pulling him farther into the depths. Matt's brain and lungs screamed for air, but he could not fight the force pulling him downwards. He looked down to see what was holding him and saw Sam's tail.

Samsire was floating leisurely in the water and he pushed Matt around to face him. Matt's stomach bubbled in anger at the alorath's betrayal. He kicked at him feebly, but the alorath only drew him closer until their noses were almost touching. Matt stared into Sam's eyes and saw that they were pleading. Pleading for his trust.

Matt realized that the alorath was breathing. His sides were heaving up and down. He foggily remembered that Sam's feathers marked his elemental abilities. Blue for water. Sam could create water. He could breathe underwater. Barely conscious, Matt tentatively drew in a breath.

He did not inhale water, nor did he inhale air. It was almost as if he was not breathing at all, but his lungs were no longer screaming in anguish. Matt laughed in disbelief and a stream of bubbles escaped his mouth. The panic had passed and Matt hugged Samsire around the neck.

"Let's go, Sam!" he cried happily, but the words came out in a burst of distorted bubbles.

Sam's sides shook with laughter, but he swam forward, his wings folded closely against his sides. This time as he twisted and twirled downward, Matt enjoyed the ride. He found that as long as he had physical contact with Sam, his power was somehow transferred to Matt so that could breathe freely. As soon as Matt let go, however, he was once again trapped in the airless depths, unable to breathe. Matt gripped tightly to Sam as he swam to the bottom of the lake. It seemed endlessly deep, yet the light from the surface seemed to shine continuously, lighting their way.

Green plants lined the rocky bottom, dancing wildly like fire. Matt did not see fish anywhere, only plants, moving as if a breeze ran through them. Samsire skimmed the lake bottom so that his belly brushed up against them. Matt reached out to touch their slimy surface.

He looked ahead to see where Sam was going and what he saw made his heart skip a beat. A stone archway stood at the end of the strange, underwater field. Matt squinted and he could see detailed carvings of waves and bubbles cut into the stone. When they reached the archway, Matt patted Sam on the neck, took a deep breath, and jumped off his back, kicking as hard as he could until he could touch it. He fingered the carvings on the cool stone for an instant and then looked through the archway.

A small stone the size of a plum was perched on a rock on the other side of the archway. It was a very clear blue-green, and its transparent surface blending in with the water around it. In the center of the stone was a mass that looked like iridescent algae.

The Water Stone.

Matt dove through the marble archway and was immediately repelled by an invisible wall. He tried again, this time placing his feet on the ground and pushing through with his shoulder. He met with the same resistance. Very aware that he needed air, Matt kicked over the top of the archway to try to reach the Stone. An impenetrable shield surrounded the entire area around the stone. Becoming angry, Matt swam back down to the front of the archway and tried to force himself through again. Yet again, his efforts were futile and he was pushed back by the invisible force.

He could not hold his breath any longer. He turned around, searching frantically for Sam, who immediately came to him and rubbed his head against Matt until he had taken several deep breaths. Turning back to the archway, Matt placed both hands on the shield, pleading for it to let him through. Desperate, he focused on his magical energy, letting it fill him up. His fingers tingled sharply, but still he could not get through.

He glanced down at the black pouch hanging from his neck, floating in front of him away from his chest. He reached up his hand and grabbed it. Immediately, warm power flooded through his body, and then the invisible barrier disappeared. He fell through the archway and extended his hand until his tingling fingertips touched the surface of the Water Stone.

* * *

Arden slowly drew both of her long, curved knives from their scabbards and examined their blades. Letting her hands drop to her sides, she walked over to Lucian who was issuing orders to Ragnar and the guards.

"Garans are vicious animals. They respond only to the commands of their masters and without that guiding force they know only their own ferocity. Do not underestimate them. They may be mindless, but they are extremely dangerous."

Ragnar and the guards rushed off to relay the information to their soldiers. Lucian looked down at Arden, mildly surprised to see her.

"I thought you had gone with Natalia," he said.

Natalia had gone to gather and hide villagers who were not capable of fighting.

Arden shook her head. "No. I'm staying here. I will fight."

Lucian nodded.

"The creatures have reached the third level, wizard!" Ragnar called.

"It is time then," Lucian said, walking quickly through the throng of assembled dwarves.

Arden followed close behind him, holding her knives tightly to her sides so as not to accidently hurt a dwarf as she walked through the crowd. When they reached the front, Lucian and Ragnar addressed the dwarves together.

"Dwarves of Oberdine!" Ragnar yelled. "It is time to protect our city, our home, our lives, from these terrible intruders! This is our home, not theirs. The king has no right to give it away to them just so that he can remain in power. Let us send these foul creatures to their destruction!"

There was a loud cheer and Ragnar took several bows, urging the crowd to cheer longer and louder. Arden rolled her eyes at the theatrics. It was clear that Ragnar loved attention, but it was imperative that they hurry. The legion of garans would be upon them in seconds.

Lucian stepped forward. "I have nothing more to say to you other than fight for your lives, your honor, and your home. May you all see tomorrow's sun."

The dwarves all stood taller and grasped their weapons with determination, and Lucian and Ragnar led them down the city street.

"What is the garans' position?" Lucian asked Ragnar.

The dwarf shrugged unconcernedly, humming merrily. Lucian gave Arden an exasperated look.

"I'll go look," Arden offered

She scampered up a set of stairs that led to the rooftop of the nearest house and crawled onto the roof. Looking over the edge, she saw a group of garans skulking toward the assembled dwarves.

"They're just around the corner!" Arden yelled down to Lucian.

Lucian nodded briskly and turned to a group of guards on his left. "Go now, before you are seen."

The head guard nodded and motioned for his soldiers to slip between two buildings and down the slope. As they disappeared, the first garans came around the corner. A collective gasp rippled through the dwarves. The garans twisted bodies with their disproportionate limbs were terrifying to behold, and as they drew closer the dwarves could see the garans' vacant white eyes, wild and crazed.

"Now!" Lucian yelled.

He and Ragnar ran, yelling, with weapons raised, toward the garans. The army of dwarves followed close behind. Before they reached the garans, Lucian raised his empty hand and swung it upward. Five garans fell backward, hit by the invisible strike. Nearby garans shrieked and the dwarves quailed at the sound, but continued running toward the creatures. The noise was thunderous as the dwarves met the garans head on. Screams and shouts filled the air.

Arden jumped to her feet. The fighting had traveled down the street and was already at the bottom of the stone step she had climbed. It would be risky to try to join the battle from there. She returned to the edge of the roof, searching for the wizard's tall frame among the dwarves.

Lucian was cornered by four garans, not far from her. He whirled around, twirling his sword before him and systematically wounding one garan after another. A garan leapt at him and Lucian flung up a shield while stabbing another garan beside him. The dwarves were not faring as well, as they struggled to hold off the garans. They already appeared to be tiring.

Arden glanced around at the other rooftops, looking for a way down so that she could help her friends. Although the building next to her was slightly shorter, there was only a narrow gap between the two buildings. She stepped to the edge of the roof, sheathed her knives, and jumped over the gap. She landed easily and ran to the edge of that roof.

There was a larger gap between the next two buildings. She stepped back and took a running jump, landing awkwardly, but managing to keep her footing. She glanced around the rooftop and saw a set of stairs. Drawing her knives, she ran down the stairs into the street. The battle waged a dozen yards ahead, and she hurriedly launched herself onto the nearest garan with both knives. The garan screamed and collapsed, black blood spilling from its wounds.

She moved toward the next garan, and it shrieked, crouching down as if to pounce. A clawed foot shot out at her legs, but she jumped out of the way. It growled and lunged at her.

Caught by surprise, Arden tried to stumble backward, but claws gouged her left shoulder. Quickly she took a step forward and slashed at the garan, but was surprised by its speed and ability. She remembered how Matt and Emmon had described the garan they'd met in the forest as smarter than any garan they had seen before.

The garan tried to lunge at her again, but her knives ended the assault before it has able to injure her again. She put her hand on her wound and pressed it to stop the bleeding. Behind her, above the din, she heard a moan and turned to see a familiar red-haired dwarf lying on the ground, badly wounded.

"Borgik!" she cried and knelt by his side.

"Hello. It's you," he croaked softly.

"Don't move. I'll go get help!" Arden told him quickly.

"No," he gasped. "It's too late for me. Tell my brother I fought valiantly."

Arden nodded, tears welling her eyes.

"Don't cry," Borgik whispered. "Don't...Look out!"

Arden turned around and stopped another garan as it leaped at her. Jumping to her feet, she fought off several more as they came at her one at a time.

"Well, well, isn't this interesting. What's a pretty little elf doing alone in battle?" a voice said behind her.

Arden whirled around and saw a tall man with an angular face and menacing brown eyes. A long burn stretched down the left side of his neck. She knew she had seen him before, but could not place where or who he was, and then she remembered being chased into Hightop by Kerwin and this man with their hoard of garans and

Agurans. It was Rock Thompson. She felt anger burn in her stomach as she thought of what this man had done to Galen. She gripped her knives more tightly.

"Oh, so we do know each other?" Rock said, watching her face and then examining the blade of his sword. "So tell me, where did your loyal friends go?"

Arden fought her fear and rage, and concentrated on the burn scar on Rock's neck. She smiled slightly, knowing that Matt had given it to him.

"Well?"

Arden continued to stare, hoping to annoy him by gaping at his weakness. Rock rubbed his neck subconsciously.

"It's not polite to stare," Rock said angrily, forgetting about the phony negotiations and lunged at Arden.

She jumped away just in time, but she could still hear the whistle of the air as the sword streaked past her ear. This was different than fighting against the mindless garans.

"Hey!" a dwarf yelled. "Leave her alone!"

The dwarf jumped on Rock's back, his burly arms closing around Rock's neck. Rock stumbled for a moment from the weight, but managed to maneuver his sword around to the dwarf's side. The dwarf's grip weakened, and Rock threw him off with disgust. Arden watched in horror as the dwarf gave one last shuddering gasp and lay still.

"No!" she cried.

Rock smiled evilly and turned toward her. "Now, it's your turn, little lady. Unless you tell me where the boy went."

Arden shook her head, staring at Rock numbly.

"Fine."

Rock moved so quickly that Arden barely had time to throw up her knives in defense. His long sword clanged loudly against her blades and with such force that she staggered. She moved quickly to block his next strike over her head, but Rock brought his sword to her side. She managed to block the strike, but lost her balance again.

She regained her footing before Rock could strike again, and she moved to attack him, but intense pain in her right calf caused her to cry out and fall to her knees. A garan's sharp teeth were buried deep in her leg. Arden stabbed at it until it released her. She looked up to see Rock lunging at her again, his sword aimed at her heart.

"You will not hurt her!"

Borgik threw himself between Arden and Rock, and the sword went into his chest. Rock swore angrily and yanked out the sword, still advancing on Arden.

He paused as Samsire's roar echoed through the enormous cavern, and his head snapped toward the cliff top, his mouth twisted into a smile. He whistled loudly and the remaining garans ran to him. Forgetting Arden, Rock ran, garans on his heels, toward the lake.

Arden turned to Borgik and grasped his limp hand. The dwarf looked up at her, smiled, and closed his eyes. Tearfully, Arden turned away, letting Borgik's hand drop out of hers. Wiping her eyes, she sheathed her knives, and looked at the area around her.

All of the garans, except for the dead, were gone, leaving only some dazed-looking dwarves. Limping, Arden moved toward where she had last seen Lucian. Shriek of garans and the sound of pounding feet reached her ears, and she climbed back up several the stairs to get out of the street. A horde of garans careened down the street, pursued by a large troop of yelling guards.

Arden watched them pass and then slowly hobbled up the street. She had to find Lucian and tell him that Rock had gone after the others. She found him leaning against a building, his sword hanging limply at his side. He had several gashes across his arms and chest, but he was alive.

"Lucian!" Arden cried.

The wizard looked up and ran toward her, his sword at the ready.

"It's okay. The garans have gone," she said quickly. "You're hurt."

"So are you," he replied. "Come, let us make sure we're not needed by the other dwarves."

"Lucian, wait! I was fighting Rock Thompson, but he heard Sam's roar. He's headed up the cliff with a pack of garans. He's going after Matt!"

CHAPTER TWENTY-FIVE

A strange new sensation coursed through Matt's body as he touched the Water Stone and the Water magic mingled with his own magic and the Fire magic. It was not overpowering, but not gentle either. It was a force of purity and power.

Immediately, Matt knew he could breathe without Sam, and he gripped the Water Stone even more firmly. Letting go of the pouch around his neck, Matt swam out under the archway. He lifted his hand and showed Sam the Water Stone. Sam scooped him up with his tail, placed him on his back, and swam swiftly toward the surface.

Matt examined the light blue-green stone for a moment before stowing it safely in the pouch next to the Fire Stone. He held on tightly to Sam's neck and as they neared the surface, he slid further up the alorath's neck until his head was nearly even with Sam's. The alorath slowed and then quietly broke the surface. Only the tops of their heads were no longer submerged.

Matt glanced around hoping to see his friends looking relieved, but circumstances had changed drastically since they had left.

Emmon was pinned against a tree by a dozen garans. There was a gash across his forehead and several long gashes down his arm. Galen's sword was drawn, and his face was very pale. Facing him was a familiar man with an angry, red burn down the left side of his neck. He smiled cruelly and lunged at Galen with his sword.

Matt's heart stopped as he saw Rock Thompson lunge at Galen, his long sword streaking toward Galen's chest. Galen moved faster, bringing his own sword up in defense, striking back hard. Rock dodged easily.

"Go, Sam!" Matt yelled, urging the alorath forward.

With a mighty leap, Samsire launched himself out of the water. Matt clung to his neck tightly as Sam spiraled wildly toward Rock and Galen. Neither Galen nor Rock had noticed them yet, both pairs of eyes locked on their opponent. Samsire skidded across the rock plateau to the left of the dueling pair, and Matt was thrown from Sam's back.

"You help Emmon and I'll help Galen," Matt yelled.

The alorath hurried toward Emmon. Matt drew his sword and jumped at Rock, who had already drawn a second sword from his hip. He easily blocked both strokes.

"You, boy," Rock hissed as he glared at Matt. "I've been waiting for you. And you." He turned to Galen. "Isn't it time you died?"

Galen's blue eyes flashed angrily and he threw himself at Rock. Rock grinned viciously, eager to fight. Matt dove at the man's other side. Again, Rock easily blocked both strikes, wielding the two swords equally well. It was almost as if he could sense their next moves and was always one step ahead.

"Get out of here, Matt!" Galen ordered him through gritted teeth.

"You're not fighting him alone!" Matt hollered back struggling to block a ferocious strike.

"That's noble," Rock snarled. "I've never liked noble people."

He swung at Matt's sword with such strength that Matt was thrown backwards. Galen battled Rock and the two swords as Matt jumped to his feet. Matt watched for a moment in frustration. Rock was too strong for him, but he had to help Galen.

He glanced down at Doubtslayer, examining the strange blade. The curved edge and small point could be useful. Matt had used it many times to disarm his opponent. Maybe he could get Rock to fall for the same trick and relieve him of one of his swords.

Matt jumped back into the battle, pulling one of the swords away from Galen. Though he was nowhere near the swordsmen that Rock and Galen were, Matt knew enough to stop Rock's blows. If only he could also find an opportunity to disarm him.

Rock's constant hammering was exhausting, and Matt's arms were growing heavy. He chanced a glance at Galen and saw sweat pouring down his face, but he showed no sign of tiring. Rock sensed Matt's drifting attention, and swung his sword toward Matt's side.

Matt realized what was happening in an instant and jumped out of the way, but the sharp point still caught his side. He felt a sharp pain and warm blood seep through his drenched tunic. He staggered slightly, but focused his mind away from the pain. It was not a deep wound. He couldn't let it slow him down. He had to stay focused and ignore it.

Matt's strokes grew sloppier and weaker as he attempted to penetrate Rock's defenses. Realizing that Matt was no longer as much of a threat, Rock began to concentrate his strength against Galen. Matt still swung at him, but his arms continued to grow heavier.

"Move, Matt!" Galen yelled suddenly, and Matt realized that Rock was swinging at his head.

Galen pushed Matt out of the way while swinging at Rock. Rock's face contorted with rage. He blocked Galen's stroke, swearing angrily, and swung at him with the second sword. Galen ducked to avoid the strike, but even Galen could not move fast enough to block the strikes of two swords. One of them sliced deeply into his right side.

A grunt of pain escaped Galen as copious amounts of blood began to flow from the wound, almost immediately coating his tunic. Galen collapsed to his knees, his sword hanging limply from his hand.

"NO!" Matt screamed.

Matt lunged at Rock. He brought up both swords in defense and Matt began to hammer at him. He could not think through the blind rage that coursed through his mind and body. He wanted only for Rock's evil to be stopped, and it burned through him.

His emotion fueled his magic and Matt felt it meld with the Fire Stone, sending energy through his body and into his sword. As his own blade collided with Rock's, the fire energy surged through Rock's sword, throwing him backwards.

"You know how to play," Rock hissed, anger flashing in his eyes.

Rock lunged back at Matt. The blades clattered and the rocks shifted beneath Matt's feet. Sam's roaring and the garans' shrieks rang in Matt's ears, even as the blood pounded through his head.

Suddenly, one of Rock's swords and his own sword locked together. Moving out of reach of Rock's other sword, Matt placed both hands on Doubtslayer and pushed with all his might. Slowly, Rock's blade began to slide down the curved edge of Matt's blade. As soon as it reached the slanted tip, Matt flung up his wrist and Rock's sword went flying through the air.

Matt felt a thrill of victory as he gazed into Rock's irate face, momentarily forgetting that Rock still had another sword. In an instant it sliced deeply into his right arm from shoulder to wrist. Matt's sword dropped from his limp fingers, clattering against the rocky ground. His legs crumpled beneath him.

Rock raised his sword above his head and swung down at Matt's head, but Galen was suddenly on his feet, wielding his sword against Rock with a terrifying blend of rage, determination, and pain on his face.

* * *

Samsire had flown to Emmon's aid just in time. Emmon's bow lay on the ground, its string broken by the garan's claws. Samsire was battling four garans at once. They were climbing all over him, clawing at his neck and wings. Samsire growled and roared as the garans clawed mercilessly at his wings, and he struggled to throw them off.

Emmon kicked at the nearest garan with all his might, knocking its sharp claws away. He dived to the right as the garan's claws grazed his shoulder. Reacting rather than thinking, Emmon looped his foot around the garan's back leg, and it stumbled to the ground. Emmon kicked upward flinging the garan hard against a tree trunk.

Pulling an arrow from his quiver, Emmon jumped at the nearest garan and stabbed it. The garan shrieked and crumpled. Emmon pulled another arrow and ran at one of the garans hanging onto Sam. The alorath swung his head around and yanked another one off his back and flung it violently against a tree. One by one Sam dealt with the vile creatures.

Years of scout training kicked in as Emmon was attacked by another garan, and he dove forward underneath the garan's belly. He kicked hard and the garan was thrown backward, landing near Samsire's claws, and Sam quickly finished him off. Emmon got to his feet.

There were only five garans left, but they were all on Sam's back and they were attacking him ferociously. Samsire staggered, bleeding from the many wounds. With a mighty shake from Sam, three of them flew off his back. Emmon was ready with his arrows, felling them one by one.

It was at that moment that they heard Matt's bloodcurdling yell.

CHAPTER TWENTY-SIX

Matt wanted to move. He wanted to help Galen, but he could not make his limbs work. Vaguely, he thought he should do something to stop his arm from bleeding so much. He tried to imagine how Galen had found the strength to launch himself back into battle.

Rock was pushing his advantage, further wearing down Galen's defenses with each stroke. It would not be long before Galen was overpowered. A look of triumph appeared on Rock's face and he pushed hard against Galen's blade.

Galen staggered, momentarily dropping his defenses. Rock did not hesitate. With one quick flick of his wrist, he cut deeply across Galen's thigh, causing him to drop to the ground.

Matt yelled again. It was torture to watch Galen collapse again, with unbearable pain on his face.

Matt shut his eyes momentarily, trying to block out the scene. He tried to calm his mind. He must help Galen and the only way he could do so at the moment was to use magic. He tried to block out the pain he felt and the fear he felt about Galen injuries. He must focus.

Rock was smiling wickedly as he moved closer to the Galen.

He began to laugh. "You are weak, warrior. Once again, you fail to defeat me. And this time you will not live."

Galen looked up at Rock dazedly, and with a mighty shout, he hauled himself to his feet, holding his sword limply. His hunched frame did not seem like a threat, but for the first time, Matt saw fear on Rock's face. Still, he had failed to defeat Galen.

But Matt knew that Galen would only kill himself faster by continuing to fight Rock.

With great effort, Galen swung his sword. Rock dodged the strike as Galen staggered. Confidence returned to Rock's face.

Matt focused his waning energy on his own weakening magic and the magic of the Fire Stone. Feeling the warmth and the strength of the melded magic spreading through his body, he let the Fire Stone take over and he threw up a shield in front of Galen so strong that its shimmering outline was visible.

With all his strength, Rock took a mighty swing at Galen. At that same moment, Samsire bellowed an earsplitting victory roar. Rock's eyes briefly flicked toward the alorath.

In that split-second of distraction, Rock's sword rebounded violently off the powerful shield, flipped backward in the air, and landed forcefully in Rock's chest.

Rock's eyes registered his astonishment. He stood unmoving for a moment and then fell to the ground.

"A...good warrior...is never distracted!" Galen managed to wheeze before he lost consciousness.

Matt released the shield, breathing heavy, ragged breaths, and closed his eyes. He opened his eyes to see Emmon kneeling over Galen.

"Galen!" Emmon cried.

No. Matt's brain could not accept it. But the anguish on Emmon's face forced him to realize the magnitude of what was happening. Pushing away the pain that threatened to overwhelm him, Matt rolled onto his stomach and pulled himself onto his knees. Holding his right arm close to his chest, he crawled to Galen.

Dimly, he could see his own bloodstained clothes as he watched Galen's chest to see if he was still breathing. He saw the faintest of movements. Matt felt a glimmer of hope. Galen was not dead yet. He could die within moments, though, and Matt needed help.

The Water Stone.

Reaching for the pouch around his neck with his uninjured arm, Matt withdrew the green-blue stone, feeling its cool surface in his palm.

Gathering all of his remaining strength, Matt focused on the stone in his palm and on the dying Galen beside him. Once again, he felt his magic and the Fire Stone magic join, and then he reached out for the Water Stone with his mind. He felt a gentle, reassuring power merge with the other magic and spread through him.

He laid the stone in his limp right hand and reached forward with his other hand to touch Galen. He focused on the soothing power of the Water Stone, but nothing happened.

Desperation filled him. He had to heal Galen before it was too late. Suddenly, he felt the power intensify and flow into his fingers. Small water droplets began to form on Matt's fingertips and fall onto Galen. Eventually, they pooled and spread across Galen's chest and down into the wound on his side. Slowly, Galen's breathing became stronger and steadier.

"It's working!" Emmon whispered.

Matt did not respond as he weakly placed his hand on Galen's thigh, where the water droplets gathered again, until the wound stopped bleeding. His own arm was throbbing painfully, and continued to bleed.

"Matt? Are you okay?" Emmon asked.

Samsire growled uneasily. Matt knew he could not stay conscious much longer, and Galen was still injured, though he did not know how badly.

"Matt! You have to help yourself now! You won't be able to save Galen if you don't," Emmon said urgently.

Matt forced the limp fingers of his injured arm to grasp the Water Stone more tightly. He felt a strange sensation up his arm, and tiny water droplets began to gather on his own wound. He watched, mesmerized, as the blood flow lessened and the pain eased slightly. He did not have the energy to heal it completely, but he began to feel better.

"Matt! Galen!"

Lucian and Arden were running toward them trailed by a group of dwarves.

"It's all right," Emmon said.

Lucian leaned over Matt, and Arden sat beside him.

"Lucian," Matt said as he slumped against Arden and she put her arm around him.

"I see you managed to find more trouble, Matthias," Lucian said with a strained smile.

Emmon explained to them what had happened. Lucian knelt over Galen, instructing the dwarves to get a stretcher, and then checked Rock's body for sign of a pulse.

"He's dead," Lucian said.

"That… is not a bad thing," Galen whispered with a weak grin.

Matt smiled. Galen was alive.

CHAPTER TWENTY-SEVEN

Matt flexed his arm experimentally. It was slightly sore and weak, but other than that it felt normal. A dwarf with long white hair stood next to his bed in the palace infirmary holding a basin of sparkling water and a wet rag.

"It should be just a little stiff and sore for a short while," she told him kindly. "The healing waters have certainly helped the process, but you seem to have healed unnaturally quickly. You see, the more healing water that is used on a person, the more likely it is that there will be some permanent weakness, so we try to use a little as necessary.

"You are very lucky," she continued. "You must be blessed with strong magical energy. In your case, we had to use very little healing water."

Matt nodded, marveling at his healed arm. A long scar stretched from his wrist to his shoulder, but it was barely noticeable. The healing water of Oberdine was truly incredible.

"You should still rest, though," the dwarf healer urged him. "You've lost a lot of blood and you are going to be weak for a few days."

Matt thanked her as he lay back on the pillow, and she smiled at him before moving to help an injured dwarf. As he shifted into a more comfortable position, he glanced over at the bed beside him.

Galen was sleeping peacefully. The healer had explained to him that Galen's wounds were so nearly fatal that they had not been able to heal him completely with the water. Using more than what they had used would have left him permanently weakened. Galen's arm was in a sling, and large, gauzy bandages covered his side and leg. He was sleeping peacefully.

Matt drifted off into a dreamless sleep, his exhausted mind and body taking advantage of the chance to rest. The trials of the day and of the weeks they had spent traveling had taken their toll on him.

"I don't know why he's sleeping," Emmon's voice said, cutting into Matt's consciousness.

"If you almost drowned, fought a man like Rock Thompson, who practically sliced your arm to pieces, and saved Galen from certain death, you'd be tired too," Arden argued.

"Well, he's been healed now! It's not like when Kerwin stabbed him and *he* was facing certain death. Galen's the one who almost died."

Matt smiled slightly as he listened.

"Why don't we just let him sleep?" Natalia offered.

"I'm sure he'll want to see it, though," Emmon said.

"You'll have to be the one to wake him, then," Arden told him.

"Fine. He'll probably strangle me, though."

"He is also listening to everything you're saying," Matt said, opening his eyes.

He smiled at their expressions and sat up in bed. "What is so urgent that you need to wake me up?"

Emmon grinned. "The rebellion is going to appoint Ragnar as the king. There's a huge gathering in front of the palace. The crowd is enormous! Of course, Ragnar roused the whole city."

Matt grinned back. "All right. Sounds like fun. It'll just take me a minute to get some clothes on with this gimpy arm, and then I'll meet you in the hall."

They crept out of the infirmary, and after Matt joined them, Emmon led them through the palace until they reached the throne room. Ragnar was standing in the center of the hall talking to Lucian, Harbin, and Myron, cook turned reluctant hero. The wizard turned as he heard their footsteps echo through the hall. He smiled when he saw them and walked over to join them.

"Hello, my young friends," Lucian said "I am glad to see you up and about, Matthias."

Matt smiled and the wizard patted him warmly on his good shoulder. He turned back to Ragnar. "Do you wish to proceed?"

"Yes," Ragnar said fervently. "All of you will need to stand beside me as I address the crowd. You, wizard, shall stand on my right."

Lucian raised an eyebrow and Matt glanced at his friends. They tried, unsuccessfully, not to smile at the sight of the small dwarf ordering around the imposing wizard. Ragnar led Harbin and Myron to the doors, and Lucian and the four teenagers followed close behind.

Guards pushed the doors open before them, and there was a tumultuous roar of applause as Ragnar walked out of the palace and faced the crowd. Matt had never seen so many people in one space. There were dwarves of every sort, young and old, male and female, rich and poor. They were grouped around a crude podium made of loose stones from damaged buildings.

Matt shrank back behind Lucian, intimidated by the size of the crowd. He felt Emmon and Arden do the same, and Natalia bowed her head, her cheeks very pink.

Ragnar, however, appeared to be very comfortable with the attention. He walked confidently up to the makeshift podium holding up his hands to stop the cheering crowd. The dwarves only cheered louder. Matt couldn't hear himself think. After several minutes of non-stop applause, the crowd finally calmed down, and Ragnar was given the opportunity to speak.

"Dwarves of Oberdine!" he yelled. "Today is a day of victory! Of triumph! We have taken back our city, our home. Never again shall we submit to unfair rule or to the claws of vile beasts and intruders! Oberdine is ours!"

There was a roar of applause and Ragnar held up his hands for silence.

"There are thanks that must be given. If not for the wizard and his companions, my loyal followers and I would still be trapped in prison. If not for them, the king's rule would never have been undone, and we would all be helpless prisoners of those vicious beasts. And so, I declare that a statue be made in the wizard's honor. A tribute to him and to his companions."

The crowd applauded again and Lucian nodded in gratitude.

"But now, I say, bring forth the disgraced king!"

The crowd parted as several dwarves carried a heavy wooden beam through the street. The fat king was balanced on it precariously, his large belly bouncing as the dwarves jostled the rail through the crowd.

"To prison!" Ragnar yelled.

The crowd roared so loudly that Matt thought his ears would burst. The crowd trailed the disgraced king as he was carried down the street to the prison. Gradually, the crowd returned to the street in front of the palace, happiness on their faces.

"Long live King Ragnar!" a dwarf shouted.

The rest of the dwarves joined in the chant. "King Ragnar! King Ragnar!"

Ragnar nodded appreciatively. The chanting was unceasing, demanding for Ragnar to be crowned. Finally, a dwarf ran up the hill from the prison, holding the king's fallen crown before him. He was pushed forward by the crowd until he reached Ragnar.

"Crown him!"

Obeying the will of the crowd, the dwarf handed the crown to Harbin, and Ragnar's second-in-command placed the crown atop the kneeling Ragnar's head. The new king rose and the crowd erupted. Several dwarves were so overcome with emotion that they fainted. Ragnar launched into a long-winded speech about the honor of being king. Matt barely heard a word as he watched the excited crowd and resisted the urge to yawn.

"Thank goodness that's over," Arden breathed afterward

"You woke me up for that?" Matt joked, pushing Emmon teasingly.

Emmon yawned. "It was fascinating, don't you think? If I ever become that boring, promise me you'll push me off a cliff."

Matt made his way back to the infirmary to check on Galen He needed to be sure that the mergling was going to be all right.

Galen was sitting up, and he had taken the sling off his arm. He looked uneasy, but relaxed visibly when he saw Matt. He grinned, his face pale.

"Galen," Matt said as he reached his bed. "You're awake."

Galen nodded and croaked, "Sure looks like it."

"How...how are you feeling?"

Galen shifted uncomfortable, wincing slightly. "All right. But...I would be dead, if it wasn't for you."

Matt felt his face go red.

"And if I recall correctly, Rock is dead, isn't he?" Galen asked hopefully. "I vaguely remember that he died, but then I thought maybe I dreamt it."

Matt nodded. "He's dead."

"That's good, isn't it?" he said with a grin. "So now, I suppose I owe you some heavy gratitude. Those were some pretty heroic deeds you performed back there. "

Matt grinned. "What did you expect me to do? Leave you to die? Tough choice, Galen."

Galen laughed, but immediately winced and clutched his side. He lay back on the bed and sighed.

"Besides, you saved my life, too. You were so heroic that you almost got yourself killed. Why is it that you can't manage to be a just a little heroic, you have to almost die being heroic," Matt said, smiling.

In a more serious voice he added, "The healers said it will take you longer to heal because your wounds were so bad. They said you're going to be weak for a while."

"So, in other words, Galen," a voice said behind them. "Pursuing deadly assassins is off-limits for a while."

Lucian stood next to the bed, smiling. "How are you feeling, old friend?"

"I've been better, but I've been worse," Galen said with a grin.

Lucian turned to Matt. "I thought I might find you here. I need to ask you for a favor, Matthias. I know that you are still weak, but I need for you to leave for Gremonte immediately."

Though he was tired, Matt answered without hesitation.

"Yes. I'll go now."

"Good. Have Samsire fly you. Before you go, return to the lake and fetch a skin of the healing water to take with you."

"Why? I can use the Water Stone to heal all of those people. It's easy to control."

Lucian looked at him sternly. "Do not think that the Water Stone is something to be trifled with, Matthias. Like the Fire Stone, the Water Stone has two different sides, a mirror of the elements they control. Fire provides warmth and comfort at times, but it is also wild and untamed and can be destructive.

"Water is the same way. The Water Stone can heal and provide sustenance for life, but it can also be incredibly powerful and dangerous. Strangely, in different ways, water can be more dangerous than fire. Can you control the waves of the sea or the rapids in a river? It would exhaust your energy, and possibly endanger your life if you were to use the Water Stone to individually heal each one of the sick.

"No. You must only use it as you use the Fire Stone, to increase your powers. In this case, you must use it to multiply the healing water that you will take with you from the lake. The Water Stone will also increase the water's power."

Matt nodded obediently and Lucian's tone softened.

"We will all meet you in Gremonte, as soon as we can. I believe the dwarves have somehow managed to breed horses here, and we can buy a few to ride back. But you and Samsire must make haste."

"We will, Lucian," Matt said. "We will leave as soon as I load my pack."

CHAPTER TWENTY-EIGHT

Matt tightened the straps of his pack and checked to make sure that the bulging water skin was safely tied to it. He and Emmon had collected it as soon as he left the infirmary. Matt turned to his friends, standing at the edge of the cavern opening. Everyone was there, except Galen, who had already said good-bye. Samsire stood next to Matt, his wings twitching in anticipation.

"King Ragnar says that this is the passage the previous king opened to allow Rock to enter," Lucian said. "The dwarves will be closing it up again, but they are waiting until we all leave."

"Good luck, Matthias," Lucian added, squeezing his shoulder. "We will meet you there as soon as Galen is able to travel."

Matt nodded. "See you all soon."

They all hugged him, careful to avoid his arm.

With a final wave, Matt and Sam walked into the dark passage. Matt created a ball of light in his palm, letting it guide them through the tunnel. Unlike the other tunnel, this tunnel sloped upward dramatically. As soon as they were near enough to the top for sunlight to begin seeping in, Matt dismissed the orb of light.

There were several scared-looking dwarves waiting for him at the mouth of the tunnel. They scurried underground when Matt smiled awkwardly at them.

The sunshine felt amazing to Matt, and he sighed as he felt its warmth on his face. He had not been in Oberdine for very long, but the mysterious light was artificial and lifeless in comparison to the purity of the sunlight that warmed his skin. He saw that a number of boulders had fallen onto the shore of the lake. The passage must have been blocked from the outside.

Sighing happily, Matt turned to Sam. He could tell he was anxious to get into the air. Matt quickly scrambled onto his back, and Sam roared gleefully. He leapt forward, letting his claws skim the lake surface until the plateau dropped off.

Matt's stomach dropped as Sam dove straight downward, paralleling the mountainside, trees blending together as they passed. The bottom appeared quickly, but Samsire waited until the last moment to pump his wings and level them out just above the treetops.

Matt laughed in exhilaration, an irrational happiness surging through his body. Samsire roared again and pumped his wings leisurely, rising higher and higher into the air.

The day passed smoothly and uneventfully. Matt entertained himself by watching the landscape change beneath them. The grass transformed from long and scraggy, to short and green, and the flat plains became rolling hills.

After a while, Matt grew tired, but he was afraid to doze while riding on Samsire's back. He forced himself to stay awake by repeating each of Dorn's clues aloud, much to Samsire's annoyance. After a few hours, when the sun was approaching the horizon, Sam began to slow, and Matt convinced him to stop for the day.

They landed in a green field where there were no landmarks in sight. Matt searched for something to start a fire, and found some dry, brittle bushes that they could burn. Using the Fire Stone, Matt pointed his fingers at the plants and two small jets of flame appeared on his fingertips.

The plants smoldered weakly. Samsire bent his head to examine it, and after a moment he took a breath to blow on the plants, but instead a stream of water shot from Sam's mouth, extinguishing the fire completely.

Samsire growled. "It seems that ever since you found the Water Stone, my Water magic is trying to outshine my Fire magic. It's difficult to control. Rather irksome and inconvenient, is what I would call it."

Matt muttered something about showing Sam what was inconvenient as he struggled to relight the pitiful fire.

The alorath grunted.

They sat in silence for several minutes until Matt, ignoring Sam's grumpiness, gently stroked the feathers on his neck. Sam's only response was to lean against Matt's hand. Matt smiled.

Matt ate a cold dinner while Sam rummaged around in the bushes for his dinner. Afterward, Sam curled up and Matt climbed next to him for warmth and protection.

As they were getting ready to leave early the following morning, Matt picked up his pack and felt fear creep down his spine. He shuddered and glanced around.

"Matt, look out!" Samsire bellowed.

Matt saw a flash of movement and then something slammed into him. He went sprawling to the ground. He scrambled to his feet, trying to find his attacker.

His breath caught in his throat as he saw the dark gray skin, protruding bones, and sightless black eyes of an Aguran.

Malik's assassins. Many times more deadly than a garan.

It loomed over him and before Matt could move away, it grabbed Matt's wrist. Searing pain crept up Matt's arm, and he squirmed desperately to free himself. The Aguran's free hand groped for the pouch around Matt's neck. Matt kicked the Aguran's chest as hard as he could, breaking its grip on his arm and sending it flying backwards.

Matt jumped to his feet and fumbled to pull his sword from his scabbard. The Aguran had recovered, but before he could reach Matt, Samsire had flown over Matt's head and landed on the creature. Sam sent it flying across the field. It let out a high-pitched screech and clambered upright like an overgrown spider. It leered at them from across the field and Matt raised his hands, preparing to attack it with magic, but it did not come at them again.

Instead, it bent its head and ran in the other direction, moving faster than Matt had ever imagined anything on two legs could move. They watched it disappear into the distance.

"What was that about?" Matt said, breathing heavily. "Why didn't it stay and attack?"

Samsire growled deep in his throat. "Maybe it was with Rock and the garans when they were following us."

"Why wasn't it with them at Oberdine, then? Why here?"

"Maybe it was following them and it was going back to report," Sam said. "I don't think it was actually trying to attack and kill you. It would have done a lot more damage than that, if it had been. Maybe it knew you had the Water Stone and tried to see if it could take the Stone from you, but gave up when it realized it would have a fight on its hands, fighting both of us."

"And now it's gone back to tell Kerwin or Malik that I have the Water Stone," Matt concluded. He looked anxiously around the fields. "Do you think there are any more of them?"

Sam shook his head. "I don't think so, but it doesn't matter. We're leaving anyway. We have to hurry and get to Gremonte before it's too late, remember?"

They were going to save Gremonte today, and nothing could stop them. The plague that Rock had taken to Gremonte would be defeated. No more would die. Matt wondered how many had died since they left. Swiftly calculating in his head, Matt realized that they had left Gremonte nearly a month ago.

Fear clutched at his heart. One had died before they had left, and a month was a very long time. The city had probably already given up hope of their return.

"Quickly, Sam!" Matt yelled.

The alorath seemed to understand the urgency in Matt's voice, and he doubled his speed, rocketing northwards. They passed over the city of Borden, a forest, and seemingly endless fields, spotting no major sights except for the Insla River. By the late afternoon, Matt noticed that Sam was tiring.

Matt was relieved when he peered into the distance and recognized the dusty fields that surrounded Gremonte.

"We're almost there, Sam," Matt reassured the alorath.

Soon, Matt could see the doors and green flags of Gremonte. Samsire landed lightly beside the gates when they reach them, and Matt leapt from his back. He faced the great stone doors uncertainly.

"Er...Open up!" Matt yelled, banging on the door with the end of his sword.

Nothing happened.

Matt tried again. "I am a friend of Lucian, the Wizard of Light!"

Again, nothing happened. Matt stomped the ground angrily. He had to get in. Desperate, he melded his power with the Fire Stone. Slowly, he created a fireball, and expanded it gradually grew until it was half the size of the doors.

Drawing deep upon his own energy, he forcefully flung the fireball at the stone doors. There was a loud bang. The stone doors were blackened and still standing, but ever so slightly crooked from the force of the blow. The grass in front of them was burning. Samsire stepped over Matt and blew a stream of water on the grass and the fire disappeared in a billow of smoke.

"That was a brilliant idea, Matt," Samsire said. "Now they *really* want to let you in."

Matt shook his head in frustration. He had to get in. Pacing, he examined the slightly crooked doors. If the ball of fire had knocked them askew, maybe if he did it again... He stepped back and focused deeply again, feeling the power burning inside of him. He pushed it to his fingertips, and grunting, he heaved another ball of fire at the doors.

He was thrown off his feet as it made contact with the doors. When he looked up the doors were crooked on their hinges, and there was a large gap between them, big enough for Matt to fit through. He smiled in relief. Sam gave him a toothy grin and butted his head against Matt's back.

"I've got to go, Sam. Thanks for everything. I'll see you as soon as I can come out, but I have to help everyone in there."

"I know. Good luck, buddy."

Waving at the grinning alorath, Matt squeezed through the gap and jogged down the dark tunnel that led into the city. The torches on the wall were a crude source of light in comparison to the magical light of Oberdine, and many of them weren't lit.

Matt ran down the path until the tunnel walls disappeared and he could see the city of Gremonte. There were two very somber looking guards sitting at the edge of the street. They spotted Matt and jumped to their feet.

"How did you get in?" one demanded.

"Blasted the doors," Matt said quickly. "I have to get to the infirmary or to Chief Golson."

"You can't just…Wait, I remember you. You were here with the wizard!"

Matt nodded urgently. "Listen, I have a cure for the sickness. Please, let me through."

"I'll lead you to the sick house!" one of the guards replied eagerly, and then he turned to his companion. "Alert Chief Golson!"

The guard led him down the street, past the silent buildings. Matt felt panic welling up in his chest. The streets were empty.

"How many have died since we left?" Matt asked.

The guard considered this for a moment. "Ten or twelve, maybe. Too many, to be sure, but not as many as it will be, if your cure doesn't work. Most of the city is sick, and there aren't enough who aren't sick to collect food and supplies. We've been living off of our reserves in the field, but we're nearly out and when that happens, we'll all die, anyway."

Matt's heart sank. What if Alem was among those dead? He had been very sick when they left. And he was old. Finally, they were in front of the stone building where the sick were staying. A few people moved slowly in and out of the building. Fear, fatigue, and illness were evident on their faces.

"The most seriously ill have been moved to the bottom floor," the guard told him as he pulled open the door. "You should go there with your cure first."

Matt nodded, feeling both terrified and hopeful. He entered the building with the guard close behind him. He found that the hall was even more crowded than it had been when he left, but it was now lined with beds with ill people, instead of crying families.

A knot twisted in Matt's stomach. Nervously, he walked down the hall until he came to the first room. He glanced inside and saw at least a dozen beds crammed against the wall. He scanned the faces of the ill, searching, and his gaze stopped at the last bed. A small, withered figure was lying against the pillows, with a bushy brown beard and a thin wisp of hair standing upright on top of his head. Alem. He was still alive!

Matt practically sprinted into the room, but was stopped by a woman bending over a bed who held up her hand. "You can't be in here. This group is all about to die."

Matt ignored her, nearly pushing her out of the way as he knelt beside Alem's bed. He dropped his pack and the guard explained to the woman who Matt was. Untying the water skin filled with the precious water of Oberdine, Matt gazed at Alem for an instant, listening to his scarce, feeble breathing. His skin was thin and sallow.

"I need a cup or basin," Matt told the woman urgently.

She disappeared into the hall and returned with a small silver bowl. Matt took it and poured several drops of water from the water skin into the basin. First, he must increase the amount of water. Just as he was about to do so, another guard appeared in the doorway, and Chief Golson barreled into the room, his thick arms tense at his side. His face was red and accusing.

"Where's my daughter, you?" Golson yelled at Matt gruffly.

"She's coming with Lucian in a few days. She's fine," Matt answered calmly. "I came first so that I could deliver the healing water of Oberdine to the ill."

Golson's red face twisted in confusion and then surprise. "You found it? The city exists?"

Matt nodded, losing his patience. "So does the water, and if you'll allow me to continue, it could heal your people."

Golson's anger disappeared and he said gruffly, "Well, proceed then. What are you waiting for?"

Hoping desperately that it would work, Matt focused on the power of the Water Stone and the water drops in the bowl began to multiply until the water level was at the top edge.

Matt gently lifted Alem's head and tilted the basin so that a trickle of water dribbled into his mouth. He carefully poured a little more into his mouth and set the dwarf's head back on the pillow. He held his breath and waited.

"Nothing's happening," Golson said.

"Wait," Matt said, though his heart was beating rapidly.

Another minute passed with no results, and Matt began to lose hope. Suddenly, Alem took a deep, unlabored breath, and slowly exhaled. He began to breathe more easily and regularly, and a hint of color touched his pale cheeks. Matt turned to look at Chief Golson, who chuckled in wonderment as the nurse and the two guards broke into a hearty cheer.

"I need buckets," Matt said, smiling. "Lots of buckets."

CHAPTER TWENTY-NINE

Matt spent the remainder of the day multiplying his small supply of water until he had filled enough buckets to administer water to the entire city.

The town's healers had gathered to examine Alem's condition, and it was decided that every patient needed to drink a cup of the water a day for at least a week until they were out of danger.

Increasing the water was tiresome work. Matt needed to control the Water Stone's power at all times - he was beginning to understand what Lucian had meant about the Stone. It was just as difficult to control as the Fire Stone even though it felt gentler when he wielded it.

By the time he had multiplied enough water for the entire town for two days, Matt was exhausted. He nearly fell asleep on the stool where he sat in the building filled with buckets. Forcing himself to stay awake, he stretched his sore arm and yawned. He had to fill at least another fifteen buckets before he would reach three days worth of supplies.

Telling himself he would complete the total supply in the morning, Matt picked up his pack and walked out into the street. Unfortunately, Golson was walking toward him, and he definitely had something on his mind. Groaning inwardly, Matt waited for the chief to reach him.

"Hello, hello! The water is still working quite well!" Golson said. "My, you look tired! Why don't you rest? But before you do, I wanted to ask you when you thought the wizard and Natalia will be returning with the others."

Eventually, Matt managed to leave the chief and his incessant questions, and he retreated to the library where they had stayed before. He collapsed in one of the comfortable armchairs and fell asleep almost immediately.

During the next two days, Matt completed multiplying the water until there was a week's supply for everyone in the city. The day following that, Matt was happy to hear that Lucian and the rest of his friends were at the city gates. A guard led him to the entrance tunnel.

Within a few minutes, Lucian, Galen, Emmon, Arden, and Natalia emerged, riding very short horses. Lucian, looking slightly disgruntled, dismounted his steed immediately. Galen was bent over his horse in exhaustion, and looked as if every step was jarringly painful.

"Matthias!" Lucian called.

Matt ran to them and told them about the success of the healing waters.

"Those are interesting horses you're riding, Lucian," Matt added, trying to suppress a grin.

"Well, the dwarves of Oberdine certainly do breed very short horses," Lucian said briskly. "Terribly fast, but terribly short."

Matt laughed, and let Galen lean on him as he got off his horse.

Lucian frowned at Galen and said to Matt. "He was a little too eager to leave. And whenever I tried to slow down, he only rode faster."

"Better than being trapped in bed," Galen said, wincing, but his eyes were twinkling. "Besides, if I'd fallen off my horse, I wouldn't have done much damage would I? Not far to fall. By the way, Matt, are those doors up there your handiwork?"

Matt grinned, and happily led them back to Chief Golson's hall where Golson embraced his daughter and gave them a rousing welcome.

"Welcome back, welcome back! As you can see, thanks to you, the city is on the mend! Yes! A festival shall be held in your honor tomorrow! The city of Gremonte is deeply in your debt!"

Everyone was happy to let Lucian do the talking, and finally, Golson allowed all but Natalia to leave his hall. They talked for a while until Galen nearly collapsed from exhaustion, and they reluctantly went off to bed.

The following day they attended a joyful festival, and many of the people who had been ill joined in the festivities. There was food of all types, meats, exotic breads, fruit, deserts, and practically every type of cheese Matt could think of. There were games and activities, but the most enjoyable part of the festival was when Alem walked out of the sick house and into the street on his frail little legs.

"Alem!" Matt cried, and he, Emmon, and Arden ran to the small dwarf.

Alem allowed them to embrace him and said gruffly. "I don't know what you are all so happy about. Who knew that all a dwarf had to do was to walk and he could get such a reception!"

Arden only hugged him harder. Matt and Emmon took his arms, lifted him between them, and paraded him over to Lucian who was sitting next to Galen on a short wall in the main square. The wizard greeted Alem almost as vigorously as the teenagers had.

The dwarf shrugged off their fussing and settled down beside Lucian, looking strangely pleased. Matt grinned at Emmon and Arden, and positioned himself against the wall next to Alem, as Natalia rushed up to them.

"Father is giving a speech in our honor," she said excitedly. "It should start at any moment."

She sat down next to Emmon, wriggling around with excitement. Emmon put his arm around her shoulders. Matt smiled genially, but really, he was quite tired of speeches. Within a few minutes, the crowd had gathered in the square where Chief Golson stood on a crate in front of his hall.

"My people!" he yelled. "We are here to celebrate the life of our city and its people. The past month, we have suffered great loss and sadness. But today, we live freely with lightened hearts. Thanks to our brave friends, our families are safe and well."

The applause was almost as loud as when Ragnar was crowned king of Oberdine.

Golson proceeded to name them each off individually and Matt shrank back against the wall, wishing it would swallow him up. He looked determinedly at his feet, feeling his cheeks burn. Finally, the chief moved on to talk about the revival of Gremonte, and Matt relaxed.

"Sounds like you've been busy while I've been gone," a voice behind him said resentfully.

Matt turned in surprise and saw a tall, red-haired boy standing behind them. "Hal!"

The rest of his companions turned as well and Emmon asked, "When did you get here?"

"Just now. My instructor told me a few days ago that you had come back to Gremonte," Hal replied as he swung his leg over the wall and sat down. "He said something about a sickness. Did I miss a lot?"

Matt looked at Emmon and they both laughed. "Just a bit."

Hal looked highly disgruntled, and turned to Galen, looking him up and down. "You look like you've been through a war."

Galen grinned. "Well, a battle, at least."

Golson speech was forgotten as they filled Hal in on their adventures.

"You haven't been the only ones having adventures," Hal said easily. "I've learned a million new things that Galen didn't teach us."

"What fun," Arden muttered quietly, so only Matt and Emmon could hear.

They tried not to smile, but Hal seemed to notice that he was being challenged. "Not only that, but I snuck away to Hightop to see Cadia."

"What?" Arden said.

Hal nodded proudly, but Arden shook her head. "That was incredibly stupid, Hal. What if you had been caught? General Barrum would have had you killed."

Matt saw Emmon flash her a warning glance. Matt couldn't agree with Arden more, but he had learned not to provoke the older boy. Arden had obviously never been on the receiving end of Hal's sword.

Hal, however, ignored her comments and said proudly, "She said she missed me and told me about the terrible place she has to sleep in…"

The rest of Hal's story was lost on Matt when he saw Galen sitting up very tall with his hands on his hips, miming Hal's moving mouth. Matt tried to turn his explosion of laughter into a coughing fit, and Alem looked at him warily.

"Not coming down with the sickness, are you, Matt?"

This only made Matt laugh harder and Emmon clapped him on the back, grinning from ear to ear himself. Eventually, Hal realized that no one was listening to him, and he directed his attention to Golson's speech, nodding solemnly at the words.

* * *

Four days later, Matt sat in the library with Galen, Emmon, Arden, Natalia, Alem, and Hal. It was nice to relax after so many weeks of traveling and strife. Galen seemed to be feeling much better, and Hal became more humble as the days wore on.

"I must say," Emmon said as he stretched out in an armchair. "If I ever hear another one of Dorn's riddles again, I might dig a hole of my own and crawl underground."

"Except for the fact that you're already underground," Galen pointed out.

"Yeah," Emmon shrugged. "But at least there's no crazy king here."

"I say, dear elf," Alem said reproachfully. "Don't insult Dorn or Oberdine. They are both-"

Lucian walked up the stairs at that moment with Raumer perched on his shoulder and several sheets of parchment in his hands.

"What's that, Lucian?" Matt asked.

"A letter from Beagan," Lucian replied. "He's graciously offered to bring the horses to Dornhelm so we don't have to ride those terribly short horses."

"Ride where?"

Lucian's gray eyes twinkled. "Wherever we must go when the time presents itself, Matthias. Although we have no leads on the location of the Wind Stone, we will need to locate it sometime in the near future."

Matt nodded slowly, thinking. There were things he wanted to do, places he needed to go that were unrelated to his destiny as the One of the Prophecy of the Elements.

"I need to return to Amaldan," he said. "Now that I have the Water Stone, I need to heal the forest and the Great Tree. Who knows what will happen to the elves if I don't?"

Emmon and Arden looked at him gratefully, but Lucian frowned. He waved the second piece of parchment in his hand.

"I'm afraid that's not possible," Lucian said grimly. "I also received a letter from one of the Amaldan falcons. It was from Lord

Balor. It says that you and all of your allies are henceforth forbidden from entering the Amaldan Forest."

"What?" Emmon yelled, outraged.

Lucian nodded. "Balor is blinded by his fear and arrogance. He believes that you, Matt, are the cause of the growing darkness there."

Matt's stomach twisted into a knot. He wanted to help Amaldan but now he could not, and he was also being blamed for the spread of the darkness. He looked at Emmon and Arden

"I don't care what Balor or any of the other elves think," Emmon told him. "I know that you're the cure, not the cause, Matt. Wherever you go, I go."

"And I'm practically an outcast already," Arden added. "I don't know if Balor would let me back even if I wanted to go. So, you can count me in."

Matt smiled at them gratefully. "I want to look for the Wind Stone or anything else that could help us stop Malik," Matt said finally. "And I want to find out who my parents are. I can't stop thinking about that old woman in Borden."

Lucian nodded approvingly. Matt turned to Galen, who was studying him carefully.

"Will there be trouble on this quest?" Galen said, smiling slyly.

Matt grinned back. "Oh, yes. I can guarantee that."

Acknowledgements

My family has been essential in the creation of *The Water Stone*. Mom, you are reader and editor extraordinaire. Your incredible enthusiasm and hard work amazes me, and I am endlessly grateful for everything that you have done for me. You are the greatest mom on the planet. Dad, thank you for always being an eager reader. You have been so supportive through this whole process, and I am thankful for your constant encouragement. Nick, you are an endless source of inspiration for my characters and my stories. I am so glad you are my brother. Also, thanks for passing on your sense of humor to your little sister.

I am so lucky to have you as my family.

CPSIA information can be obtained at www.ICGtesting.com
Printed in the USA
LVOW08s1404300114

371660LV00001B/36/P